KILLER
TAKE ALL

KILLER TAKE ALL

A DUFF MACCALLISTER WESTERN

WILLIAM W. JOHNSTONE

and J. A. Johnstone

P

PINNACLE BOOKS
Kensington Publishing Corp.
www.kensingtonbooks.com

PINNACLE BOOKS are published by

Kensington Publishing Corp.
119 West 40th Street
New York, NY 10018

PUBLISHER'S NOTE
Following the death of William W. Johnstone, the Johnstone family is working with a carefully selected writer to organize and complete Mr. Johnstone's outlines and many unfinished manuscripts to create additional novels in all of his series like The Last Gunfighter, Mountain Man, and Eagles, among others. This novel was inspired by Mr. Johnstone's superb storytelling.

All Kensington titles, imprints, and distributed lines are available at special quantity discounts for bulk purchases for sales promotions, premiums, fund-raising, educational, or institutional use. Special book excerpts or customized printings can also be created to fit specific needs. For details, write or phone the office of the Kensington sales manager: Kensington Publishing Corp., 119 West 40th Street, New York, NY 10018, attn: Sales Department; phone 1-800-221-2647.

PINNACLE BOOKS, the Pinnacle logo, and the WWJ steer head logo are Reg. U.S. Pat. & TM Off.

ISBN-13: 978-0-7860-4360-6
ISBN-10: 0-7860-4360-1

First printing: April 2020

10 9 8 7 6 5 4 3 2 1

Printed in the United States of America

Electronic edition:

ISBN-13: 978-0-7860-4361-3 (e-book)
ISBN-10: 0-7860-4361-X (e-book)

Author's Historical Note

In 1886 Thomas Sturgis, a rather substantial cattle-man in northeast Wyoming, suggested to Union Pacific that a local company be created to lay tracks from Cheyenne, Wyoming, into northern Wyoming and Montana. Thus, the Cheyenne and Northern Railway was established. The initial investors included Thomas Sturgis, as well as the first president of the Cheyenne Club, a man named Phillip Dater.

The eventual goal of the railroad was to build all the way north to connect with the Northern Pacific line in Montana, but the immediate target was Fort Laramie, which would include the settlements of Wal-bach, Chugwater, and Uva, as well as some of the more substantial ranches in the area, such as the Goodwin, Davis, and Sturgis ranches. After a year and a half, the line was constructed 125 miles north, but there it stopped. Union Pacific took over the line in 1887, and in 1890 Union Pacific created the Union Pacific, Denver and Gulf Railway, which incorporated the Cheyenne and Northern as well as several other short-line railroad companies.

After a series of mergers and adjustments, the railroad was finally merged into the Burlington Northern system in 1981. Then in 1995, Burlington Northern merged with the Santa Fe Pacific to form the BNSF Railway, one of the U.S. Class I railroads serving especially the western half of the country, with a rail network of 32,500 route miles in 28 states.

The C&FL (Cheyenne and Fort Laramie Railroad) of our story (as well as the machinations and participants of its building) is fictional, though its existence is inspired by the early history of the Cheyenne and Northern.

Chapter One

Chugwater, Wyoming

Thad Gorman counted out twenty-six dollars for Bob Guthrie, owner of Guthrie Lumber and Supply. "Here's what I owe you, Mr. Guthrie." Gorman smiled. "I got a good price for my wheat, and I thank you for carrying me on your books."

"Ahh, it's all part of doin' business, Thad. Why, most of the ranchers and farmers run a tab with me." Guthrie chuckled. "And I run a tab with my suppliers. Did Sue come to town with you?"

"Oh yes, Sue and the two young'uns. They're over at the mercantile now. She's payin' off Fred Matthews and stockin' up with things we been puttin' off till we had the money."

"What about Slocum? Did he come into town also?"

"I expect he'll be in tonight. I just got paid myself, so I haven't paid him yet."

"How's Slocum workin' out for you?"

Gorman chuckled. "Well, he's not the friendliest feller I've ever known, but his work has been all right."

"You were a good man to hire him," Guthrie said.

"Not everyone would be willing to hire someone like Drury Slocum, a man who had spent five years in prison."

"I guess so. But it seems to me like ever'one deserves a second chance. Anyway I guess I'd better go pick up Sue 'n the kids before they spend all my money."

When Gorman stepped into the Matthews Mercantile a couple of minutes later, he was greeted by a little girl who held out a doll. "Papa, look what I have! Isn't she beautiful?"

"I suppose so, but she isn't as beautiful as you are." Gorman smiled at Ethel, his six-year-old daughter.

"Huh, there's nothin' beautiful about a doll," Jimmy said. He was Gorman's nine-year-old son. "I got me a pocketknife," he added proudly.

It took half an hour for the farm wagon loaded with purchases to reach the family farm. When they drove into the yard, they were met by Drury Slocum, Thad's farmhand and only employee.

"Did you get the money for the crop?" Slocum asked.

Gorman smiled. "Drury, you see all the things we bought while we were in town. Do you really have to ask that question?"

"I'll take care of the team," he said as he began to disconnect the two gray mules from the wagon.

"Mr. Slocum, would you like to take supper with us tonight?" Sue asked.

"Nah, soon as I'm paid I'll be goin' into town."

"Look at it this way, Drury. You have to eat. If you eat with us, you won't have to spend money for food in town," Gorman said.

"Yeah," Slocum said. "Yeah, that's right, ain't it?"

* * *

An hour later, Slocum came into a house that was redolent with the aroma of fried chicken, biscuits, mashed potatoes, and gravy.

"Drury, are you ready to be paid?" Gorman asked.

"Yeah."

Gorman reached over to the sideboard where lay the three hundred seventy-five dollars he had been paid for his wheat crop.

"I'll be giving you thirty-five dollars," Gorman said. "The extra five dollars is a bonus."

"I'll take it all," Slocum said.

Gorman smiled. "Yes, I didn't think you would turn down the extra five dollars."

"No, I mean I'll take all the money." Slocum pulled his pistol and pointed it at Gorman.

"Mr. Slocum, what are you doing?" Sue called out, her voice high-pitched with fright.

Slocum didn't answer. He pulled the trigger, shooting Thad Gorman in the chest from point-blank range. The bullet lodged in Gorman's heart, killing him instantly. Slocum then turned his gun on Gorman's screaming wife and crying children, firing three more times.

With the four members of the Gorman family lying on the floor, Slocum grabbed two pieces of chicken and two biscuits and left the house.

Slocum was in the Wild Hog Saloon later that same evening. His plan was to be very visible in town, then when word came that the Gorman family had been murdered, he would have the alibi of having been in town. That way, he wouldn't have to go on the run. But something he overheard from a nearby table caused him to change his mind.

"It was the hired hand that did it. Mrs. Gorman was still alive when Duff MacCallister 'n Elmer Gleason stopped by to buy some hay from 'em. She told 'em it was their hired hand that done the killin'. They tried to bring her into town but she died before they could get her to the doctor."

Not everyone in the saloon knew that Slocum worked for Gorman, and those who did hadn't noticed that he was there. Slocum got up and went through the back door as if going to the privy.

He had no horse of his own, nor did Thad Gorman. Slocum had come into town riding one of the two mules Gorman owned. He had considered stealing a horse, but he didn't want to take a chance. He needed to get out of town as quickly as possible.

But the mule wouldn't cooperate.

"Get up, you worthless, long-eared galoot!" Slocum said, trying to urge the mule into a gallop.

He headed south, and no matter what he did to force the mule into a gallop, it wouldn't respond. Then, quite unexpectedly, the mule balked, bucked, and threw Slocum off its back. The mule decided to run then, leaving Slocum stranded on the road.

Sky Meadow Ranch

"There is someone in the mine," Wang Chow said to Duff and Elmer Gleason the next day. Wang was speaking of a gold mine, played out now, that sat at the extreme north end of Sky Meadow.

"How do you know?" Elmer asked.

"Tracks go into mine but do not come out," Wang said.

"Well, let 'im snoop around," Elmer said. "He won't find anything, and if he does, we can give him a commission for finding it."

Before Duff had built Sky Meadow, before even he and Elmer Gleason were friends, Elmer had discovered and was working an old mine that had been abandoned by the Spanish more than a hundred years earlier. Legally the mine and all proceeds belonged to Duff, but he shared the money with Elmer, and Elmer invested back into the ranch so that he was not only the ranch foreman, but a junior partner.

"Elmer, have you considered that it is nae someone looking for gold?" Duff asked in the heavy Scottish brogue that he had not lost in all the time he had been in America.

"Well, who else could it be?"

"Perhaps it is the one who murdered *Xiānshēng* Gorman," Wang suggested.

"I'll be damned. That's what you was thinkin' too, ain't it, Duff?".

"Aye."

"Well then, maybe we should go have us a look," Elmer suggested.

"I'll go in first," Elmer said when they reached the mouth of the mine. "There don't nobody in the whole world know this mine better 'n I do." He was justified in making such a comment, since he had actually lived in the mine for almost six months.

Elmer went in first, surrounded by a bubble of golden light cast from the torch he had lit. Duff and Wang followed, but were just outside the light.

"All right, mister, you can just stop right there!" a voice called from the darkness before Elmer.

"Who the hell are you?" Elmer asked.

"It don't matter who I am. You're in light 'n I ain't."

Elmer started to reach for his gun.

"Uh-uh," the voice said from the darkness. "I already got my gun out, 'n if you pull that 'n of your'n, I'll shoot you." Slocum appeared then, holding a pistol in his hand and pointing it at Elmer. "You know who I am, Gleason?"

"Yeah, Slocum, I know who you are. What I don't know is why the hell you are here. After what you done I figured you'd be long gone by now. Hell, ever'body figured that."

"Yeah, I would be if that damn mule I stole from Gorman hadn't throwed me 'n run off. You got a horse here?"

"What if I do? I ain't goin' to let you have it."

Slocum's laugh was short and without any real glee. "You think I'm askin' you for it? I ain't a-askin'. I'm goin' to kill you 'n take it." He extended his hand and pulled the hammer back.

A bright muzzle flash lit up the mine even beyond that of the flickering torch, and the sound of the gunshot was almost deafening in the closed-in area. The gun flew from Slocum's hand as Duff and Wang suddenly appeared. A narrow wisp of smoke curled up from the end of the Enfield Mark 1 pistol Duff was holding.

"We'll be for taking you in now, Slocum," Duff said.

"How you plannin' on gettin' me there? Like I said, I ain't got no horse to ride."

"You can walk, can't you?" Elmer asked.

"What do you mean, *walk*? It's five miles to town," Slocum complained.

"You don't have to walk if you don't want to," Elmer said. "We can drag you into town."

Chapter Two

Chugwater, two weeks later

The courtroom was filled to capacity for the murder trial of Drury Slocum. Wang Chow had testified to finding Slocum hiding in the abandoned mine on Sky Meadow, and Elmer had just testified to finding, along with Duff, the bodies of Thad Gorman and his family. At the moment, Duff was on the witness stand.

"Tell the court if you would, please, the condition of the bodies when you and Mr. Gleason found them." Jim Robison was the prosecuting attorney.

"Mr. Gorman and the two wee ones were already dead," Duff said. "Mrs. Gorman was nae yet dead, but she died before we could get her to the doctor."

"Did she say anything before she died?"

"Aye."

"What did she say?"

"She said 'twas the black-hearted Slocum that shot her."

"Objection, Your Honor, to the term *black-hearted*." Milton Gilmore was the court-appointed defense attorney for Slocum.

"Sustained," Judge Goff said.

"Do you see Slocum in this room?" Robison asked.

"Aye, he is sitting at the defense table."

"Thank you. Your witness, Mr. Gilmore."

Gilmore stood, but he didn't approach the witness. "Mr. MacCallister, did you actually see the defendant shoot Thad Gorman or any of his family?"

"Nae, I dinnae see such a thing."

"Thank you, no further questions."

Robison eschewed any redirect, and as Gilmore had no witnesses for the defense, he began his summation.

"Remember this," he said, holding up his finger to emphasize his point to the jury. "Both Mr. Gleason and Mr. MacCallister testified that they did not, personally, see the defendant shoot the Gorman family. We have only hearsay evidence from someone who cannot be questioned. Hearsay evidence is not enough to convict, and without proof beyond a doubt, you must acquit."

Robison gave the closure for prosecution. "We have the sworn testimony of two witnesses who heard, in her dying testimony, the declaration that Mrs. Gorman and her entire family had been shot by Drury Slocum. In addition, three hundred and seventy-six dollars was found on Slocum's person when he was arrested. Where did he get such a sum of money?

"Mr. Gorman was paid four hundred twenty-five dollars for his crop. He paid Guthrie Lumber twenty-six dollars, which left him with three hundred and ninety-nine dollars. Mrs. Gorman spent twenty-four dollars at Matthews Mercantile, which left Gorman three hundred seventy-five dollars. That money was not found at the house and it wasn't found there because it was in Slocum's pocket.

"Prosecution rests, Your Honor."

"Jury may retire to consider the verdict. Court is in recess," Judge Goff said with a rap of his gavel.

Less than ten minutes later, Marshal Bill Ferrell, acting as the bailiff, shouted out to the court. "Oyez, oyez, oyez, this court is about to reconvene, the honorable Judge Amon T. Goff presiding. Everybody stand until the judge is seated."

Judge Goff came out of the back room and took his seat at the bench.

The trial of Drury Slocum had taken no more than an hour, and the jury's deliberation lasted only five minutes. Then the jury sent word that they had reached a verdict, thus causing the court to be reconvened.

After taking his seat, Judge Goff, who had a splotchy red face and a rather prominent nose, adjusted the glasses on the end of his nose then cleared his throat. "Would the bailiff please bring the prisoner before the bench?"

Marshal Ferrell walked over to the defendant's table and looked directly at Slocum. "Get up," he growled. "Present yourself before the judge."

Slocum made no effort to move until Martin Gilmore stood and urged Slocum to stand as well. Gilmore remained standing at the defense table while Slocum approached the judge.

"Mr. Foreman of the jury, have you reached a verdict?" Judge Goff asked.

"We have, Your Honor."

"What is the verdict."

"Your Honor, we have found this sidewinder guilty of murderin' Thad Gilmore, his wife, and their two innocent children," the foreman said.

"You damn well better have!" someone shouted from the gallery.

The judge banged his gavel on the table. "Order!" he called. "I will have order in my court." He looked over at the foreman. "So say you all?" he asked.

"So say we all," the foreman replied.

The judge took off his glasses and began polishing them as he studied the prisoner before him. "Drury Slocum, you have been tried by a jury of your peers and you have been found guilty of the crime of murder and robbery. Before this court passes sentence, have you anything to say?"

"Yeah, do your damndest, you red-faced, hook-nosed ass," Slocum growled.

"Hang 'im! Hang 'im right here!" someone from the gallery shouted.

Judge Goff pounded his gavel again until, finally, order was restored. He glared at the defendant for a long moment, then he cleared his throat once again. "Drury Slocum, it is the sentence of this court that a gallows be built so that you may be hanged, such act to bring about the effect of breaking your neck, collapsing your windpipe, and, in any and all ways, squeezing the last breath of life from your worthless, vile, and miserable body. And may the Good Lord have mercy on your soul, because I do not.

"This court is adjourned," he said with a rap of his gavel.

One week later

It had rained earlier in the day, and though the rain had stopped a couple of hours earlier, the sky was still gray. The newly built gallows stood in the middle of

Clay Avenue between Second and Third Street, a harsh-looking construction with a single rope and loop hanging from the crossbeam.

It was 11:15, lacking forty-five minutes of the hour appointed by Judge Amon Goff that sentence was to be carried out for Drury Slocum.

At the moment, the prisoner was standing at the barred window of the jail looking out toward the gallows.

Marshal Ferrell went to Slocum's cell. "I know it's a little early for lunch, but under the circumstances, if you want anything to eat, now would be the time to ask for it."

Slocum looked toward the marshal with a glare. "Now why the hell would I want to eat anything?"

"I just thought I'd make the offer. Would you like a drink?"

"Whiskey?"

"If you'd like."

"Yeah, I would like some whiskey. I doubt that I have enough time left to get a good drunk on, but I'd sure as hell like to try."

"One drink," Marshal Ferrell said.

"All right. I'll take what I can get."

Out in the street, a crowd was beginning to gather. Some had come just for the morbid fascination of watching someone die, but most were there just to see justice done. Thad and Sue Gorman had been well-liked. Their murder, and the murder of their two small children, was incentive enough even for the most sensitive of souls to watch their killer be hurled into eternity.

"They say that the Chinaman who works for Duff MacCallister is the one who found the tracks leadin' into the mine," said someone in the crowd. "I can't think of his name."

"His name is Wang Chow, 'n I don't care if he is a Chinaman. He's a damn good man in my book. 'N yeah, he is the one that found 'im," a second man said, confirming the first.

"I'll say this. Ole' Slocum sure picked the wrong place to try 'n hide out," another said. "Duff MacCallister is the last person you'd want a-comin' after you."

"Where is MacCallister? I'd like to go shake his hand."

"He ain't here, nowhere. I done looked."

"Why ain't he here? He's the one that catched up with Slocum. You'd think he'd be wantin' to see this, wouldn't you?"

"Maybe he gets a little queasy from watchin' some-one hang. Lots of folks do."

"Not me. After what Slocum done to them nice folks, I want to see his neck stretched out 'bout six more inches, 'n I want to see his eyes pop near plumb out of his head."

"Here he comes!"

Every eye in the crowd turned toward the jail and they saw Slocum, flanked on one side by Marshal Ferrell and on the other side by Ferrell's deputy, Thurman Burns. Reverend E. D. Sweeny of the Church of God's Glory followed behind. By the time they had climbed the thirteen steps to the scaffold floor, Nigel Black, the hangman, was already there.

Marshal Ferrell stepped out to the front of the gallows platform, cleared his throat, and began to read. "Draw nigh and listen. Drury Slocum, having been tried before a jury of his peers, was found guilty of the heinous murder of Thad Gorman, Sue Gorman, Jimmy Gorman, and Ethel Gorman. Having been found guilty I, Amon T. Goff, Circuit Judge of Laramie County, sentence Drury Slocum to death by hanging. Sentence is to be carried out at the stroke of noon on the fifth day of this month."

The marshal folded the paper and looked out over the crowd, which represented nearly three hundred spectators. "Having been given the time and date of the execution, I, Marshal Bill Ferrell, have carried out my duty and delivered Drury to the place where he is to be hanged by the neck until dead."

Ferrell turned toward Slocum, who was standing on the trapdoor with his arms tied to his sides. The mask had not yet been put over his head, and the expression on his face could best be described as resigned.

"Does the prisoner have anything to say?" Ferrell asked Slocum.

"Is there anything I can say that would stop this hangin'?"

"No."

"Then no, I ain't got nothin' to say."

"Would you like the preacher to say a few words for you?"

"No."

Ferrell looked at the hangman. "Mr. Black, you may carry out your assignment."

Black started to put the mask over Slocum's head.

"I don't want that. I want to look right into the faces of all those who have come to—" Slocum stopped and stared at one man in the crowd. "You're here? I didn't think you would be here, but thank you. I'm glad you came."

The crowd was still wondering about Slocum's strange remark when the trapdoor was sprung. There was a collective gasp as the bottom half of his body dropped through the opening. He turned one quarter of a turn to the left then hung there with his tongue extended and his eyes open and bulging.

Some in the crowd grew sick.

Chapter Three

Three months later

Meagan Parker was sitting with Duff MacCallister at "their" table in Fiddler's Green Saloon. Although it was a saloon, it was considered a decent enough establishment that no stigma was attached to women who visited. She was discussing with Duff the prospect of taking some cattle to market

"According to the *Cheyenne Weekly Leader*, top steers are bringing eighty-seven dollars a head." She put some figures to a piece of paper and looked up with a broad smile. "Sixty-five thousand, two hundred and fifty dollars. That is, assuming we can get every head to the railroad without losing any of them."

"Sure 'n there's nae *we* in this, Meagan, as you will nae be for goin'," Duff replied.

"Are you forgetting, Duff MacCallister, that of the seven hundred and fifty head you'll be driving to Cheyenne, seventy-five of them are mine?"

"Aye, 'tis a ten percent owner of Sky Meadow you be, Meagan, 'n you are nae for letting me forget that."

"Duff, you aren't saying that you don't like having me as a partner, are you?" Meagan asked with a pout.

"Nae, lass, nae!" Duff said quickly, reaching over to lay his hand on Meagan's. "Sure 'n 'tis no finer partner I would be wantin'."

Biff Johnson laughed out loud. "Duff, I do believe the beautiful Miss Parker has her bridle on you." Biff, who had served with Custer in the Seventh Cavalry, was owner of Fiddler's Green. He had been standing close enough to overhear the conversation.

"'N would you be for tellin' me, Sergeant Major, if there be a more beautiful lass for me to submit to?"

"You've got me there, Duff, because I sure can't think of one."

"Here comes Elmer," Meagan said.

Like Meagan, Elmer was a partner in the ranch.

"Did Wang come into town with you?" Duff asked.

Wang Chow's absolute loyalty to Duff was earned when Duff kept him from being lynched. The offense for which he was being lynched was being Chinese while riding with a white woman.

"Nah, I left the heathen back at the ranch to get the cows gathered for the drive tomorrow."

Neither Duff nor Meagan questioned Elmer's use of the word *heathen.* They knew that Elmer and Wang were very close friends and would take a bullet for each other.

"Elmer, would you do me a favor and leave seventy-five of the cows behind?" Meagan asked.

"What?" the question came in unison from Duff and Elmer.

"Meagan, are you for saying that you don't want your cows to go to market?" Duff asked.

"Oh, I want them to go, all right. But since you won't let me go with you, I suppose my cows and I will just have to go on our own. I'm sure I can get someone to help. It's only a three-day drive, after all."

Elmer chuckled and shook his head slowly. "Duff, m' boy, I think the woman has got you caught in a vise."

Duff chuckled as well. "Meagan, let me ask you somethin', m' darlin'. Would you be for wanting to make the drive to Cheyenne with us?"

"Oh, well, now that you have asked so nicely . . . yes, I would love to make the drive with you. And now, if you'll excuse me, I'll go down to the shop and make some arrangements for it to be kept open without me for the next few days." She stood, leaned over, and gave Duff a quick kiss on his forehead, then hurried out of the saloon.

Duff watched her leave, then saw that Elmer and Biff were looking at him with a bemused expression on their faces. Duff held up his finger, then wagged it back and forth. "You dinnae have to say a word. I had it in mind all along to take her. 'Twas just giving her the chance to stay home if she wanted to without feeling guilty about it."

Biff chuckled. "Duff MacCallister, when has Meagan ever felt guilty about anything?"

After supper on the first evening of the drive when most of the others had bedded down for the night,

Meagan, who had been unable to fall asleep, decided to go for a walk. Within a few steps from the camp, she was enveloped in the darkness, and the night air felt good as it touched her skin with the softness of a lover's kiss. The sky above was filled with stars from the several very bright ones, to those of lesser intensity, down to small but still identifiable individual specks of light, and finally to a dim film where individual stars couldn't be seen but there was an awareness of their presence within that barely perceptible glow.

The cows, having spent the entire day moving, were quiet, some lying down while just as many were standing motionless but at rest. An owl landed nearby and his wings made a soft whirr as he flew by.

Meagan came to a small grass-covered knoll then looked down upon Bear Creek, the water a dark streak except for where the flowing stream broke over rocks, causing white feathers to form. The contrast between the dark water and the white swirls made the stream even more beautiful at night than it was by day. She sat down in the grass and pulled her knees up under her chin. The constant chatter of the brook soothed her, and she was enjoying the contemplative silence—a silence that was soon interrupted.

"Tell me, lass, would you be for wanting some company?" a voice asked.

"Oh, so now the man who would keep me from making the drive wants to spend some time with me?" Meagan teased, smiling back at Duff, who was climbing up the little hill toward her.

"What are you doin' out here so late?" he asked as he sat down beside her.

"I couldn't sleep."

"It has been a long day for you, Meagan, 'n 'twas early enough you had to get up this morning to come from town so you could be at the ranch in time to make this drive with us. I can nae imagine you having trouble falling asleep."

"I know I shouldn't be having any trouble sleeping, but my mind is so full of thoughts that sleep won't come."

"What is it you are thinking?"

Meagan smiled at him. "Duff, never ask a woman what she's thinking. She might tell you, and then you'll have no place to run."

"Och, 'tis silence I'll keep then," Duff replied, returning the smile.

The long moment of quiet was broken only by the soft sound of the flowing creek.

Meagan broke the silence. "Duff, do you miss Scotland?"

"Aye, lass, 'twould be lyin' if I said I didn't miss it. But there is nothing back there for me now, 'n if I were to return to Scotland, 'tis thinkin' I am that I would be for missing this place even more than I miss Scotland." He reached over to take Meagan's hand. "And 'twould be much more than a place I would miss."

"It's nothing we'll ever have to worry about. I don't intend to ever let you go." Meagan chuckled softly. "If I have to, I'll hog-tie you to keep you here."

Wang had made a private sleeping area for Meagan by dropping canvas down from the sides, front, and back of the hoodlum wagon. She had no idea what time it was when she finally crawled under the wagon but imagined that it must be eleven or later.

As she lay there listening to the snoring of a few of the cowboys who were sleeping nearby, she thought of her relationship with Duff. She loved him, and she was certain that he loved her. Meagan's sister Lisa, who lived in Rongis, Wyoming, had asked her on more than one occasion why she and Duff had never married. Lisa was married and often extolled the virtues of matrimony.

Marriage was always there, just beneath the surface in their relationship. They had never overtly spoken about it, but each knew that the other often thought about it. Back in Scotland, Duff's fiancée had been murdered on the night before they were to wed. Meagan knew that Skye McGregor would always occupy a chamber in Duff's heart, and she felt no jealousy over that. She thought of it only as proof that a man like Duff was capable of a love so intense that it could never die.

Was there room in his heart for another love as deep as the first? She was certain that there was, but she had no intention of forcing the issue. It would happen, when it would happen.

The next morning Duff was awakened by the smell of coffee brewing, bacon frying, and biscuits baking. In addition to Elmer and Wang, six cowboys were on the short drive: J. C. Jones, Larry Wallace, and Bill Lewis, who were Duff's permanent hands, and Eddie

Marshal, Merlin Morris, and Vernon Mathis, who were hands he had hired just for the drive.

Wang was the cook, but to say that he was just a cook was a huge understatement of the Chinese man's actual position. He was a cook, an assistant foreman to Elmer Gleason, a man of intense talent and abilities as a mechanic and technician.

More important, he possessed the most unique fighting skills of any that Duff had ever seen. Wang never used guns, but in a life-or-death situation one could never have a more valuable ally than Wang, nor a more dangerous foe.

"How come it is that in all the time you been here, you ain't never learned how to make grits?" Elmer demanded. "You're supposed to be my friend, but you ain't never made no grits for me."

"Grits look like very small grains of rice," Wang said. "I think if you eat rice it will be same."

"No, it ain't the same thing, you heathen celestial," Elmer said in frustration. "It ain't the same thing at all."

Duff approached just as the two friends were engaged in an argument that had become routine between them.

"I'm just disappointed that Wang has nae made neeps 'n haggis for us," Duff said.

"Argh, no!" Elmer called out. "Wang, you go ahead and cook all the heathen food you want, as long as it'll keep you away from that . . . that poison Duff calls food."

* * *

The next day the drive covered ten miles without incident, finding a place with water and grass that would keep the cattle contented. While two of the cowboys kept watch on the herd, Duff, Meagan, Elmer, and the remaining drovers settled down for the supper Wang had prepared.

"What we should have brought with us is one of Vi's pies," Duff said.

"We did," Meagan said. "I have four of them back in the hoodlum wagon. That should be enough to feed the entire crew. I was just looking for the best time to bring them out."

"Meagan, you brought pies?" Elmer asked.

"Two cherry pies and two apple."

"What a good thing for you to do. I'll tell you what. If Duff don't never marry you, I will."

Duff laughed out loud. "Aye, 'n what makes you think that any lass would be for wantin' to marry an old former pirate?"

"They's some out there that would," Elmer insisted. "'N you can mark my words on that."

"Vi would marry you," Meagan said.

"Why would Vi Winslow want to marry me?" Elmer asked. "She's much too grand of a woman to get tied up with the likes of someone like me."

"Don't put yourself down so, Elmer. You're as fine a man as I've ever known," Meagan said.

"I, uh, had better go check on the cows," Elmer said.

"What did I say that upset him?" Meagan asked as he walked away, quickly disappearing in the night.

Duff chuckled. "You dinnae upset him, lass, you

embarrassed him. Someone like Elmer isn't used to having someone say nice things about him."

"Well he should get used to it. I really do believe that he's as fine a man as I've ever known."

"Aye, 'n I'll nae be for disagreeing with you. Still, 'tis a hard thing for a man such as Elmer to be hearing people say good things about him."

Meagan smiled. "Yes, I can see that now. I shall try and be less effusive in the future."

One by one the other cowboys drifted off until only Meagan and Duff remained by the fire. A trapped gas bubble in one of the burning logs burst with a quite audible pop, and it sent some bright red sparks riding a heat wave up into the night sky to mingle with the stars.

One of the cowboys watching the herd began to sing.

> *It was early in the month of May,*
> *The rosebuds they were swelling;*
> *Little Jimmy Grooves on his deathbed lay*
> *For the love of Barbery Allen.*

> *He sent his servant into the town*
> *Where she'd been lately dwelling,*
> *Saying, "Bring to me those beautiful cheeks,*
> *If her name be Barbery Allen."*

"Oh, who is that singing?" Meagan asked.

"That would be Bill Lewis."

"Why, it's beautiful. I had no idea you had someone who could sing so well."

For the next few minutes Duff and Meagan stared quietly into the fire as they listened to the song.

So slowly, slowly she got up
And slowly she came a' nigh him
And all she said when she got there
Young man I believe you're dyin'

Oh yes I'm low, I'm very low
And death is on me dwellin'
No better, no better I never will be
If I can't get Barbery Ellen

Chapter Four

New York City

The Poindexter Railroad and Maritime Corporation occupied a six-story building on the corner of Fifth Avenue and 53rd Street. Preston Poindexter, the founder and president of the company, was one of the wealthiest men in America. At the moment he was standing at the window of his sixth-floor office, looking down at the traffic on Fifth Avenue—carriages, freight wagons, and trolley cars. His son, Jacob Poindexter, was sitting on a leather sofa in the same office.

Preston turned away from the window to talk to him. "Jake, would you mind telling me why in the world you want to go out west? There is plenty enough for you to do right here in New York."

"I'm twenty-two years old, Pa. Are you ready to put me in charge of your shipping company? Your railroad, perhaps?"

"Well no, I couldn't do that, Jake. I've got very good men in those positions, and you hardly have the experience to take on such a position of responsibility right now."

Instead of being defensive about such a remark as Preston thought he would be, Jake smiled.

"Thank you, Pa, you have just made my point. I am barely qualified to keep fresh coffee in the offices. That's why I want to take about a year to see the country and get a little experience."

"Why kind of experience?"

"Life experience," Jake said. "Pa, you started your career as a merchant mariner, you went from bosun's mate to captain, to owning your own ship. Once you and some of your crew were shipwrecked on a deserted island where you were stranded for three months. You've told me that being on that island and having to fight just to stay alive taught you more than anything else you had ever experienced. And now you own a shipping line and a dozen feeder railroads, and are one of the most successful business tycoons in America."

"It wasn't just me, Jake. There were eight of us on the island, and everyone filled a valuable role, especially the bosun." Preston was silent for a moment. "Truth is, I don't think any of us would have survived if not for the bosun."

"Yes, but you still profited from it. Unlike you, I've never had a similar experience."

"God in Heaven, Jake, you aren't saying you want to be shipwrecked, are you?"

Jake laughed. "I'm hardly saying that. But Pa, I'm starting out life as a very wealthy man. You know yourself that I have done nothing to earn this. I was born into luxury, I have never wanted for a thing, and I appreciate all you have done for me, I really do.

But I want to . . . no . . . I *need* to do something on my own. I want to come back and work for you, but when I do come back, I want to be an asset to you, not an obligation."

"And you think that getting some of these . . . these life experiences you're talking about will benefit you?" Preston asked with a stern, almost challenging expression on his face.

"Yes, Pa, I do."

The stern expression on Preston's face melted away to be replaced by a wide smile. "I believe so too, son, and I'm proud of you for thinking so. We're going to have to convince your mother to accept the idea of you being out on your own for a while, but as long as she knows that you'll not be moving out west for good, I'm sure that we can win her over. Where are you going, do you have any idea?"

"I'm going to Chugwater, Wyoming."

"You're going where? Chugwater, Wyoming? I've never even heard of the place."

"I had never heard of it either until I saw it on the map, way out there in Wyoming all by itself. And there was something about it, perhaps its isolation, which intrigued me. That's where I want to go."

"Can you reach this place . . . this Chugwater, by railroad?"

"No, but Cheyenne isn't too far away. I can take a train to Cheyenne, then when I get there I'll buy a horse and ride the rest of the way."

"Yes, that's a very good idea." Preston chuckled. "To tell you the truth, son, I envy you. I very much miss the adventures I once had. You have no idea how much I would like to get away from the boardroom, even if for no more than a few months."

"Oh, for heaven's sake, Pa, don't do that. Why, this company would collapse if you weren't at the helm."

"Ha. I thank you for your vote of confidence, but there's no real danger of that. Not as long as we have Norman Jamison. Mr. Jamison knows where all the skeletons are buried, so to speak, and as a matter of fact, he speaks for me. So while you're gone, if you need anything—money, influence, anything at all— you just get in touch with Norman. He may well be the most competent man I've ever known. I pay him an exorbitant salary because when the time comes for me to retire, I will want him here to help you take over the helm."

"Mr. Jamison is a good man, that's true, and he has already been very helpful to me," Jake replied.

"By being helpful to you, do you mean the time you got drunk and peed in the Union Club fountain and Norman kept it out of the papers?"

"Yes, I . . . Pa, how did you know that? Did Mr. Jamison tell you? He swore that he wouldn't."

"And he didn't. It was the maître d' of the club who told me."

"I'm sorry if you were embarrassed by it."

Preston laughed. "Son, why should I be embarrassed by it? I'm not the one who pissed in the fountain, you are. I would think you are the one who would be embarrassed."

Jake laughed as well. "You're right. I was embarrassed."

"What do you say that we go talk to your mother

now? I think if both of us discuss this with her that she'll not oppose the idea."

Unlike Preston Poindexter, who was a self-made millionaire, his wife Emma Marie was a Culpepper. Richard Culpepper had come to America in 1643 and was one of the founders of Scituate, Massachusetts. The Culpeppers were now a wealthy family from the Brahmin caste of New England. She had upset her family by marrying beneath her class even though Preston Poindexter's wealth was many times that of the Culpepper holdings.

"Oh, Jacob, you aren't serious. You actually want to go out into that godforsaken Wild West for who knows how long?"

"Yes, Mother, I do." At Emma's insistence, Jake addressed her as Mother, not as Ma, Mom, or Mama.

"It will be good for him, Emma," Preston said. "And it isn't as if he were going by wagon train into the great unknown. He'll be going by train. He won't be beyond the reach of telegraph, and I'll make certain that he has enough money to get by."

"I will be fine, Mother. You don't have to worry about me."

"All right. I suppose I won't be able to stop you. But, please, Jacob, be careful," Emma said, holding open her arms to invite an embrace from her son.

When Jake and Preston returned to the office, they went in to see Norman Jamison, who held the title of executive secretary of Poindexter Railroad and Maritime Corporation, or, as it was more generally called, the P R and M. Preston explained what Jake had in mind.

"Well now, that sounds like a very exciting proposition. Even the name 'Chugwater' evokes a sense of mystery," Jamison replied.

"Yes, sir, I must say I am looking forward to it," Jake replied.

"Norman, I want to give him some operating money. It's good to have an adventure, but it's even greater to have an adventure and money."

Jamison laughed out. "Indeed it is, sir. Do you have a sum in mind?"

"I was thinking in the neighborhood of twenty-five thousand dollars."

"Yes, that's a very nice neighborhood. But may I make a suggestion?"

"Of course."

"I would suggest that he take no more than five hundred dollars in cash, and the rest of the money can be deposited by wire in a bank in Chugwater."

"Yes, that's an excellent idea," Preston agreed.

"First, of course, I'll have to learn if Chugwater actually has a bank, and I can do that by sending a few telegrams. Give me some time to work on that, say, a day?"

"Sounds fine to me," Preston said. "You're not in that big of a hurry, are you, Jake? You can wait a day or two until Norman has everything set up for you?"

"Yes, sir. I'll need to tell some of my friends good-bye anyway."

Goodwin Ranch

It would take three days to drive the cattle from Sky Meadow Ranch to the railhead at Cheyenne, and while Duff and the others had spent the first two nights camped out, before leaving home they had made arrangements by telegraph to spend the third night at the Goodwin Ranch.

When Duff turned his cattle out on Goodwin range. the group of Black Angus stood apart from the Herefords of Goodwin's ranch. They did so not only in appearance, but also because the Sky Meadow cows tended to stay in familiar company so they remained in a cohesive group, apart from the Goodwin Ranch cattle.

"If they stay like this, we won't have no trouble in roundin' 'em up when we get started out again in the mornin'," Elmer said.

"You dinnae have to worry about the creatures staying together," Duff said. "Angus are a proud breed and they prefer their own company."

"Meagan is visiting with the Goodwins, is she?"

"Aye. The Goodwins have invited us for dinner tonight, you, Meagan, and me."

"Well, I 'preciate it, but I reckon I should eat with the men tonight. If anythin' comes up, why, I'll be there to handle it."

"Tell me, Elmer, is it being there to handle anything as may come up the reason, or is it that you just dinnae want to come?"

"You got me there, Duff. I ain't got no doubt but that the Goodwins is just real decent folks 'n all, but they seem a little too highfalutin for me. So, iffen it's all the same to you, well, I'd just as soon not go."

Duff chuckled. "All right. Dinnae you be worryin', lad, I'll be for comin' up with some excuse for you."

"Yeah, I figured you could do that."

"It's too bad Elmer can't come," John said at dinner. "That old man has some of the most fascinating tales to tell. He fought in the war, he was a fur trapper, he lived with the Indians. And to look at him, you would never know that he's been all over world."

"Aye, for he was a sailor."

"Ha. I wouldn't be surprised if somewhere he hadn't been a pirate."

Duff laughed as well, and though he didn't share it with John, Duff knew that while Elmer had never been a pirate on the high seas, he had actually ridden the outlaw trail for a while.

"Meagan, I hope you'll find the bed comfortable tonight," Edna said.

"Edna, I spent the last two nights on the ground under the hoodlum wagon," Meagan replied with a little chuckle. "Believe me, I'll be quite comfortable." She had been given the spare bedroom for the night.

Duff would be spending the night in the bunkhouse, though Elmer, Wang, and the others would be sleeping in the barn where there was plenty of straw to pad their sleeping rolls.

"Have you had any trouble moving your cows?" John asked.

"Nae, 'tis been an easy drive so far," Duff said.

"I'll be taking my own cows down to Cheyenne soon," Goodwin said. "It's too bad we don't have a railhead here. It would be so easy to just take them down to the track and put them on the train."

"Aye, but 'tis only one day for you to make such a drive, 'n but four days from Sky Meadow, so I can nae complain."

"That's true," Goodwin agreed. "A one-day drive, or even a four-day drive, is nothing. I didn't start here, you know. After the war many stray cows wandered around down in Texas belonging to whoever had the energy to lay claim to them. A few friends and I rounded them up and drove a herd of five thousand from Texas, intending to take them all the way to Missouri. When we got there we found out Missouri had a quarantine against all cows coming from Texas because of the tick fever. None of our cows were infected, but we had to take them to Abilene to get them on a train, and by the time we were finished, we'd been on the trail for two months." He made a scoffing sound. "And here I am, complaining about a one-day drive to the railhead in Cheyenne."

"Och, 'tis nae complaining, 'tis only discussing. When I first came here to start my own ranch I chose your ranch 'n the Davis ranch as the models for Sky Meadow."

Those two ranches were large enough that they'd appeared on all the maps of Wyoming when Duff first arrived in America. Now Sky Meadow was listed as well.

"Tell me, Duff, have you got your cows booked?" Goodwin asked.

"Aye, 'tis a buyer waiting for them."

"What are you getting for them, if you don't mind my asking?"

"Eighty-seven dollars a head," Meagan replied proudly, answering before Duff could.

"Eighty-seven dollars? That is a very good price. I'm only getting sixty-five dollars a head for my Herefords."

"Sure 'n haven't I been for telling you to switch to Angus?"

"Duff is on a one-man crusade to get every rancher in America to switch to Angus," Meagan said.

"Nae, lass, for if everyone would switch to raising Angus, we would lose the advantage we have. 'Tis only m' friends I'm trying to bring around."

"Then I consider it a compliment that you've asked me," John said with a smile.

Lula Belle and her daughter brought the meal in then and began setting the plates before the diners.

"It's lamb chops," Edna said. "I know that John considers me a traitor for eating lamb, but I love it so"

"Well John, you can call me a traitor or a heathen if you wish, but I love lamb as well," Duff said as he looked at his plate with eager anticipation.

Chapter Five

Poindexter Building

"My boy, I have been talking over your situation with Norman this morning, and he has come up with an idea," Preston said when Jake showed up in the office the next day. "Do you think Norman and I could interest you into turning your personal adventure into a business venture?"

"Well, yes, I suppose so. But what do you have in mind?"

"I would like for you to build a railroad."

"What?" Jake replied, shocked by his father's answer.

Preston glanced toward his Executive Secretary. "Norman, would you like to tell him what you told me?"

"I'll be glad to. Jake, come into the operations room and take a look at the map with your father and me, and I'll show what we have come up with," Norman invited.

Jake followed the men into the operations room, which was the largest room on the floor. It had long planning tables and maps of all the sea routes, as well as maps covering every Poindexter Railroad operation.

Poindexter owned no long-distance railroads; rather

he owned a dozen local railroads called spur lines that generally connected to track systems belonging to other companies. He had to pay a connection fee to the main line in order to operate them, not only when the connection was made, but also a commission on the traffic that was generated as a result of the connection.

In some places the Poindexter Railroads didn't connect to any other railroad right-of-way but merely connected a few of the towns in more remote areas. Making a medium or large town the hub meant it could deal with towns that may be separated by as many as a hundred miles. Although Poindexter didn't have to pay commissions because they were not connected to the larger railroads, they weren't as profitable.

"Look, you are going here, to Chugwater."

Though Jake had located the town many times on his own, he made no comment as Norman pointed it out to him.

"As you can see, Chugwater sits almost exactly halfway between Cheyenne and Fort Laramie. If we were to build a railroad from Cheyenne to Fort Laramie, it would make sense to set up our operating headquarters right here, in Chugwater. Such a railroad is bound to get some business from the army. In addition, we go through these three ranches, Goodwin, Davis, and Sky Meadow. They must be very large ranches or they wouldn't be depicted on the map, and I'm certain we can do business with them. Also our railroad would go through Walbach, Chugwater, Uva, and finally Fort Laramie. It looks to me like that would be about"—Jamison began to measure the distance on the map—"oh, I'd say a hundred and twenty miles. At ten thousand dollars per mile, we could build this railroad for one million, two hundred thousand dollars."

"One million, two hundred thousand? Oh, my, that is a lot of money. Do we have enough cash on hand to finance such an operation?" Jake asked.

Jamison chuckled. "Tell him, Mr. Poindexter."

"I'll be glad to. Son, we don't have to worry about the cost, because we won't be paying for it."

"Oh, I see. You are going to try and get the residents to pay for it," Jake said. "Won't that be pretty hard sell to get them to do that?"

"No, it's even better than that. We are going to let the government pay for the railroad from Cheyenne to Fort Laramie."

"Yeah, well, that'll be a pretty good deal, I suppose. But tell me, how are we going to get the government to pay for it?"

"They will pay for it by giving us land grants that we can sell, and they will grant us the power of eminent domain by which we can acquire the route for practically nothing."

"Why would the government do that?"

"America is a big country, Jake. It's to the government's advantage to reach as much of it as possible by track, so they encourage entrepreneurs in the building of railroads," Jamison explained.

"I had no idea this was how it was done," Jake said.

"Since you are going out there anyway, I'm going to put you in charge of building this railroad," Preston said.

"You want me to build the railroad? Pa, are you sure?"

"I've got confidence in you, son. All you need to do is develop a little confidence in yourself."

"You won't have to do it alone," Jamison said. "I have already arranged for you to be met in Cheyenne by a man named Roy Streeter. He'll probably be alone when he meets you, but he has been instructed to round up all the people you will need."

"You mean railroad construction crew?"

Jamison shook his head. "No, the actual construction will come later. The first and most important part of building the C and FL Railroad will be in getting title to the land you will need, not only the right-of-way but the sections of land that will used for financing the project. You'll need to stake out those claims, as well as make arrangements with the residents already there to acquire their land by act of eminent domain."

"C and FL?"

"Cheyenne and Fort Laramie Railroad," Preston said. "I came up with the name, but since you'll be building the railroad you can come up with a name of your own if you don't like that one."

"No, I like it fine. But Mr. Jamison, about this eminent domain thing," Jake said, letting the words hang without closing the question.

"What about it?"

"Doesn't that mean taking land from existing owners, even if they don't want to sell it to us?"

"It does," Jamison agreed.

"But won't we make enemies that way?"

"We may make some enemies," Jamison agreed, "but in the long run the railroad will be of such benefit to all the other residents in that area that we will be welcome. Even those who will have to give up their land to us will eventually come around. And if you encounter too much resistance, well, you'll have men to help you overcome whatever resistance you might face. Just don't give up until the job is done."

"What do you mean I'll have men to help? Mr. Jamison, are you suggesting that there might be physical confrontations?"

"I'm not only suggesting it, I'm saying there most likely will be. It has certainly happened before. But remember, you will be in the right, because you will have the law on your side."

"So, these men you are talking about will be like vigilantes? How is that even legal?"

"Vigilantes have no authority, these men will. In a manner of speaking, you could consider them as deputy U.S. Marshals. Actually, they will be railroad police, and the U.S. Marshals have recognized the authority of their operation."

"Has something like this ever resulted in . . ." Jake paused to form the question. "Well, I'll just come right out and ask it. Could there be shooting?"

"There have been shootings before, yes, and it could happen again. But you, personally, need not get involved with that part of it. That's why you will have a cadre of railroad police to handle that for you."

"Pa, you are willing to trust me with all this?" Jake asked.

"Yes, son, I am. That is, if you are willing to give it a try."

"Thanks, Pa." He took a deep and determined breath. "I'm ready for this."

* * *

From the *Chugwater Defender:*

Duff MacCallister and the Cattle Market

Duff MacCallister, the largest rancher in Chugwater Valley, is currently taking a small herd of Angus cattle to a buyer in Cheyenne. The Angus breed was introduced to the valley a few years ago when Mr. MacCallister founded his ranch, Sky Meadow. Originally from Scotland, it was while still a resident of that country that he first began to raise Angus cattle and indeed, Scotland is the country credited for developing the breed.

MacCallister is highly regarded by the citizens of Chugwater, not only for being the agent of an improved economy, but also because he has frequently brought outlaws to justice. The most recent example of that was in the role he and two of his employees played in capturing Drury Slocum, the despicable scoundrel who so brutally murdered the Gorman family, the mother and father and two children.

This newspaper is happy to report that the villainous reprobate Slocum will murder no more as he went to the gallows to pay the penalty for his misdeeds.

Immediately after reading the article three days ago, Grant Slocum had gone to Cheyenne, intending to be there before MacCallister arrived. Grant had been in the crowd when Drury was hanged. It was one of the ironies of life that because of a difference of opinion between the two men, seeing Drury being led to the gallows was the first time Grant had seen his brother in over two years.

"You're here? I didn't think you would be here, but thank you. I'm glad you came." Drury had said when he saw him. Those were the last words Drury spoke in his life.

As Grant sat eating the biscuit and bacon being served for breakfast in the Bella Union Saloon, he thought about why he was in Cheyenne. The disagreement between the two brothers had been so intense that at one time Grant had contemplated killing Drury himself. So, why hold it against a man who did what he had once thought about doing?

Grant answered his own question. Anything that had happened in the past between the two brothers no longer mattered. As far as he was concerned, Drury had made a moment-of-death reconciliation, and for that reason, Grant felt obligated to avenge his death.

Goodwin Ranch

Duff and Meagan took their breakfast with the Goodwins, though if Meagan hadn't been along, Duff would have preferred to eat in the ranch kitchen with his men and those who rode for the Goodwin brand.

Elmer and Wang were eating with the others.

"I ain't never seen no Chinaman cowboy before," said Woody, one of the Goodwin hands.

"Oh, Wang ain't just a cowboy," Elmer said. "He's a Shaolin priest."

"Shaolin? What kind of church is that?" Woody asked.

"It must be a Catholic church, seein' as they're the

only ones what's got a priest," figured one of the others, a man called Poke.

"Uh-uh, that ain't so. Episcopal churches, they got priests, too." This observation was made by Elmer. Then he laughed. "No, him bein' a priest don't have nothin' to do with a church. It's sort of a special Chinese kind of thing and you have to go to school for a long time to learn how to fight real good. And then once you learn, they call you a priest."

"What do you mean learn how to fight? You don't learn to fight, you just sort of fight, don't you?" Woody asked.

"Hit Wang," Elmer said.

Wang, who was enjoying his breakfast, was seemingly paying no attention to the conversation about him.

Woody frowned. "What do you mean, hit him? Why would I want to do that?"

"Because I just want to show you that you can't."

"I don't want get him mad at me."

"He won't get mad at you, on account of even if you try, you won't be able to hit him."

"Ha. So if I tell 'im I'm goin' to hit him, what will he do, run away?"

"Don't tell 'im, just go over there 'n try 'n hit 'im when he's not expectin' it. You won't be able to, but you can at least try."

"If I sneak up behind 'im, 'n don't say nothin' to 'im, I'll be able to hit 'im, all right," Woody insisted.

"I'll give you a dollar if you can do it."

"A dollar? I don't never bet that much money, but it's awful temptin'."

"It's not a bet," Elmer said. "If you can't do it, you

don't have to give me nothin', but if you can do it, I'll give you a dollar."

"Hey, Woody," Foster said. "Come 'ere."

Woody, Foster, and Poke held a quick conference, speaking so quietly that Elmer couldn't hear them. Then they separated and began to approach Wang, Foster from the left, Poke from the right, and Woody from behind.

Elmer watched and smiled at whatever plan they had concocted.

"Hey, Wang, I got somethin' I'd like you to look at," Foster said.

Wang looked toward Foster, just as Poke ran toward him. Woody, taking advantage of the distraction, snuck up from behind and quickly and quietly swung at him with an open hand. He didn't actually want to hurt Wang, he just wanted to prove that he could, and win the dollar.

Sensing that Woody was there, Wang ducked just far enough to avoid Woody's hand, grabbed the arm and, using Woody's momentum, turned him so that he and Poke collided.

Wang turned toward Foster. "What do you wish me to see?"

"I, uh, that is . . ." Foster said, stunned by what he had just seen.

Elmer laughed out loud.

Half an hour later, Elmer, Wang, and the other Sky Meadow drovers joined Duff and Meagan out in the south pasture. The air resonated with the bawling and the rumble of cattle activity. The sun shining down on the 750 gathered Angus caused a pungent smell, actually more of an odor at first, though it was a scent to which the men who worked around cattle quickly adjusted, so that it became a familiar part of their lives.

When all the drovers were in position, Elmer rode up to Duff and Meagan, both of whom would be riding at the head of the herd.

"We're ready to go," Elmer reported.

"You want to move us out, Meagan?" Duff grinned.

Meagan smiled back, then turned her horse about so that she was facing the drovers. Standing in the stirrups, she let out a loud call. *"Eeeee-yah, yip, yip, yip, hoo-yah!"*

Her call was answered by all the other drovers with shouts and whistles so that the herd, spurred on by all the noise, began their slow but steady movement south toward the cattle pens at the Cheyenne railhead.

Chapter Six

Cheyenne

The drive from Goodwin's Ranch was easy and uneventful, and they reached Cheyenne by midafternoon, stopping about a mile north of the city limits.

"Elmer, I'll be for leaving the herd here in your hands while Meagan and I go in and make arrangements for the sale."

Leaving the herd, Duff and Meagan rode on ahead. Viewed in comparison to Chugwater, the town of Cheyenne was a metropolis. Both sides of the street were lined with multi-story masonry buildings, some of which were as high as four stories. A stagecoach from the Black Hills Stage & Express Line, its team of six horses standing quietly, obediently, was taking on passengers from the stagecoach depot.

They could hear the bawling of cows as they approached the pens. Unlike the smell of cattle on the move or even on the range, this odor was quite pungent due to the fact that the cattle were confined, and their droppings were concentrated.

Dismounting in front of the office, Duff and

Meagan stepped inside to the reception area, where a very thin man with a sharp nose and light blue eyes sat behind a desk. A sign on his desk identified him as Stan Feeler, and he looked up as Duff and Meagan approached.

"Yes?"

"I would like to meet with Mr. Heckemeyer," Duff said. "I've a herd of Angus just outside of town, and I've had a telegraphic exchange with him, so he'll be expecting me."

"What's your name?"

"MacCallister. Duff MacCallister."

Feeler lifted a receiver from a telephone box, then turned the crank. "Mr. Heckemeyer, there is a Duff MacCallister here to see you. Yes, sir." Putting the receiver back in the hook, he pointed to one of four doors that opened from the reception area. "He's in there. You can go on in."

Duff knocked lightly on the door and, receiving an invitation, opened the door then followed Meagan inside.

"Mr. MacCallister, what do you have for me?"

"I have seven hundred and fifty Angus, and 'tis holding them I am, just north of town. Before I bring them in, I wanted to be sure that you had space for them."

"Oh, yes indeed, we have space for them. Angus, you say? Well, they're bringing top dollar right now, about—"

"Eighty-seven dollars per head," Meagan said, interrupting Heckemeyer.

Heckemeyer laughed. "That is absolutely correct, young lady. You have done your research."

"It wasn't hard to do. I read it in the paper."

"Come with me and I'll show you which pens I have reserved for you."

Duff and Meagan followed Heckemeyer outside, where he called out to someone who was leaning against the corral fence. "Creech, show Mr. MacCallister where he is to bring his cows."

"What cows would them be, Mr. Heckemeyer? I don't see no cows." Creech was a few inches shorter than Duff, with close-set dark eyes, dark hair and eyebrows, and a short, scraggly black beard.

"They'll be here shortly, as soon as I know where to be taking them," Duff said.

"You ain't American, are you, MacCallister? But you ain't Mexican neither. I don't know as I've ever heard nobody that talks like you do."

"I'm Scots."

"Scott? I thought Mr. Heckemeyer told me that your name was MacCallister."

"Scots means that I'm from Scotland."

"Scotland, yeah, seems to me I've heard of it, but don't know nothin' about it, or where it is. Anyhow, when you get the cows, we can put 'em in here."

"I'll be for bringing them now," Duff said as he and Meagan remounted.

"What an ill-mannered person this man Creech is," Meagan said. "He didn't even acknowledge my presence."

"Aye, he was a bit impolite," Duff agreed. "But we'll nae be seeing much o' him."

It took less than fifteen minutes to reach the herd where they were met by Elmer.

"Did we get what we were thinkin' we would get?"

"Aye. Your share will come to almost ten thousand dollars."

Elmer smiled broadly. "Well, what are we doing just standin' aroun' like this? Let's get these here cows to market."

"We'll take them down Snyder Street," Duff said. "That's a quiet street, but we must keep them bunched tightly so as not to be for causing any trouble."

"If we keep 'em bunched too close, it's goin' to stretch out the herd a long way," Elmer said.

"I've done some calculations," Meagan said. "If we keep them six abreast, we'll have a line about two hundred fifty yards long. Staggering the men will let us have someone on one side or the other every twenty-five yards. We should be able to keep them under control that way."

Elmer laughed out loud. "Whooee, Duff." He jabbed his finger toward Meagan. "Now that is one smart little lady there."

"Aye," Duff agreed with a wide smile. "Meagan is a lass of uncommon intelligence. "

"Wang, Jones!" Elmer shouted and Wang and Jones came riding up. "We need to get the herd moving." Elmer gave the two men Meagan's explanation as to how the cows were to be moved.

The residents of Cheyenne were used to seeing cattle being driven through town, though the fact that these were Angus rather than Herefords did draw a little extra attention. Many stood out in their front

lawns to watch the cattle pass. Several young boys
ran down the street keeping pace with the parade
until it reached the Union Pacific tracks. There, the
punchers swung the line of cattle to the left and
crossed a sidetrack just before they approached the
cattle pens which were about 150 yards west of the
freight depot.

Creech, Heckemeyer, and Feeler were waiting for
them. Feeler was perched on the fence next to the
gate, and he had a tablet and pencil in his hand.

"We need to control the entry into the pen so that
Mr. Feeler can count them," Heckemeyer said. "I
think we can get them all in in little over half an
hour."

"Aye, we'll manage the herd for you till all the creatures are in," Duff said.

"Mr. Heckemeyer, would you mind if I sat on the
fence on the opposite side of the gate from Mr. Feeler
so I could also make a count?" Meagan asked.

"I have no problem with it at all." Heckemeyer
smiled. "In fact, it'll be good to have a backup count."

"All right. Let's bring 'em in!" Elmer called loudly.

Prodded by the drovers, the cows started in through
the gate, which was only wide enough to allow four at
a time to enter.

Just over half an hour later, Feeler gave his report.
"I counted seven hundred and fifty two."

"Does that match your count, Miss Parker?" Heckemeyer asked.

"I have exactly seven hundred and fifty."

"It could be that I counted a couple of them
twice. Thank you for your honesty, young lady." This
from Heckemeter.

* * *

The First Bank and Trust of Cheyenne was but one block north of the Union Pacific Depot on 16th Street, and there Duff presented the draft Heckemeyer had given him for the cattle. The draft was for sixty-five thousand, two hundred and fifty dollars, and Duff asked for one thousand dollars in cash, the remaining money to be transferred by wire to the Bank of Chugwater.

"Gentlemen, 'tis thanking you I am for a job well done." Duff said as he gave each of the drovers one hundred dollars apiece. For the three men who worked for him full-time, the one hundred dollars was a bonus in addition to their regular salary. He gave Wang two hundred dollars. Fifteen percent of the money actually belonged to Elmer, and he, like Meagan, left the money intact to be moved by wire transfer to the Sky Meadow account at the Bank of Chugwater.

"We'll see you when you get back," Elmer said as he and the others started back to the ranch.

Duff and Meagan weren't returning right away. They had taken a room in the Interocean Hotel and were going to stay one more night in Cheyenne to attend a performance at the Cheyenne Opera House.

"Your share comes to a little over sixty-five hundred dollars," he said later that evening as he spread butter on his roll during dinner in the dining room of the hotel. "You'll be for putting it in your shop?"

"I will do no such thing," she replied. "Didn't you say that you needed a new barn and corral fencing at the ranch?"

"Aye, but there's nae need for you to be for spending any of your money for such a thing."

"You forget, Duff MacCallister, that ten percent of that ranch belongs to me. And as I am taking ten percent of the profits, then I'll be responsible for ten percent of the expenses as well."

"Will you be now? 'Tis glad I am to hear you say that, Meagan, for it makes me think you'll not soon be wantin' to be for runnin' away from me."

Meagan put her hand on Duff's hand and smiled across the table at him. "Duff," she said in throaty voice. "We have taken only one room at the hotel. How far can I run?"

"Aye, you make a good point," Duff agreed.

"I'm really looking forward to attending the opera," Meagan said. "I picked up the playbill. Let me read to you what it says.

"*Olivette* is a comic opera in three acts. It is a romance story about a young woman named Olivette, who is in love with Valentine, but is engaged to a sea captain, who she refuses to marry. When Valentine secretly weds Olivette, the sea captain declares that Olivette is his rightful bride and he has Valentine is arrested. Olivette is disowned, but eventually her marriage to Valentine is upheld."

"Och, I can tell you from my time at sea, you dinnae want to get involved with a sea captain."

Meagan smiled. "And here I've always thought that a sea captain would be quite a romantic figure. But you're right. It's much better to be involved with a Scotsman."

"Aye, lass, 'n you'll nae be for forgetting that."

* * *

"Oh, isn't it beautiful?" Meagan asked an hour later when she and Duff entered the theater.

A huge chandelier hung from the very high, vaulted ceiling, with its fifty-two electric bulbs providing very bright lights. The railings were upholstered with plush red silk. The woodwork was ornately carved, and there were three cathedral windows at the rear of the balcony with 600 colored glass panes. The grand stairway to the balcony was built of hardwood, ash, and black walnut. When Duff and Meagan took their seats, they were looking at a drop curtain portraying a Roman chariot race, illuminated by an array of very bright footlights that stretched across the stage.

The orchestra began the overture starting with flutes and drums. Then the sea captain took the stage, singing of how he had come to claim Olivette as his own.

As Duff and Meagan were enjoying the opera, Lou Creech, the employee at Heckemeyer's Stock Exchange, had invited his friend Joe Rudd to his room in the boardinghouse where he lived.

"I was there when he brung the cows in, 'n I heard Heckemeyer, Feeler, 'n MacCallister talkin' 'bout the money. He got near sixty-five thousand dollars for them cows."

"Yeah, that's a lot of money, all right," Rudd said.

"'N we're goin' to take it from 'im," Creech added.

"How we goin' to do that?" Joe Rudd asked. "I seen

'em bring them cows in. They was at least half a dozen men with 'im, maybe even more."

Creech smiled. "No, they ain't with 'im no more. They all went back soon as the cows was delivered. Only ones that didn't go back was MacCallister 'n the woman that come with—'em. Pretty thang she is, too," he added, digressing for a moment. Then he returned to the subject. "Anyhow they're over in the opry house now, the man 'n woman I mean, a-watchin' 'em a show. I heard 'im tellin' Heckemeyer about it. They ain't plannin' on startin' back till tomorrow mornin'. Him bein' the one that owns all the cows, well you just know that he'll be a-carryin' all the money on 'im."

"'N you're a-sayin' that they's just the two of 'em?"

"Yeah, just two of 'em, 'n like I said, one of 'em is a woman."

"Damn. We can wait for 'em out on the trail 'n pick 'em off real easy," Rudd said.

"That was my thinkin'," Creech said.

"Sixty-five thousan'?"

"That's what he got paid for the cows."

"That's more money than I ever seen all put together in my whole life," Rudd said.

"What you plannin' on doin' with all your money when you get it?" Creech asked.

"I don't know. I can't stay here with all that money 'cause folks would start to askin' questions. So I reckon I would go someplace else where they don't nobody know me, 'n then just start spendin' the money. What are you goin' to do?"

"It's like you said, they can't neither one of us stay here once we got all that much money, 'cause folks will start wonderin' how it is that we come up with it.

So what think I'm goin' to do, is I'm goin' to go some'ers else 'n buy me a saloon, maybe in Nevada or California or maybe even in Arizona. 'N I'm goin' to have me some whores a-workin' there, 'n I'll be able to drink all the beer 'n whiskey I want, 'n take any 'o the whores upstairs anytime I want 'cause they'll all be a-workin' for me, 'n they can't tell me no, on account if they do I can fire 'em," Creech said.

Rudd laughed. "Yeah, that sounds like a good idea. Maybe we ought to go into business together. That way we can get a bigger saloon with more whiskey 'n more whores. 'Course, we got to get the money first."

"Yeah, well if we play our cards right we won't have no trouble a-doin' that," Creech said.

After the opera, Duff and Meagan walked through the dark for the two blocks between the Cheyenne Opera House on 18th Street and the Interocean Hotel on 16th.

"Sure 'n it all came out just fine in the end with the girl getting the man she wanted instead of the evil ship's captain," Duff said.

"What about *this* girl?" Meagan asked. "Will I get the man I want?"

"Meagan, when you are ready to be for leavin' your dress shop so as to become Queen of Sky Meadow, I want you to be for knowin' that m' heart and m' doors are open to you.

"What about tonight?" Meagan asked. "Will your door and your heart be open tonight?"

"Meagan, innocent lass that you be, I can only take

it that you've nae idea of the shameful proposal you have just made."

Meagan looked up at him with a wanton smile on her lips. "Duff, m' lad, you are for knowin' that 'tis not all that innocent I am, 'n 'tis with full understandin' o' the scandal of m' words that I did speak with you," Meagan said in a perfect imitation of Duff's brogue. "Sure, for 'tis into m' own bed that I'm invitin' you."

Duff laughed then reached out to put his arm around her shoulders and pull her closer to him as they approached the front of the hotel.

"'Tis a wanton lass you be, Meagan Parker, 'n with a Scottish brogue, too. 'N I'll have you be for knowin' that 'tis every bit to my liking."

Chapter Seven

Chicago, Illinois

    TRAIN ARRIVES CHEYENNE 11PM
    THURSDAY STOP HAVE MEN READY

Just short of one thousand miles east of Cheyenne, the *Pacific Flyer*, which had left Grand Central Depot in New York two days earlier, was pulling out of Chicago. Jake Poindexter, who had a private compartment on the train, was sitting at a table in the club car, looking through the window at the dark outside. He could see the squares of light projected from the windows as they slid along the ground, matching the better-than-thirty-miles-per-hour speed of the train.

A man approached his table. "You're Jake Poindexter, aren't you?" He was clean-shaven, and wearing a black broadcloth suit.

"Yes, I am. Do I know you?" Jake asked with a puzzled expression on his face.

"I remember you from the football game we

played. I was with Michigan. You played for the Harvard eleven."

"Yes, yes, I remember that game. It was the first western team we had ever played. We beat you, I believe."

"And beat us rather thoroughly, I'm sad to say. We were a lot of inexperienced players without teamwork, depending entirely on individual play. Our halfbacks, I believe, were equal to any we met, but our line was weak, the men being light and having little experience. Most of us had never played in a match game and some of us had never seen a copy of the rules." The young man extended his hand. "My name is Collins, Ed Collins. It's an honor to meet you, without having to tackle you. As I recall, that was rather difficult to do," he added with a friendly smile.

"Well, I'm happy to say that my days of getting tackled are well behind me. Say, Ed, why don't you join me for a drink?" Jake invited.

"Thank you. I would glad to," Collins said, sitting across from Jake.

Jake raised his hand to signal the porter.

"You are from New York, I believe," Collins said. "What are you doing this far from home?"

"I'm going to Chugwater, Wyoming."

"Chugwater? That sounds interesting, but I must admit that I've never even heard of the place. Why are you going to such a remote location?"

"You might say that it is my last leisurely experience before I settle down. Oh, wait, that's not entirely true.

As it turns out there will be very little leisure in this adventure. I will also be building a railroad."

Collins chuckled. "Don't you mean your father will be building the railroad? I am very familiar with Mr. Preston Poindexter and the Poindexter Railroad and Maritime Corporation. Everyone is."

"Well, let's just say that I will have my father's backing, but I am proud to say that it is I who will be building the railroad. However I wouldn't be truthful if I didn't say that I'm also feeling some apprehension over the project."

"So you're going to be building the railroad, are you? I must confess that I'm having a difficult time picturing you out in the hot sun, swinging a sledge hammer," Collins said.

Jake laughed. "Oh, heavens, when I say I'm going to build a railroad, I don't mean that I am physically going to be laying track."

"Then I don't understand. How will you be building a railroad if you aren't actually building it?"

"When the time comes to start the actual construction I'll hire people to lay the rails and swing the hammers. But there's a lot to be done beforehand in securing the financing and acquiring the right-of-way. And I'll be able to do that with this." Jake took an envelope from his jacket pocket and handed it to Collins.

"What is this?"

"It's a letter appointing me as my father's surrogate in all business deals, especially in securing government grants and the power of eminent domain." Jake pulled the letter from the envelope. "Here, perhaps this will explain."

POINDEXTER RAILROAD AND MARITIME CORPORATION
Fifth Avenue, New York, N.Y.
PRESTON C. POINDEXTER, *President*

Assignment of Authority

Know you all by these presence that I, Preston Clark Poindexter, President of Poindexter Railroad and Maritime Corporation, do appoint the holder of this letter, my son Jacob Byron Poindexter with power of attorney to exercise eminent domain, acquire government land grants, deposit and withdraw funds from the Poindexter account at the Bank of Chugwater, and do all such as must be done in the building of a railroad from Cheyenne, Wyoming to Fort Laramie, Wyoming.

My hand and seal:

"Tell me about this eminent domain and government grant thing. What does that have to do with your building a railroad?"

"Oh, it has everything to do with it," Jake said excitedly. "Here, let me buy you dinner and I'll explain it all to you."

"Well, that's very generous of you," Collins replied. "Thank you."

"It must be very expensive to build a railroad," he said a few minutes later as the two men enjoyed a meal of fried trout.

Jake explained the concept of government financing to his new friend.

"So what you are saying is, you can make a lot of money building a railroad," Collins said.

"Oh, yes, and the beauty is you can make money while building it, and of course once it is built, you can make money from the operation of the railroad."

"No wonder Preston Poindexter is so wealthy," Collins said. "You are a lucky man to have him as your father."

"You're right. It is just a matter of luck. I've certainly done nothing to earn it." Jake smiled. "But now that I am going to be put in charge of building the C and FL Railroad, I hope to rectify that."

"C and FL?"

"Cheyenne and Fort Laramie."

"Yes, C and FL indeed," Collins replied.

"I must say, Ed, I'm glad you dropped by. It's good to have a friend on such a long journey."

"It is at that," Ed replied with a warm smile.

Cheyenne

Having breakfast in the dining room of the Interocean Hotel the next morning. Meagan poured coffee for Duff, then for herself. "Thank you for changing your mind and allowing me to come to Cheyenne."

Duff chuckled. "Allowing you to come? Sure 'n it seems to me like you had all intentions of coming whether it be with me or by yourself."

"Well, that's true," she said with a broad smile. "But I'm sure that being included was much better than it would have been if I had tried to bring seventy-five cows all by myself."

"Aye, 'twould have been a difficult task for a wee lass such as yourself. 'N after the great pleasure you gave me last night, 'tis more than happy I am that you are here with me."

"Duff!" Meagan said, her cheeks flaming red. "That's not something we should be talking about in public."

"Sure, lass 'n I'm for talking about the opera we saw. What do you think I'm talking about?"

"I . . . uh . . . never mind," Meagan said in chagrin.

Duff reached his hand across the table to take hers. "Lass, I've nae wish to embarrass you. Every moment we spend together is a pleasure for me' 'n I've nae wish to ever do a thing that would cause you to be uncomfortable."

The expression on Meagan's face changed from one of chagrin to one of contentment. "I hope the opera wasn't the only thing you enjoyed last night," she said with a sensual smile.

Their intimate moment was interrupted by the arrival of the waiter, bringing their breakfast.

"Ah, good," Duff said. "Eat hearty, lass, for 'tis my intention to get all the way back today, 'n we'll likely have naught but jerky in the saddle for our lunch."

Having followed Duff from the moment he'd reached Cheyenne, Slocum had stood nearby, watching as the cattle had been loaded into the holding pen. He had been in the bank, ostensibly waiting to convert a twenty-dollar bill into twenty ones, when he overheard Duff making arrangements to send the money back to Cheyenne.

You'll never make it back to get that money, he'd thought, even as he'd wished there was some way he could get to it. After learning that MacCallister was staying at the Interocean Hotel, Grant Slocum had taken a room there, as well.

During breakfast, he studied MacCallister and the woman who was with him.

They would be returning to Chugwater today, and Slocum intended to meet them on the road. He would have the advantage because the two men had never met. He had started out with the intention only of killing only MacCallister but realizing that the woman would be going back to Chugwater with him, Slocum knew that he would have to kill her as well. A moment later, he decided that she might turn out to be a bonus. After all, she was a very pretty woman.

As Duff and Meagan ate their breakfast and Grant Slocum watched them while contemplating their fate, about eight miles north of town Creech and Rudd were already in position and waiting alongside the road. They had arrived before sunrise, and Rudd was dozing.

"Wake up," Creech said, shaking him by the shoulder. "What if they was to come by now 'n you're asleep? What good would you do me?"

"I wasn't asleep," Rudd said. "I was just restin' my eyes is all."

"Keep your eyes open is all I'm sayin'. Maybe thinkin' 'bout all that money will keep you awake."

* * *

Less than a mile south of where Creech and Rudd were waiting, Duff and Meagan were riding at a smooth, rhythmic pace. Just below a trot, it was swift and ground eating.

"Wouldn't it be nice if we had a railroad from Cheyenne to Chugwater?" Meagan asked.

"Why Meagan, 'n would you be for saying that you don't like riding with me?"

"What? No, I'm not saying that. But if we were on a train now, we could be sitting on cushioned seats, sitting close together I might add, and it would take only about two hours. Also we could eat in the dining car, rather than sit in a saddle chewing on a piece of leather."

Duff chuckled. "So you think jerky is leather, do you? 'N here I've selected the choicest cuts for you to enjoy."

Meagan laughed. "Tell me, Duff, exactly how does one go about selecting the choicest cuts of jerky?"

"Oh, 'tis easy if you know how to go about it."

At that very second Duff and Meagan's conversation was interrupted by the sound of two gunshots. One bullet came so close to Duff's head that he could hear the buzz of its passing. Meagan cried out and fell from the saddle.

"Meagan!" Duff shouted as he leaped from the saddle. He saw blood on her upper arm and even as there were two more shots, marked by the dirt that was kicked up near them, Duff put his hands under her shoulders and dragged her off the road and down into a small drainage ditch that ran parallel to the road.

Meagan grunted in pain.

"I'm sorry," he apologized, taking a closer look at the wound. "Looks like it just cut a groove in your arm. I know it's painful, but 'tis not all that bad."

"So you say. You aren't the one with a hole in your arm."

Despite their situation, Duff chuckled. "Now I know you'll be all right."

"MacCallister!" someone called from the other side of the road. "Give us your money, 'n we'll go away."

"Money? What money?"

"The sixty-five thousand dollars you got from Hecke-meyer."

Duff recognized the voice as the man who had shown him the pen to be used. "Is this Creech?"

"Yeah, this is Creech. And I know you got the money, 'cause I seen you get it."

Grant Slocum had been trailing Duff and Meagan, having followed them from Cheyenne. The sound of the shots startled him, and he stopped to listen, wondering if there might be some way he could capitalize on what was happening just ahead of him.

Duff, having no idea that he had adversaries ahead and behind him, spoke to Meagan. "I've got an idea," he said quietly.

"What kind of idea?" Meagan asked.

"I'm going to let them shoot me."

"That doesn't sound like much of an idea to me. As a matter of fact, it sounds foolish."

"Trust me."

"I trust that you aren't seriously going to let them shoot you," Meagan replied.

"Pull your pistol and be ready."

"Be ready for what?"

"Lass, would you just be doin' it?"

"All right," Meagan replied, doing as Duff asked.

"Creech!" Duff shouted.

"Yeah, what is it? You're goin' to give us the money?"

"I'm nae going to give you anything! You killed my woman 'n now I'm goin' to kill you!"

Meagan gasped, and Duff put his finger across his lips. "Be quiet. Don't say anything no matter what you see or think you see."

"What are you going to do?" Meagan whispered.

"Just be ready." He shouted again. "Creech! You killed my woman, 'n I'll be for comin' after you now."

Duff looked at Meagan and she nodded to indicate that she was ready. Then he stood up and started running down the road, not toward Creech, but parallel to and very close to the ditch. He threw a shot toward where he had seen the puffs of gun smoke. It wasn't an aimed shot, but there was no need for it to be.

"I'm coming after you, Creech!" he shouted again.

There were two more gunshots.

"Uhn!" Duff called out, and slapping his hands over his stomach, he fell, then rolled down into the ditch.

Meagan was shocked and started to call out, but

she saw Duff looking back at her and holding his hand out as if asking her to be silent and wait. She realized then that this was all a ruse.

"We got the diry devil!" This was Creech's voice.

"Think he's dead?"

Duff didn't recognize the second voice.

"If he ain't dead yet, he soon will be. Now that he knows who I am, I can't let 'im stay alive. Let's go finish off both of 'em, take the money, 'n get outta here."

"He said the woman was already dead."

"We'll make sure. Let's go shoot 'em both."

Having dismounted when he heard the first shots, Slocum advanced up the road, hoping to be in position to take advantage of the situation. He had heard the latest exchange of gunfire and the conversation between someone named Creech and whoever was with him.

Had they actually killed MacCallister? Whoever Creech was, he was convinced that Duff MacCallister had the money from the sale of his cattle. Slocum already knew the money wasn't on him, but these two men thought MacCallister had the money, and that was all the incentive they needed to kill him.

Slocum turned around and started back toward his horse. He didn't need to be seen by Creech and the other man right now. Once they discovered that MacCallister had no money, they were going to be in a very foul mood. Besides, MacCallister was dead, so there was no need for him to hang around.

* * *

Duff could hear Creech and the other man climbing down from the slight rise where they had been waiting, then start across the road. He held out his hand toward Meagan, signaling for her to be ready. Meagan nodded back at him, then raised her pistol and pulled back the hammer.

"I seen 'im drag the woman in over there," Creech said, pointing. "You go shoot 'er a couple more times, 'n I'll make sure MacCallister's dead. Then we'll get the money 'n get on out o' here."

The two men approached the edge of the road, then they reached the ditch and raised their pistols.

"Now!" Duff shouted, pulling the trigger even as he called out.

Meagan responded instantly, and Creech and Rudd were dead even before they had time to be surprised.

Fifty yards down the road, Grant Slocum heard the latest outbreak of gunfire and he smiled. That would be the assailants finishing off MacCallister and the woman. On the one hand, Slocum was satisfied that MacCallister was dead, and he didn't even mind that he didn't personally kill him. But on the other hand, he regretted that he had no opportunity to take advantage of the woman who had been with him. She was one very good-looking woman, and he felt a little tingling in his groin as he thought about what might have been.

* * *

Back at the site of the ambush, Duff, totally un-aware of the presence, or even the existence, of Grant Slocum, climbed up from the ditch and checked on the two who had attacked them. Both men were dead.

"Stay there," Duff said. "I'll go get our horses."

"Duff, we can't leave them just lying here in the road."

"You're right. I'll get their horses too, 'n we'll take them on into Walbach, which is just another few miles. That's closer than going back to Cheyenne, and when we get there we can have a doctor look at your wound."

Chapter Eight

Duff located the horses the two outlaws had picketed and took them down to where the men lay dead in the road. He had no way of knowing which outlaw belonged to which horse, but it didn't seem to make any difference to the animals, so he draped the bodies across the saddles. Leading the horses, he and Meagan continued north to Walbach, which was only about three miles farther.

The little town had grown up where once had stood the army post of Camp Walbach. The post had been disbanded some time before, but the town remained. Duff and Meagan received no small amount of attention from the citizens as the four horses—two with bodies draped across the saddles and one ridden by a woman whose arm was red with blood—rode into town. The little caravan stopped at the marshal's office.

"Duff MacCallister!" the marshal said stepping out of his office with a welcoming smile of greeting. "What brings you—" he stopped in midsentence when he saw the two bodies and Meagan's bloody shirt-sleeve. "Good Lord, what happened?"

"Hello, Marshal Coats. We were accosted on the road by these two brigands who were bent upon robbing us," Duff said.

"Are these the only two?"

"Aye."

"Trying to rob you, you say?"

"I sold my cattle in Cheyenne, and they thought I had the money with me."

"Yes, I remember you bringing the herd through a couple of days ago," The marshal looked again at Meagan's wound. "Ma'am, are you in much pain?"

"Not too much," Meagan replied.

"She's a brave young lass," Duff said. "But I would like for a doctor to have a look at her wound."

"We don't actually have a doctor in town, but Miz Willis comes the closest to one, I reckon. She has potions and remedies for nigh onto ever'thang a person can come down with, 'n she has treated more 'n a few gunshot wounds," Marshal Coats said. "If you'd like, I'll send for her. If nothin' else, she can get you bandaged up good enough so's you can go on into Chugwater 'n see the doctor there."

"Yes, thank you. I would appreciate that."

Mrs. Willis was in her late sixties but still very active. The widow owned the boardinghouse in town, which, because there was no hotel, were the only accommodations available for anyone who needed them. Validating Marshal Coats's comment that she was the closest thing to a doctor they had in Walbach, she brought her medical bag with her.

"I hope you have another shirt to wear, dearie, because I'm about to tear this 'un off."

"In my saddlebag."

"I'll get it," Duff offered.

It took only a few minutes for Mrs. Willis to clean the wound, then apply a fresh bandage. "You're going to have to have the wound sewed shut. When you get back to Chugwater, you need to see Dr. Taylor first thing soon as you get there."

"Yes, thank you. I will."

As soon as Mrs. Willis was finished administering her treatment, and after assuring Marshal Coats that he would be available if anyone needed to discuss the incident in which the two men were killed, Duff continued on with Meagan to Chugwater. The trip took them another five hours, and it was quite late in the afternoon when they stopped in front of a low, brick building with a sign out front that read V. SCOTT TAYLOR, M.D.

Duff dismounted first, then went over to help Meagan down.

"Oh, for heaven's sake, Duff, I'm not crippled. I can get down myself."

"Aye, I know that, but 'tis only that I like holding you close to me."

"Oh, well why didn't you say so?" Meagan asked with a little smile, relaxing her body to the degree that helping her down required quite a bit of physical contact.

Dr. Taylor met them out front. "I got Marshal Coats's telegram saying that Meagan had been shot. Come on in. I'm all ready for you."

"Thank you, Dr. Taylor."

"Are you in any pain? Would you like some laudanum?"

"I have very little pain. But the truth is I don't know if I would want any laudanum anyway. I'm a little frightened of that stuff."

Dr. Taylor shook his head. "Yes, it's good to be frightened. Laudanum is most effective for easing pain, but it has a brutal side effect, in that it is very easy to get addicted to the drug. All right, come on in, and let me have a look."

Meagan peeled out of her shirt without any sense of shame or embarrassment.

"Mrs. Willis did such a good job of applying the bandage that I almost hate to take it off, but I have to examine the wound." Dr. Taylor used a pair of scissors to cut through the cloth then opened it as carefully as he could to minimize any pain. "Ah, good. The bullet cut a channel but didn't involve any arteries or muscle structure. You'll be good as new in no time."

A few minutes later Meagan looked down at the stitches Dr. Taylor had just applied.

"I'll put another bandage on and you can come back in about a week for me to look at it again and remove the stitches. As long as you keep it clean and sterilized, you won't have any trouble with it," Dr. Taylor said.

As they left the doctor's office a little later, Meagan asked, "Duff, if I bought a pie from Vi, do you think you could get Elmer to take it down to Mrs. Willis?"

"Aye, 'twold be no problem for him to do so. I'll be for asking him tonight when I get home."

"Would you like a drink before you go back?" she

asked. "We can stop in Fiddler's Green, and it'll be my treat since I have recently come into some money."

Duff chuckled. "Aye, that you have. All right, lass, I'll let you buy me a drink."

They dismounted in front of the saloon, tied their horses off, and went inside, where they were met immediately by Biff Johnson.

"Meagan, how is your arm?" Biff asked.

"How did you know about my arm?"

"Hodge Deckert told me. He told everyone."

"Does the telegrapher nae know the meaning o' the words 'private telegram'?" Duff asked.

"Don't be hard on him, Duff. You know that Hodge thinks the world of you and Meagan. He's just concerned, that's all."

"I'm sure he didn't mean anything by it, Duff." Meagan chuckled. "And it's nice to know that there are people who actually care."

"There a lot of people who care, Meagan," Biff said. "Oh, Duff, by the way you have some happy troopers working for you. Some of them have come in here since they came back, and they much appreciated the bonus you gave them." He chuckled. "And since they gave me their business, I appreciate it as well. You and Meagan find a table. I know what you'll be drinking, and I'll have Kay bring them to you."

"Kay?"

"That's right, you haven't met her yet, have you? She's my newest hostess."

Unlike the Wild Hog, which was the other saloon in Chugwater, the young women who worked at Fiddler's Green were hostesses, not soiled doves, although they did wear provocative apparel. When a young and very attractive woman approached the table a moment later bringing a glass of scotch from Duff's personal bottle for him and a sauvignon blanc for Meagan, her attire displayed all her attributes.

"Biff said you are new here," Meagan said. "Kay, is it?"

"Yes, ma'am."

"What brings you to Chugwater, Kay? I mean we are a little off the beaten path here, aren't we?"

"Yes, ma'am, I suppose it is. I'm originally from Jackson, but I left there. I was in Cheyenne when someone told me about this place, so I thought I might come up and see what I thought of it."

"What's the verdict? What do you think about us?"

"Oh, I think it is beautiful here. Just beautiful."

"So do I."

At that moment Kay noticed that two new customers had come into the saloon. "Oh, would you all excuse me? I need to get to work."

"Of course," Meagan said.

"Miss Kay is a most bonny lass," Duff said.

"She is at that. You know what? She would make a very good model for me to show off some of my designs."

"You wouldn't be for stealing her from Biff now, would you?"

"No, of course not. At least, not full-time. I'm sure Biff and I could work out some arrangement, and it would be a source of extra income for the young lady."

"Aye, I think that would a good thing for her."

Cheyenne

It was just growing dark when Roy Streeter rode into Cheyenne. He wasn't alone. Seven men—Jalen

Nichols, Bo Hawken, Dusty Caldwell, Morris Butrum, Hank Mitchell, Clete Dixon, and Pogue Flannigan— were with him.

"What time does the train get in?" Flannigan asked.

"Not until eleven o'clock tonight," Streeter said.

"What the hell? Do we have to wait down at the depot until then? That's almost midnight."

"There's no need for all of us to have to meet 'im. I'll do it by myself. The rest of you can wait in the saloon," Streeter said.

"Yeah, that sounds like a pretty good idea to me," Hawken said.

Streeter went into the Bella Union Saloon with the others, and while they flirted with the bar girls and drank rather heavily, Streeter needed to be sober when he met the train. He limited himself to two beers, drank them slowly, and kept an eye on the large stand-up clock clearly in view. When the hands on the clock indicated that it was a quarter till eleven, he drained the last of the beer, then stood up.

"You goin' to meet 'im now?" Hawken asked."

"Yes. You boys stay out of trouble," Streeter said. "I don't care how long you stay here tonight, but meet me for breakfast at the Railroad Hotel no later 'n seven o'clock tomorrow mornin'."

"Yeah, we'll be there," Hawken said. "If I have to, I'll tell the woman to wake me up at six tomorrow."

"What woman are you a-talkin' about, Bo?" Caldwell asked.

"I don't know," Hawken replied, glancing out at the several young women who were working the bar. "I ain't quite figured out yet which one of 'em it's goin' to be."

Streeter left to the sound of the other men laughing at Hawken's comment.

It was a short walk to the depot and when he arrived and checked the depot clock he saw that he still had a little over ten minutes remaining before the train was due to arrive. Going into the large Union Pacific Depot, he stepped up to a four-sided desk that created an enclosure in the center of the grand court. Signs on each of the four sides of the enclosure identified it as an information desk.

"Have you heard anything on the westbound? It's supposed to arrive at eleven o'clock," Streeter said. "Is it on time?"

"Yes, sir, we received a telegram about an hour ago," the man replied. "It should arrive exactly on time."

"Thanks."

Streeter took a seat in the waiting room, all the while maintaining a close eye on the clock. At exactly three minutes before the train was due, he stepped out onto the platform. At many of the smaller towns, Streeter knew, the arrival and departure of the trains was always a major event, and sometimes almost half the town would turn out, even for a train arriving as late as this one.

But Cheyenne was big enough that several trains passed through each day, and the population had grown sufficiently jaded that the arrivals and departures went mostly unnoticed except by those who had business with them. Roy Streeter stood on the platform with but a handful of others.

He could hear the train—a distant mournful whistle, followed by a chugging sound of working steam—

before he could see it. Then the train appeared around the curve in the track a quarter of a mile east of the station. Initially all that could be seen was its large, mirrored headlamp projecting an insect-filled beam into the darkness before it.

The train chased the beam of light on into the station and rolled by with steam venting from the drive cylinders and flaming coals falling from the firebox to leave a glowing path between the rails. With a pipe clenched between his teeth, the engineer was leaning out of the window looking ahead for the mark to stop. The train ground to a halt, but it wasn't quiet as steam continued to be vented, and hot journals and bearings made clicking sounds as they cooled.

Three cars back from the engine, the conductor stepped down, then took out his pocket watch and examined it in order to determine how long the train could sit in the station. A porter jumped down and placed a stool by the bottom step of the passenger car, then he stood by ready to offer assistance to anyone who might need it. Finally the arriving passengers began to step down.

Streeter held up a sign he'd printed out— POINDEXTER—when he saw two men approaching him. Unlike Streeter, who was wearing denim trousers and a red flannel shirt, the men coming toward him were wearing suits and bowler hats.

"I am Jacob Poindexter," said one of the two men. "Would you be Mr. Streeter?"

"Yes."

Jake smiled. "Ah yes, Mr. Jamison told me that I could count on you to handle things for me."

"Yes, sir, I got the telegram."

"And you have assembled the men?"

"Yes, sir, I done that too. I told 'em to meet us at the Railroad Hotel for breakfast tomorrah mornin'. I kinda suggested that you'd be buyin' the breakfast."

"I see no reason why I can't. Oh, by the way, may I introduce a new friend? This is Ed Collins. We met on the train. He has agreed to come to work for me as my executive assistant."

"It's good to meet you, Mr. Collins," Streeter said, extending his hand.

Chapter Nine

Instead of going out to his ranch, Duff had spent the night in town. He wanted make sure Meagan was recovering from her wound without any difficulty. He also intended to go to the bank the next morning so he could transfer funds to Meagan's and Elmer's accounts.

Elmer had come into town early. While they were waiting for the bank to open, Duff, Meagan, and Elmer were having breakfast at Vi's Pies. Owned by Vi Winslow, an attractive widow in her midforties, it was a full-service restaurant, but she was known for her pies. Thus the name of her establishment.

"How are you feeling this morning?" Elmer asked Meagan.

"I'm feeling well, thank you. My upper arm is a little sore, but it isn't too bad."

"I've been shot a few times my ownself so I know what it feels like," Elmer said.

Just as they were finishing their breakfast, Vi came over to the table with a small box, which she set before Elmer. "It's an apple pie."

"You're givin' me an apple pie?"

"Oh, no, I bought the pie for Mrs. Willis," Meagan said. "She's the lady who tended to me after I was shot. I thought it would be a nice gesture and I was hoping you would deliver the pie for me."

"Well, I don't know," Elmer said. "Good-lookin' woman, is she?"

"Elmer!" Vi said, snatching the pie away from him.

"Now, Vi, you know that I ain't got eyes for nobody but you."

"That's more like it," Vi said with a smile as she put the pie in front of him again.

"I mean, it ain't that you're all that good-lookin' but that don't really matter none, 'cause I ain't never knowed anyone that could make pies as good as you do."

Vi laughed and shook her head. "You're incorrigible."

After breakfast Duff, Meagan, and Elmer walked down to the bank where Duff verified that the money had been wire transferred and arranged for Meagan's and Elmer's percentages to be deposited into their personal accounts.

"I must get back to the dress shop," Meagan said.

"And I need to get this pie delivered," Elmer added.

The departure of his two friends left Duff alone so he stepped down to Fiddler's Green. It was too early for him to have an alcoholic drink, but Biff served hot coffee all morning, and it was a good way to catch up with things before he returned to Sky Meadow.

Biff was sitting at a table with Fred Matthews, owner of the mercantile, and Charley Blanton, editor of the *Chugwater Defender.*

"Hey, Duff, come over here and listen to this," Biff called out.

"Listen to what?" Duff asked.

"Charley says we're gettin' us a railroad."

"What?"

"It came over the AP wire this morning," Charley said. "I haven't put the paper out yet, but I have written the article if you'd like to read it."

"Aye, I would like to read it."

Chugwater to Get Railroad

Poindexter Railroad and Maritime Corporation has announced its intention to build the C&FL Railroad, a feeder line that would connect Cheyenne with Fort Laramie. And though the railroad would be a tremendous asset to the U.S. Army at Fort Laramie, it would also be a boon for the towns of Walbach, Chugwater, and Uva through which sites the railroad would run.

According to the announcement, Jacob Poindexter will be in charge of the operation. This newspaper has not heard directly from the Poindexter Corporation, nor from Mr. Jacob Poindexter, but the Bank of Chugwater has received a rather substantial deposit in Mr. Poindexter's name.

"This is great news!" Duff said.

"If the money is on deposit here, that means that this Poindexter person will more 'n likely make his headquarters here, don't you think?" Biff asked.

"Aye, that seems likely," Duff replied.

"Well now, that's going to be very good for the town," Biff said. "And I mean even before the railroad gets built. If Chugwater is going to be the headquarters, there's going to be a lot of business done here."

"I wonder when he'll get here."

"Soon, I hope." Charley smiled. "This won't just be good business for the commercial enterprises in town. I can see news copy coming from this for the next six months or so."

"We should call a town meeting," Fred Matthews said.

"What for?" Biff asked.

"If we're going to have a railroad coming through town, and especially if we are going to be the headquarters for the railroad, there's a lot of things we can do to get ready for them. And to help them, if that's needed."

"I agree. Where can we hold it?" Charley asked.

"Well, if we're going to have a meeting, how about right here at Fiddler's Green?" Duff suggested.

"You would have to close the bar during the meeting," Fred said to Biff.

"That's all right. If you had the meeting somewhere else, it's more 'n likely there wouldn't be that many people in the bar anyway. This way as soon as the meeting's over, people will be wantin' to have a drink to celebrate. And if we really are goin' to get a railroad, that will be somethin' worth celebrating."

"Good. I'll put the announcement in the paper." Charley said.

* * *

Charley put the announcement in the same edition of the paper in which he ran the story about the railroad being built. Even those who hadn't read the announcement soon learned of it, as news of the town meeting spread quickly, so quickly that by two o'clock the next afternoon, the scheduled time and day of the meeting, well over a hundred people had gathered at the saloon.

Several of the local businessmen were present. Several women were in attendance, too, mostly those who were businesswomen. Biff's wife Rose was sitting with Meagan. Like Duff, Rose was Scottish, though the two had never met until after Duff had arrived in Chugwater.

Duff and Elmer were sitting with several valley ranchers who, because they didn't represent the town, chose to sit together in a rather large group.

Brad Houser of Twin Peaks noticed Reverend E. D. Sweeny of the Church of God's Glory was also present. "Preach, ain't you somewhat a-skeert that God's goin' to send a lightnin' bolt to strike you down for bein' in a saloon? I mean in case you ain't heard, you bein' a preacher man 'n all, the sergeant major does serve spirits in this place," he teased.

"I'm quite aware than Mr. Johnson serves liquor here. But my boy, from what I have read in the Bible, Jesus didn't turn water into sody pop," Sweeny replied, and those within hearing distance laughed.

"Reverend Sweeny, would you be so kind as to say a prayer to get us started?" asked Mayor C. E. Felker, who was known to most as "Daddy."

"Now, Daddy, why'd you go 'n do that?" Jonas Perkins of the JP Ranch asked. "We come here to talk about gettin' us a railroad, not to listen to some long-winded sermon."

"Lord!" Reverend Sweeny began, saying the word loud enough to preclude any further discussion on the subject, "let us conduct this meeting with hope, courtesy, and understanding. Amen."

"That's it?" Perkins said. "All right, Preach, you done just fine. Now, let's get on with the meetin'. Who's goin' to conduct it?"

"How about Daddy Felker? He's the mayor," Biff suggested from his spot behind the bar.

"All right," Mayor Felker replied. "This meeting is underway."

"I have a question," liveryman Lonnie Mathers asked. "Has anyone actually seen this Jake Poindexter person? Or heard from him?"

"We haven't met him, nor heard from him personally," said Bob Dempster, the new banker ever since Joel Montgomery had moved to Big Rock, Colorado. "But I can attest to the fact that twenty-five thousand dollars has been deposited in the bank with Jacob Poindexter being the one authorized to access the account. The money was deposited by wire, and he won't be able to draw any money from it until he comes in and physically opens the account, so I think we can be reasonably certain that he will be here."

"Is he actually coming to build a railroad?" Fred Matthews asked.

"The name on the account is Cheyenne and Fort Laramie Railroad," Dempster said.

"Gentlemen," Daddy Felker said, then corrected himself. "Ladies and gentlemen, I would say that is all the proof we need that the P R and M Corporation has every intention of building a railroad right through Chugwater. As we are about halfway between Cheyenne and Fort Laramie, it stands to reason that we will be the focus of the entire operation."

"I have an idea," Mathers said. "Suppose we find an office and make it available to Poindexter while he's here."

"What if he doesn't want to rent an office?" Perkins asked. "He may have other plans for the money."

"No, you don't understand. When I say we make an office available to him, I mean we will pay the rent."

"Why would we want to do a thing like that?" Brad Houser asked.

"To show him that we welcome him and will do all that we can to help bring the railroad into fruition," Daddy Felker said.

"Good idea," Marshal Ferrell said. "I agree."

"There is an empty office next to mine that you can use. I was thinking of using it as a legal library." Martin Gilmore was the lawyer who had defended Drury Slocum. No one held that against him though, as he had been appointed to the position by the court.

"You shouldn't have to come up with it all by yourself," Charley Blanton said. "The rest of us can pitch in and help with the rent."

Gilmore held up his hand and smiled. "That won't be necessary. He is going to need a lawyer and this will put me in good with him."

"Mr. Mayor," Meagan said.

"Yes, Miss Parker?"

"I think we should have a reception for him."

"A reception?"

"Yes, perhaps dinner, a few words to let him know that he is welcome, and maybe even a dance."

"You're not plannin' on that bein' just for all the highfalutin' businessmen in town are you?" asked David Lewis, owner of the Trail Back. "I know my hands out at the ranch would very much like to come to such a thing."

"As the railroad will be for everyone, the reception should also be for everyone," Meagan said.

"Then that is exactly what we will do," Charley Blanton said.

"Does anyone have any idea when Poindexter plans to arrive in Chugwater?" Daddy Felker asked.

"I'll see what I can find out," Charley offered.

Corporate office of P R and M Corporation

Jamison stepped into Preston Poindexter's office, carrying a little yellow sheet of paper. "We have heard from your son," he said.

Preston got a worried look on his face. "Oh, he's all right, isn't he?"

"Yes, sir, I think he is doing just fine." Jamison started to hand the telegram to his employer, but Preston waved it away.

"No, read it to me if you would, please."

Jamison cleared his throat and began to read. "Chugwater citizens pleased stop offered help stop having reception, stop. Jake."

"How about that?" Preston said. "They are giving a reception. Jake is representing us quite well, don't you think, Norman?"

"Yes, sir, I do."

CHUGWATER WELCOMES JAKE POINDEXTER
AND THE C&FL RAILROAD

The banner stretched across Clay Avenue fluttered in the breeze as Mayor Felker extended the welcome of the town. "Mr. Poindexter," he said to the young man who occupied a position of honor on the platform, "as mayor of the city of Chugwater I want to extend the welcome of our citizens to you and to your associates." He nodded toward Roy Streeter and the seven men who were standing in the front row with him.

"We are honored to have our town be selected to play such a prominent role in the construction of the new railroad, and we will do everything we can to make P R and M Corporation's investment in time and money profitable for the company and beneficial to the residents of Chugwater and Laramie County.

"And now if you would sir, we would like to invite you to say a few words."

"Hear, hear!" someone shouted from the crowd as the young guest of honor stepped out to the front of the platform.

"Ladies and gentlemen of the fair city of Chug-water, my associates and I thank you for this warm welcome. Over the next few weeks you will be seeing a lot of us as we begin laying out the route for the Cheyenne and Fort Laramie Railroad. Such an oper-ation, requiring the acquisition of land as it must, may from time to time cause a bit of disagreement to arise between us, but when we consider the greater good for all parties involved, I'm absolutely certain we will be able to resolve any differences that may come up."

The reception was held in the ballroom of the Dunn Hotel, and at the moment Colonel Gerald Royal was in conversation with Duff and several others. As Commandant of Fort Laramie, the colonel had accompanied the Sixth U.S. Infantry Band to take part in the welcome reception.

"It will be a fine thing to have a railroad connect the fort with the Union Pacific," Colonel Royal said. "To tell the truth, the post is so isolated between the Northern Pacific north of us, and the Union Pacific to our south that I don't how much longer we'll be able to keep Fort Laramie open."

"You know something I was wondering about, Mr. Poindexter, is why are you stopping at Fort Laramie?" Charley Blanton asked. "Wouldn't it be more productive to extend the railroad and connect the Union Pacific with the Northern Pacific?"

"That's a very good question and I'm sure that it will be eventually. But we would have to negotiate connecting rights with the Northern Pacific, and for now we only have connecting rights with the U.P. We will go ahead and make that connection as soon as possible, but in the meantime we are going to have to acquire, by land grants and eminent domain, the right-of-way for the track that we will be laying."

"Eminent domain?" asked Merlin Goodman. Owner of Mountain Shadow Ranch, he'd sat with Duff and other ranchers at the town meeting. "What is that?"

"It means that we have the right to buy any land we need to secure the right-of-way, and the current land owner cannot refuse to sell to us."

"The hell you say! What if you decide you want to buy Mountain Shadow, and I don't want to sell it?"

"If you refuse to sell it, the government will confiscate the land and give it to me." Jake explained.

"You mean just take the land?" Perkins asked.

"Oh, it's not quite as bad as that. The government won't take your land without paying you something for it."

"That's not right. There's no way they could do such a thing!"

"I'm afraid he can, Jonas," Martin Gilmore said. "It's part of the Fifth Amendment."

"I thought the Fifth Amendment said you didn't have to talk if you didn't want to," Marshal Ferrell said.

"Yes, that too. One of the things I had to do while studying law was remember the Fifth Amendment. It says 'No person shall be held to answer for a capital, or otherwise infamous crime, unless on a presentment or indictment of a Grand Jury, except in cases arising in the land or naval forces, or in the Militia, when in actual service in time of War or public danger; nor shall any person be subject for the same offence to be twice put in jeopardy of life or limb; nor shall be compelled in any criminal case to be a witness against himself, nor be deprived of life, liberty, or property, without due process of law; *nor shall private property be taken for public use, without just compensation.*'

"It's that last line, called the 'taking clause' that enables Poindexter to take whatever property is needed for the public good. And I think all of us here agree that the railroad is for the public good."

"Yeah, well, I don't know about that. To be honest, I'm beginning to wonder if this railroad is going to be such a good thing after all," Perkins grumbled.

"Don't come to any hasty decisions," Martin Gilmore said.

The reception continued, complete with a fine meal, music, and dancing. Most of the citizens of the town considered it to be a celebration, for all would welcome the railroad. It was only the few who had been a party to the discussion of eminent domain who were unable to put aside a little niggling concern as to where this would lead.

Chapter Ten

When the train arrived in Cheyenne it was met by Ed Collins and Roy Streeter.

"I don't see 'em," Streeter said as they watched the arriving passengers leaving the train.

"That's because you aren't looking in the right place," Collins said. He pointed to a cattle car that was attached to the train. There, several Chinese passengers, men and women, were exiting the car without benefit of ramp or step. They had to jump down onto the platform, and because it was rather high, exiting the car wasn't an easy task.

"There they are," he said.

Collins and Streeter went down to meet them. Everyone had exited the car except two men, and they were passing down the belongings.

"Do any of you speak English?" Collins asked.

"I am Cong Sing," the oldest of the Chinese said.

"You have come to work for the railroad?"

Cong Sing placed his hands together, prayer like, and bowed his head, slightly. "*Shi*. Yes," he translated quickly.

"I've got a wagon and team of mules for you. Get your people loaded and I'll show you where to go."

"When will work begin?" Cong Sing asked.

"It will begin when I tell you it will begin," Collins replied.

"*Shi*," Cong Sing said, again placing his hands together and bowing his head slightly.

Doty Simmons drove a freight wagon for Matthews Mercantile and he was returning with a load of goods from Cheyenne. He was about a mile south of Chugwater when he was surprised to see a dozen or more Chinese camped alongside the road. He stopped his wagon and stared at them for a moment. They had a campfire going and a pot hanging over the fire. The group consisted of men and women, some of whom were drinking from a cup, a couple were eating, and the others were sitting or lying on the ground.

Simmons thought about approaching them and asking what they were doing here, but there were so many of them that if they took his questioning wrong, it might be dangerous for him. He snapped the reins against the team and hurried the wagon on, passing them by without looking into the eyes of anyone. As soon as he reached Matthews Mercantile he backed the wagon up against the dock.

As the dockhands began unloading the wagon, Simmons walked down to the marshal's office. "They's a bunch o' Chinamen just outside o' town," he told Marshal Ferrell.

"What are they doing there? Did you ask?"

"No, I, uh, well the truth is I didn't feel that it would

be right for me to go up 'n ask 'em anything. It don't look like they're doin' nothin' more 'n just sittin' around out there, like they're waitin' on somethin' to happen. 'N here's the strange thing. They ain't got no horses, no wagons, nothin'. Looks like they musta walked. I can't figure out no other way they coulda got there."

"Yes, well thanks for tellin' me."

"You goin' to go out there 'n see what it's all about?"

"Yes, I'll take care of it."

After Simmons left, Marshal Ferrell walked down to Lu Win's Restaurant, intending to ask Win to come with him to question the Chinaman to see why they were there. When he went inside he smiled in relief when he saw Wang Chow sitting at a table drinking tea.

"Wang, can I talk to you for a moment?"

"Yes. Sit and drink tea with me as we talk."

"Uh, do they serve coffee in here?"

Wang called out to a young woman, speaking to her in Chinese, and a moment later she appeared with a cup of coffee, putting it before the marshal with a pretty smile.

"Wang, there's a bunch of Chinamen that's camped just outside of town," Marshal Ferrell said. "Do you know anything about them? Who they are? How they get there? And what they are doing there?"

"I do not know of this," Wang replied.

"Well I was wondering, that is if you don't mind, if you would go with me to talk to 'em 'n find out what this is all about. I mean you bein' a Chinaman 'n all, they'd more likely talk to you than they would to me.

'n even if they did talk to me, chances are that I wouldn't understand nothin' they was sayin' anyway."

"I will come."

When Wang and Marshal Ferrell reached the encampment, the air was redolent with the smell of cooked pork. There were a dozen men and half again as many women. All the men were seated, while the women were cooking.

One of the men stood, then approached Wang and Marshal Ferrell as they dismounted. Putting his hands together, he dipped his head, then spoke. *"Wènhòu xiānshēng. Báirén shì jiànzhú lǎobǎn ma?"*

"Meíyou," Wang answered. *"Nǐ jiào shénme míngzì."*

"Cong Sing."

"What was all that?" Ferrell asked.

"His name is Cong Sing. He wanted to know if you were to be their construction boss. I told him that you were not."

"Construction boss for what? How did they get here?"

For the next few minutes Wang and Cong Sing spoke, their conversation followed closely by the others. Finally Wang turned to Ferrell to give him a report on what was said.

"They are here to build the railroad. They came by train to Cheyenne, where they were met by someone and brought here by wagon. The person who brought them left them here and said they would be contacted later by someone who will be their boss."

Ferrell smiled and nodded. "Yes, tell them I know about the railroad, but I know nothing about who is to meet them. Tell them they can wait here and they will not be bothered."

Wang translated for Ferrell, then, exchanging good-byes, he and the marshal rode back into town, leaving the Chinese railroad construction crew behind.

Home of Preston Poindexter, Manhattan's Upper East Side

"I'm really proud of Jake, and I think you will be, too," Preston said.

"I suppose I am," Emma Marie said. "But, Pete, I am worried so about him being out there in the middle of nowhere."

Preston, who was known as Pete to his family and close friends, he said, "There's no need for you to worry about him. He sends me a telegram just about every other day keeping me apprised of what is going on. Why, he has already hired a bunch of Chinese workers, and we wouldn't do that if he hadn't made enough progress in all the initial planning and survey-ing to get the project underway."

"How is he doing?" Emma Marie asked. "Is he eating well? Is he staying healthy?"

Pete laughed out loud, then reached over to lay his hand on hers. "Why, he's probably healthier than he has ever been in his life. And why not? He's living in the wide-open spaces. Emma Marie, believe me, there isn't a young man in the entire country who wouldn't willingly change places with him right now. He wanted some adventure. He's having the adventure of a life-time, and the best thing about it is, it isn't a wasted adventure. He's accomplishing something. He's build-ing a railroad."

"I know he is, and I know I'm just being foolish worrying about him so. I suppose it's just a mother's worry is all."

"I'll tell you what I'll do. I'll send a telegram tomorrow that will come directly from you. All you have to do is tell me what you would like to say."

"I would like for you to tell him that his mother loves him, and wants him to be very careful."

"All right, I'll see to it that the telegram is sent first thing tomorrow."

"No, wait. That might embarrass him." Emma Marie held out her hand and smiled sheepishly. "Just tell him that I am very proud of him."

"I can do that," Pete said.

Chapter Eleven

"It's time to start confiscating all the free range and buying the more choice land that we want," Collins said. "I expect there will be a lot of people who aren't going to be very happy about what's going on, and that's where you and our railroad police come in."

"Takin' in all this land like this, how is it that it ain't stealin'?" Bo Hawken asked.

"Hell, it *is* stealing," Collins replied with a little laugh. "However, this stealing is legal. Poindexter explained it all to me."

"Damn, who was smart enough to come up with somethin' like this?" Streeter asked.

"Who have we got on watch?" Collins asked.

"Hawken 'n Butrum."

"Bring Butrum back in. One is all we need," Collins said.

"All right."

"Boys," Collins said with a wide smile. "Let's start making some money!"

* * *

Two days later, Roy Streeter, Jalen Nichols, and Clete Dixon were driving about fifty head of cattle toward the main part of Pitchfork Ranch when they were stopped by a cowboy known only as Dirt.

"Looks to me like them's Pitchfork cows," Dirt said.

"Yeah." Streeter pointed to the brand. "That's what we figured when we seen this brand that looks like a pitchfork."

"All right. So now you know, just where is it that you boys think you're a-goin' with 'em?" Dirt asked.

"We're gettin' 'em off C 'n FL land," Streeter said.

"C 'n FL land? What are you talkin' about? Where is this C 'n FL land?"

"This here is C 'n FL land," Streeter said with a wide sweep of his arm. "We're on C 'n FL land right now. So are you. 'N so are these cows, which is why we're pushin' 'em back."

"The hell you say." Dirt pointed to the north, the direction from which the cattle were coming. "That land there belongs to the Pitchfork, all the way to Lone Tree Crick. You ain't got no claim to it, 'n you ain't got right to be moving Pitchfork cows around, neither."

"This here ain't actual Pitchfork land. It belongs to the government," Streeter said, again taking in the area with a wide sweep of his arm. "Right now Pitchfork is usin' it as free range, but it's pretty soon goin' to belong to us by government grant. And when that happens, we don't want none o' Pitchfork's cows on it."

"Why the hell would the government be a-givin' you the land?"

"Because we're building a railroad," Streeter said.

"Yeah, I heard that you're buildin' a railroad, ever'one knows that, but that don't give you no right to just come in 'n start takin' the land 'n runnin' off the cattle."

Streeter's smile was without humor. "Yeah, it does."

"We'll just see about that," Dirt said. Turning his horse, he galloped back to the main house where he found Dale Allen, owner of the Pitchfork, watching one of the other hands working on the pump.

"Damn, Dirt, what's got you in such a frenzy?" Dale asked.

"It's the North Range, Mr. Allen," Dirt said. "They's some men from the railroad that's come 'n drove off all the cows we got up there. They say the North Range don't belong to you no more. They say the government has took it 'n give it to the railroad."

Over the next several days, more "right-of-way" land was acquired, not only from the ranchers in the immediate vicinity of Chugwater, but along the entire route from Cheyenne to Fort Laramie. So far Sky Meadow had not been affected.

"'Tis thinking I am there is nae way I'll be for avoiding this," Duff told Biff as the two of them shared Biff's personal table in Fiddler's Green.

"I don't know, Duff," Biff said. "When all this started everyone was all excited about it. But Dale Allen of the Pitchfork, then David Lewis of Trail Back, and Webb Dakota of Mountain Shadow . . . all three of 'em have seen a lot of their land taken."

"Aye, but to be fair, Biff, 'tis not their land that's

been taken so far. 'Tis only the free range, 'n since all the free range belongs to the government, we've been sort of borrowing it in the first place."

At that moment Charley Blanton came into Fiddler's Green then stepped back to the table where Duff and Biff were visiting. "Good afternoon, gentlemen. Do you mind if I join you?" Charley was carrying a roll of paper which was obviously too long to be a proof sheet for the newspaper.

"Please do." Biff held up his hand. "Kay, a glass of wine for Mr. Blanton."

"Yes, sir, Mr. Johnson," the pretty young hostess replied.

"You bein' the newspaper editor 'n on top o' things, 'tis sure I am that you know the land being taken from Allen, Lewis, and Dakota," Duff said, making it a statement, rather than a question.

"Yes, I know. Believe me, I know," Charles replied.

"What's that you're carrying?" Biff asked.

"Something I want to show you," Charley said as he accepted the wine Kay brought to the table. "First, I want to know what you two think about all the land grabbing that's been going on."

"'Tis becoming a bit disturbin'," Duff said. "But to be fair, we were warned about it before they started."

"Yes, well it's considerably more than a bit disturbing, I would say," Charley replied. "I don't know what it means, or if it means anything at all, but Dempster told me that over fifty thousand dollars has been deposited in the bank to the Poindexter account."

"Well, I would think that's a good thing. It means

that the ranchers are going to be compensated for the land that's been taken."

Charley shook his head. "Yes, but the money has been deposited, and some of it withdrawn, which is somewhat strange because no land has actually been taken by eminent domain yet and no work has started, so where is the money going?"

"Aye, I can see why that might be a puzzle."

"Biff, you asked what this paper is. I'm going to show you, and you'll see that this is even more puzzling than the withdrawal of the money." Charley unrolled the document he was carrying, which proved to be a map, and spread it out on the table. "The Land Grant Act of 1864 provides railroad developers with alternating sections on either side of the tracks as well as all the minerals underneath all that land.

"Now this is the most logical route from Cheyenne to Fort Laramie." Charley traced out the route with his finger as he spoke. "Through Walbach, across Lodge Pole Creek, through the Goodwin Ranch, through the Davis Ranch, across Bear Creek, through Sky Meadow, across Horse Creek, through Chugwater, then across Box Elder and Cherry Creeks to Uva, then alongside the Laramie River to the Platte River and Fort Laramie. Wouldn't you agree?"

"Aye, 'tis clearly the best route," Duff said. "It's the shortest, and it doesn't have to cross any mountain ranges."

"I'm glad you agree. But now look at the land grants they have confiscated so far. Two thousand acres that was being used as free-range graze for Pitchfork, a thousand acres from Mountain Shadow, and three thousand acres of free rangeland being used by Trail Back. And, you said no mountain range? Here are two thousand acres from the Snowy Range, and another two thousand from way up here in the Laramie Mountain Range. Now, let me show you how the tracks would have to go in order to follow these land acquisitions."

With his finger, Charley traced out several zigzags on the map, in some cases several miles away from the most logical route.

"What the hell?" Biff said. "That makes no sense at all."

"Maybe it does," Charley said. "Take a look at these acquisitions I told you about, and see if anything stands out for you."

Biff put his finger on the southern tip of the Laramie Mountains. "Isn't there a working silver mine here?"

"Good observation, Biff. Indeed there was a working silver mine there, but it turns out the claim wasn't properly filed, and now it belongs to the C and FL Railroad. And here, here, and here are some of the best grazing lands in all of Wyoming, plus, of course, a very good and continuous source of water. But, as you can see, none of these sections are along the most logical route."

"That's very interesting," Duff said.

"Yes, I thought you might find it so," Charley replied.

"I wonder what it means," Biff said.

"I'm beginning to think it means some chicanery with the way this railroad is doing business." Charley rolled the paper back up. "And I intend to find out just what it is."

Corporate office of P R and M

"Norman, another fifty thousand dollars?" Pete asked.

"That's what Jake is requesting," Jamison replied.

"I don't know about this," Preston said. "We've already invested more money than I had planned, and now he wants another fifty thousand dollars? Maybe I should take a trip out there just to see what is going on."

"Oh, I wouldn't do that, sir," Jamison said.

"Why not? We're bleeding money here. It can't just go on unchecked."

"Mr. Poindexter, you have sent Jake out there to get some experience. You say yourself that, someday, he will be running the company. If you go out there to check up on what he's doing, you will totally destroy his confidence."

"I don't know," Preston said.

"Think about it, sir. We can keep an eye on it from here. Soon, I think, we can start selling off the land that we have already acquired from the government. And once the railroad is built and in operation, why, you'll recover this money in no time."

"I suppose you're right." Preston chuckled. "But that boy has to learn that the secret to running a successful business is that you take in more money than you spend."

Jamison chuckled as well. "I think the time will come, and soon, when Jake realizes that so far all the money has gone out, and none has come in. That will be a lesson that he'll learn, painfully perhaps, but he will learn it."

"I hope you're right."

"Of course I'm right. He's your son, isn't he? That means he has come from good stock."

"I guess I'm not really that worried about it," Pete said. "You're still young enough so that when the time does come for Jake to take over the company, you'll be around to advise him. I'll be counting on you, Norman."

"I won't let you down, sir. I'll do everything I can to keep him on the right track."

"Norman, hiring you is one of the most intelligent things I have ever done since I started the company."

"I much appreciate the compliment, sir."

"How much track have we laid, so far?"

"According to the latest report, we have acquired the connection rights from the Union Pacific and have laid enough track to get us ten and one quarter miles north of Cheyenne," Norman said.

"Ten and one quarter miles," Pete said with a smile. "By damn, maybe Jake is going to work out all right. Ten and a quarter miles. I like it, not only that we have advanced that far, but also because his reports have all been so detailed."

"Indeed, sir," Norman agreed.

"I think we could drink a glass of wine in toast, don't you?" Pete asked.

"Oh, I think it would be perfectly fitting to do so," Jamison agreed with a willing smile.

Chapter Twelve

Chugwater

When Duff stepped into the Bank of Chugwater to withdraw some money, he was greeted by the teller, Otto Hirsh.

"Good afternoon, Mr. MacCallister."

"Hello, Otto, 'n would you be for telling me how Mary and your two daughters are doing?"

"They're doing quite well. Thank you for asking. Your usual one hundred dollars, I suppose?"

"Better make it two hundred dollars. I've some purchases to make today." Duff replied as he handed the teller his bank draft.

"Two hundred it is, sir," Otto said as he began counting out the money.

"Duff, could you come in here to visit me for a moment?" The call came from Bob Dempster, who had stepped from the door of his office.

"Aye, Bob, I'll be right there," Duff replied.

He stepped into the office a moment later as Dempster was pouring two cups of coffee. He held out a cup to Duff, then made a motion for him to sit down.

"I just got a wire transfer for another fifty thousand dollars to be deposited to the railroad account this morning," Dempster said. "That gives them a working account of over a hundred thousand dollars. Of course, only about twenty thousand is present in actual cash, but they have access to the entire amount."

"That's a lot of money," Duff said.

"Yes, it is."

"'Tis to be hoped that with that much money, they be for startin' the building of the railroad soon, 'n quit with their takin' land from the ranchers."

"Yes, I'm hoping they get started soon. If they do, I think it might stop some of the grumbling and dissatisfaction that's beginning to grow."

Duff, who had an appreciation for Chinese cuisine, had agreed to have lunch with Wang at Lu Win's Restaurant. Stepping into the restaurant, Duff was assailed by the piquant aroma of Chinese cooking. He was looking forward to the meal when he saw Wang and Lu Win's very pretty daughter, Mae, speaking with a Chinese man he had never seen before.

"*Xiānshēng* MacCallister, this is Cong Sing," Wang said.

"He's with the construction party you told me about?"

"*Shi*. He is troubled because there is no work for them to do."

"Well, I don't see how there can be any work yet, seeing as they have nae even surveyed the route." Duff smiled. "Mr. Sing and the others can just enjoy a paid vacation while they wait."

"They are not being paid," Wang said. "And they are running out of food. *Xiansheng*, may I make a request?"

"Aye, Wang, of course you can."

"I would wish to bring them out to Sky Meadow. Perhaps we can find work for them to do until they begin to build the railroad."

Duff reached out to put his hand on Wang's shoulder. "Of course we can, Wang. Tell Mr. Sing and his friends they are welcome and we will pay them and provide food."

Wang turned to speak to Sing.

"Nín hé qítā rén kěnéng huì yǔ wǒmen yīqǐ shēnghuó hé gōngzuò. MacCallister Xiānshēng shì yīgè fēicháng hǎo de rén."

Sing smiled, then, putting his hands together, made a slight bow toward Duff.

Duff chuckled. "I take it that you told him he could come to Sky Meadow?"

"He also told him that you are a very good man," Mae Win said. "And I agree."

"Wang, didn't you tell me that they have no horses?"

"That is true. They have no horses."

"Then we'll take some wagons from Sky Meadow to pick them up."

Again, Wang spoke to Sing, and again Sing smiled, and bobbed his head toward Duff.

"Oh, and before you go, ask Mr. Sing to stay and have a meal. I will pay for it."

After another exchange of words, Wang turned back to Duff.

"He will not eat."

"Oh? Why will he nae eat?"

"He says he cannot eat while the others remain hungry."

"How many others are there?"

"There are seventeen others. In addition to Cong Sing, there are eleven men and six women."

Duff turned to Mae Win. "Miss Win, prepare lunch for eighteen. Wang, you and Mr. Sing go bring them in. We can bring the wagons into town for them after they have eaten."

Wang told Sing what Duff said, then Sing's eyes opened wide in pleasant surprise.

"Wǒ zhǎo bù dào gèng hǎo de nánrén," Sing said.

Again Mae interpreted Sing's words.

"Mr. Sing, speaking of you, said that he has found no better man."

"Nǐ bù huì, yīnwèi méiyǒu bǐ MacCallister xiānshēng gèng hǎo de rénle," Wang replied.

"And Wang said that he will never find such a person for there is no better man to be found than you."

"Och, and now I am embarrassed by the flattery, even though it be in Chinese. Wang, you go help Mr. Sing bring his people in. I'll ride out to the ranch 'n have Jones 'n Wallace bring in the wagons."

Clete Dixon and Pogue Flannigan were just coming out of the Wild Hog Saloon when they saw Wang and Sing coming into town, followed by every member of the construction group, men and women. They were carrying all of their belongings with them.

"What the hell, Pogue? Ain't that them Chinamen that Collins hired to work on the railroad?" Dixon asked.

"Yeah, it sure looks like 'em. 'Course, all Chinamen look alike," Flannigan added with a little laugh.

"Wasn't they s'posed to stay outta town?"

"Yeah, I think that's what Collins said."

"Then what do you think they're a-doin' here?"

"I don't know. Why don't you ask 'em?"

"Yeah, I think I will. Hey!" Dixon shouted at them as they came by. "What the hell are you Chinamen doin' comin' inter town? Wasn't you all told to stay where you was till we said we was ready for you?"

"Who are you?" Wang asked.

"It ain't none o' your business who I am," Dixon said. "You just answer my question. You was told to stay outta town till we need you, 'n I know for certain we don't need you yet." Dixon pointed back in the direction from which the caravan had come. "Now get your yellow asses back where you belong."

"You have not paid them, and you have not given them food. They have come to town to eat."

"Yeah? Well how is it they plan to eat, iffen they ain't got no money?"

"Duff MacCallister is paying for their food."

"That ain't good, Clete, MacCallister payin' for 'em like that," Flannigan said. "If he buys 'em food 'n it comes down to who they are goin' to be loyal to, why it's liable to wind up bein' MacCallister instead of us."

"Yeah, you're right," Dixon replied. "You, Chinaman," he said to the one he had been talking to. "What is your name?"

"I am Wang Chow."

"Well, Wang Chow, seein' as you can speak their lingo, I want you to tell all these heathens to get the hell back to where they was 'n to wait for us there. We'll come for 'em when we're ready for them."

"They have no food."

"Yeah, you already told me that, but what the hell has that got to do with anything? Tell 'em to kill a rabbit or somethin'. Feedin' 'em ain't our problem till they actual start workin' for us."

"They will eat here."

"The hell they will," Dixon said, pulling his pistol.

Seeing Dixon pull his pistol, Flannigan did as well.

"Now the only reason I ain't goin' to shoot you is 'cause I want you to see us when we commence to shootin' Chinamen. Oh, did I say Chinamen? I see some women in that group, 'n I expect I'll start shootin' them first. Then, after I've kilt a few of 'em, I'm goin' to kill you. Now, are you goin' to tell 'em what I'm sayin', or—"

That was as far as Dixon got. Moving so fast that neither Dixon nor Flannigan were aware of what was happening, Wang snatched both of their pistols away from them. Then, as they were still trying to figure out what had just happened, Wang took Dixon down with a kick to the side of his head, and Flannigan with a blow to his chin from the heel of Wang's hand.

There were exclamations of surprise and appreciation from nearly all of the Chinese workers, as well as from several citizens of the town who, because of Dixon's loud talk and their proximity, had been witnesses to the event.

As Both Dixon and Flannigan lay on the ground, Wang, who had dropped their pistols when he attacked them, picked the guns back up and removed the cylinders. Thus disarmed, he slipped the pistols back into the holsters of the two unconscious men.

"We will eat now," he said to Sing.

The construction party had not been able to understand what was said in the confrontation but they were aware that Wang had just saved their lives. At Wang's invitation, they filed into Lu Win's Restaurant, where the plates, chopsticks, and food had already been laid out for them. With a happy shout, everyone rushed to the tables.

"How come you reckon the railroad hired them, but ain't give none of 'em any money yet, 'n ain't feedin' 'em neither?" Elmer asked Duff as they rode back into town alongside the two wagons driven by J.C. Jones and Larry Wallace.

"'Tis nae a question that I can answer, Elmer, but it does seem a bit of a queer way to be doin' business."

"Hell, Duff, there ain't nothin' these people has done yet that don't seem a queer way of doin' business if you ask me."

When they arrived in town they parked the wagons of front of Lu Win's then went inside, where Duff, Elmer, Jones, and Wallace joined the others for a meal.

It was Mae Win who told Duff about the incident

between Wang and two of the railroad police. "All the Chinese people now know what I know," Mae said with a proud smile. "Wang is a hero."

"Aye, Wang is indeed a hero."

"Wang says that you are a hero," Mae said with a big smile.

"Yeah, well, that heathen ain't always right, but I reckon he's right about this," Elmer teased.

Wang held his hand out toward Duff, and when he opened it, Duff saw two revolver cylinders.

Duff chuckled. "Poindexter is in his office. I'll take these to him. I expect his men will be wanting them back."

Of the two bunkhouses at Sky Meadow, the smaller one was occupied by J. C. Jones, Larry Wallace, and Bill Lewis, the permanent hands. The other, much larger, was for the temporary hands. The Chinese construction workers moved into this structure, and though there was no way of providing privacy for the women, that didn't become a problem. The new guests were happy to have a place to stay and a means of earning their keep.

Over the next few days Duff's eleemosynary gesture actually turned into a boon for him as his new temporary employees had many useful skills, from carpentry to blacksmithing, to gardening. They also cooked their own food.

"How long do you think it'll be a-fore they start in on buildin' the railroad?" Elmer asked.

"And 'tis it that you are anxious to be rid of them, Elmer?"

"What? No, far as I'm concerned they can stay as long as they want. We're gettin' jobs done that's been goin' a-wantin' for a long time now."

"I cannae tell you how long it will be before construction begins, or even if it will begin," Duff said.

"What do you mean, if it will begin? Are you sayin' you don't think they are goin' to build the railroad?"

"Nae, I'm just sayin' there's somethin' mighty peculiar about it all."

"Yeah, well now, that's somethin' that you 'n me both agree on."

Chapter Thirteen

So far the only land that had been acquired was the free rangeland that had been part of the government land grant. There had been no purchases by right of eminent domain, but that was about to change when four riders representing the C&FL rode up the JP Ranch road leading to the house that belonged to Jonas Perkins. Their knock on the door was answered by Jonas's wife, Eunice.

"You, you're Jake Poindexter, aren't you?" Eunice asked. "I remember you from the reception."

"Yes, ma'am, I am. Would Mr. Perkins be in, by chance?"

"No, he's down on the creek bottom. Some beavers are building a dam, and he and one of our hands have gone down there to tear it down." She smiled. "I hate it that we have to undo all the work the beavers have done. Bless their little hearts, they do work so hard at it. But when they dam up the creek it stops the flow and keeps the water from going on downstream to Mr. Goodman."

"Yes, I can see how that might be a problem. Thank you, we'll go down to the creek to see him."

* * *

Jonas Perkins was standing knee deep in the water and his arms were submerged to the elbows as he was working to take apart the dam. The beaver construction wasn't that hard to dismantle, because they had found it right away. A couple of beavers were watching him from the creek bank and they were whining their disapproval at him.

Perkins looked over at the protesting beavers. "I'm sorry, fellers, but you're just going to have to find some other place to build your dam."

"Mr. Perkins, they's some riders a-comin' this way." Kistner was sixteen, was the youngest of all the cowboys who rode for the JP brand.

"Some of our boys?"

"No, sir, 'n they ain't none of 'em from Mountain Shadow neither. I don't have no idea who they are."

Mountain Shadow was the neighboring ranch.

"I wonder who they are and what they—" Perkins stopped in midsentence as he recognized the four approaching riders. He climbed up out of the creek then stood there with his legs wet from the knees down and with wet forearms and muddy hands. "Never mind. I know who they are. They are from the railroad that's goin' to be built."

"What is it you reckon they want?" Kistner asked.

"I don't know exactly, but I have a feelin' this is goin' to be trouble." Perkins waited until the riders were right upon him. "What can I do for you, Poindexter?"

"Well, for one thing you can stop tearing down that beaver dam."

"We have to tear it down." Perkins chuckled. "I know

it might look like a bother to someone who ain't used to ranchin', but we have to do this. If we don't take it down, it'll stop the flow of the creek."

"Whether or not it stops the flow of the creek is no longer your problem, Mr. Perkins."

"What do you mean, it's no longer my problem?"

"We are taking eight hundred acres of your land, and all of it is adjacent to the creek."

"Oh, yeah, I've heard how you have took land from Allen, Lewis, and a couple others. But this here land you're a-talkin' about now ain't free rangeland. This here is my land, 'n I have the title, free and clear."

"Yes, this isn't like our other land acquisitions. The government can't give this land to us, because, as you said, you own it. That's why we'll be buyin' the land from you."

"Well, I appreciate your offer to buy, Mr. Poindexter, but I couldn't hardly sell this land. If I was to sell it, I couldn't keep on ranchin', seein' as this here creek provides most o' the water that I need for my cows."

"Mr. Perkins, I believe you might remember the discussion we had at the reception you and your friends were so generous to provide for us. I told you then that we would be acquiring land for the railroad."

"Yeah, and you done took a lot of it too, so much of the free rangeland that some of us is beginnin' to worry 'bout whether we're goin' to have enough graze for our herds." Perkins gave sort of a dismissive wave with his hand. "We can understand that you got a right to that land and we're willin' to trade some of it off for gettin' a railroad. But this that you're talkin' about now ain't free rangeland. It's like I said, this here strip you're talkin' about belongs to me, 'n I don't have no plans on sellin' it."

"I'm afraid it doesn't matter whether you want to sell it or not. We will take it by eminent domain."

"I don't know what this eminent domain thing is that you're talkin' about, but I'll tell you again so's that you understand. I don't have no intention of sellin' my land, 'n I ain't a-goin' to sell it."

"And I'll tell you again, Mr. Perkins, it doesn't matter whether you want to sell it or not. I have the law on my side, and that means if I want to buy it there is nothing you can do to stop me. And, Mr. Perkins, I want to buy it."

"Look here, are you tellin' me that the law says that even iffen I don't want to sell my land to you, I have to do it?"

"That is exactly what I'm telling you, Mr. Perkins."

Perkins felt his stomach rise to his throat, and he felt so light-headed that he believed he was about to pass out. He walked over to his horse then put his hand out to the saddle to support himself. As he did that, his hand came very close to the rifle he had in his saddle sheath.

All four riders pulled their pistols then and pointed them at him.

"Step away from that rifle, Perkins!"

"I . . ." Perkins said. He seemed to feel his body rising up through his head, and the next thing he knew Kistner was on the ground beside him, bathing his face with a wet handkerchief.

"What . . . what happened?"

"I don't know," Kistner answered. "One minute you

was standin' there talkin' to Mr. Poindexter 'n the next thing I knowed you just up 'n fell down."

"Where are they?" Perkins said. "Where is Poindexter 'n the others?"

"I don't rightly know," Kistner said. "When you fell down like you done, I come over to see about you. Poindexter 'n the others just rode off like it didn't make no never mind to 'em whether you was alive or dead."

Perkins sat up and looked around. "All this," he said in a strained voice. "They're a-takin' all this."

"You think you can ride all right, Mr. Perkins? 'Cause if you think you can ride all right, I'll get you back home 'n you can go in the house 'n maybe Mrs. Perkins can look out for you some," Kistner said anxiously.

"Yes, son, I'm sure I can ride if I can get mounted."

"I'll help."

From the *Chugwater Defender:*

IS THE C&FL RAILROAD A FRAUD?

There was universal approval and celebration when it was announced that the Poindexter Railroad and Maritime Corporation would be building a railroad from Cheyenne to Fort Laramie. A railroad would mean much for Chugwater and the citizens of the Chugwater valley, and so great was our appreciation of the coming of a railroad that the bacchanalia seemed appropriate.

But this newspaper would like to point out

to all our readers that so far not one rail of
track has been laid, not so much as one
hundred feet of roadbed has been cleared. In
fact the Chinese construction crew that the
C&FL brought for the task was left abandoned
outside of town, languishing without pay, even
without food until Duff MacCallister offered
them shelter, food, and employment at Sky
Meadow Ranch.

So far not so much as one mile of right-of-
way has been surveyed. And it is this, the lack
of survey of the route, which has raised a
question as to the actual intent and purpose of
the railroad.

The relationship between the C&FL and
citizens of Chugwater began on a high note,
with the reception and gala where we met
Jacob Poindexter. There, we listened to his
promise of a golden future of mutual growth
for the railroad and those whom it would
serve. He is the son of the founder of the
company, so one would think that we could
not be better represented. So, what have Mr.
Poindexter and the others been doing? They
have been acquiring land.

"Oh," you might say. "What is so unusual
about that? Will they not require land before
the building can begin?"

What is so unusual about it, my friends, is
the type and locations of the land they have
acquired, all without benefit of a route survey.

Here are a few examples. They have
confiscated rich and well-watered grazing
land from the Goodwin Ranch and the Davis

Ranch, as well as from the Pitchfork, Mountain Shadow, and Trail Back ranches. They have also recently made their first grab of land by use of eminent domain. I do not use the term grab loosely, for they have taken, by such maneuver, that part of the JP Ranch that abuts Bear Creek. This creek not only provides the JP with water it needs, it also furnishes water to Mountain Shadow, which is the ranch adjacent to the JP. Mountain Shadow is able to benefit from the creek because Jonas Perkins, being a good neighbor, has always seen to it that the creek is free of any debris that would obstruct its free flow.

Ah, but it doesn't stop there. Land has also been acquired from the Snowy Mountain Range and the Laramie Mountains, both areas known to be rich in mineral deposits.

Discerning readers will notice, right away, that the locations of these tracts of land are in no way contiguous, but are in fact separated from each other by no small distance. In the case of the Snowy and Laramie Mountain Ranges, the two parcels of land are separated by almost 100 miles.

In order for a railroad to qualify for free land under the provisions of the Land Grant Act of 1864, the railroad must pass over the land thus acquired. The distance from Cheyenne to Fort Laramie by the most direct and obvious route is 110 miles. If the C&FL Railroad actually utilizes the land it has so recently acquired, the same law that enabled them to acquire the land will also dictate that the tracks must be laid across or immediately adjacent to the granted land.

Such an irregular route would add 437 miles to the trip from Cheyenne to Fort Laramie.

It therefore should be obvious that the C&FL has something in mind other than building a railroad for the citizens of Chugwater Valley. To that end, I suggest that the name of the C&FL be changed from the Cheyenne and Fort Laramie Railroad to the Cheaters and Fraud Lies.

There should be an investigation launched, and soon.

"Did you read this?" Jalen Nichols asked, showing the newspaper article to Streeter.

"Yeah," Streeter said. "I seen it. The boss seen it too."

"What does he think about it?"

"He thinks we should ask Blanton not to write any-more articles like that."

"That's it? We should just ask him not to do anymore and he'll stop?"

Streeter smiled. "It all depends on how we ask him."

Chapter Fourteen

The effect of the article in the *Defender* was immediate, and it divided the residents into two opposing groups. Those who lived in Chugwater, as well as the towns of Walbach and Uva, still believed that the benefits of having a railroad outweighed any questionable activities in which the C&FL might be engaged. After all, the acquisition of land did not affect them.

"So what if the railroad does take a roundabout route from Cheyenne to Fort Laramie? Wouldn't that just mean more of our area is served?" Martin Gilmore asked.

"You have been hired as their lawyer," David Lewis said. "Of course you are going to defend them."

As the discussion continued, the rural residents—the ranchers, famers, and miners—saw the negative aspects of the oncoming railroad. Many of them had already seen the available free range disappear and having grown their herds to take advantage of this additional grazing area, they were now faced with the possibility of having to divest themselves of many head of cattle. Because it would be a distressed sale, they would lose a significant amount of money.

The relationship between the merchants and citizens of the town and the ranchers and farmers, which had always been very good, became strained to the point that frequent arguments erupted. Ranchers and businessmen, cowboys and employees of the city businessmen, men and women who had been very good friends, were barely speaking now.

Local businessmen Archie Jones and Bert Emerson were sitting together in the Wild Hog Saloon, discussing the situation.

"The ranchers and farmers and such are going to keep on messing around until the people who are building this railroad are liable to just give up and quit," Jones said. "And if they do that, that'll leave us without a railroad."

"Well, Archie, I want a railroad to come here same as you do. If we were to get a railroad, there's no doubt in my mind but this town would double in size within the next five years. That means my business would just about double, same as yours and ever'body else's. But, you have got to look at it from the ranchers' 'n farmers' point of view, too."

"You mean because they're having to give up some of their land? Hell, Bert, half of what they've been using doesn't belong to them anyway. It belongs to the government, and that means it belongs to us. If you ask me, they're just being selfish about it."

"Some of the townspeople are supporting the ranchers," Bert said. "Fred Matthews is, so are Bob Guthrie and Biff Johnson. I mean, when you think about it, the ranchers and cowboys have always supported all the businesses in town."

"Hell yeah, Johnson would," Archie replied. "All the ranchers and nearly all the cowboys go to Fiddler's Green when they come to town. But as far as I'm concerned, Biff Johnson is being as selfish as the ranchers and farmers are being. And have you been reading what Charley Blanton has been writing in his newspaper? Hell, he's come right out and called the railroad people nothin' but a bunch of crooks."

"Well, you have to admit, Archie, that what Blanton has written about some of the things the railroad has been doing is pretty bad. I mean, look at it from Perkins's point of view. They have completely cut his ranch off from water, and he didn't have any say-so about it at all."

"It couldn't be that big of a surprise, though," Archie said. "If you recall, when they first came we were told that they could make you sell your land if they needed it for the track."

"What if they said they wanted to run their track through your meat market? You would have no choice but to sell," Bert said, continuing his argument.

"Well, yes, but they wouldn't take it without paying me for it. Same as they're doin' with Perkins."

"They would pay you, yes. But you wouldn't be able to set the price. They would pay you what they decided your market is worth."

"That's nothing I've got to worry about, anyway. The track won't be comin' through Bert's Meat Market. It does make you think a bit, though. I wonder what the ranchers are going to do."

"I hear that they will be holding a meeting tomorrow night. I guess we'll find out what they plan then."

* * *

It was after midnight when Streeter, Dixon, and Nichols came into town riding down Clay Avenue. There were streetlamps at the corners of Third, Fourth, and Fifth Streets, but their illumination covered little more than the intersections. The three men appeared and disappeared in the little golden bubbles of light as if they were apparitions, now visible, now invisible.

Not one window in the entire town showed light. Even the saloons were dark. There was no sound except the quiet thud of hoofs falling on the dirt road.

"There it is," Streeter said, speaking quietly. He pointed to the small dark building on the corner of Fifth Street. Enough light came from the streetlamp to read the sign that was painted on the front window.

CHUGWATER DEFENDER
Serving the Chugwater Valley
CHARLES BLANTON, *Publisher*

"Well, sir, you ain't goin' to be servin' the Chugwater Valley much longer," Nichols said, and he chuckled as he began pouring kerosene on the side of the building.

Dixon stood out front, looking up and down the street.

"Is it all clear?" Streeter asked.

"Yeah, it's all clear."

Streeter snapped his thumbnail against the head of a match, causing it to light. He held it against the lowest board on the side of the building then was rewarded by seeing a little line of blue flame flare up from the bottom edge. He watched for just a second until he knew it had caught, then he walked back out to mount his horse, which was being held by Dixon.

"All right, boys. Let's go."

When they reached Bluff's Road at the extreme north end of town, they turned to look back. They could see a bright, wavering orange flame lighting up the darkness.

"Well, I don't reckon that runt will be printin' no more stories about us," Streeter said with a satisfied chuckle.

Just across the street from the newspaper office and about half a block down, twelve-year-old Judy Sinclair was awakened by something, surprised and a little frightened to see the walls of her bedroom bathed in a flickering orange glow. When she looked out her window she saw a building enveloped in flames.

"Mama! Papa! Fire!" she shouted.

Abe Sinclair, Judy's father, was not only a stage-coach driver, he was also a volunteer fireman, and he came running quickly into his daughter's room. "Where? Where is the fire?"

Judy pointed. "It's the newspaper, Papa!"

Abe Sinclair's first reaction was one of relief that it wasn't their house that was on fire. His second thought was also of relief when he realized it was a business building and not a private home that was burning. That meant that there was little likelihood anyone would be in immediate danger.

* * *

Several other citizens had been awakened by the fire just as Judy had, but by the time Abe Sinclair and the other volunteer firemen could be rallied, there was nothing they could do to save the newspaper office. They had no recourse but to throw water on the Chugwater Seed and Feed Store building, which was the newspaper office's closest neighbor. Fortunately the office was on the corner, so the Chugwater Seed and Feed Store was the only building at risk, and, by the prodigious effort of the townspeople, it was saved.

Although many had witnessed the fire and the effort to keep it from spreading, just as many townspeople were totally unaware of the fire until the next morning. As the sun lifted above the eastern horizon, the smell of smoke and burnt wood permeated the street. It was still early in the morning, but already a gathering of forty or so people stood in the middle of the road looking at the charred remains. Charles Blanton, who had not gone to sleep since the fire, was poking around inside seeing what was left of the building. From time to time he would pick up blackened items for a closer examination then discard them in frustrated disgust.

"I don't know what it's goin' to be like without a newspaper in town," one of the bystanders said.

"Wonder how the fire got started? You don't reckon ole' Charley left a lantern burnin' do you?"

"No, he wouldn't do nothin' like that."

"If you ask me, somebody burnt it down," another said.

"What? Why would anybody do a thing like that?"

"What do you mean why would someone do somethin' like that? You've read some of them stories he's wrote."

"What makes you think it was arson?" Marshal Ferrell asked later that morning when Charley expressed that sentiment to him.

"What else could it be?" Charley asked. "I didn't have any lit lanterns in the building, there was no lightning strike, and it certainly wasn't spontaneous combustion."

"*Spon* what?" the marshal asked, showing his confusion over the term.

"Look, Bill, you've read some of my articles," Charley said.

"Ha, that I have. They have been some stem winders, I'll say that."

"I've made Poindexter and his crowd angry, and they paid me back by burning down my newspaper office."

"Now, you ought not to be so quick as to make a charge like that, Charley," Ferrell said. "The truth is, your stand on the railroad has made a lot of people in town mad. They are afraid that you might cause the railroad to change their mind and not come through the town. So if you really think it was arson, who is to say it wasn't one of the people from town?"

"Hell, Bill, the number of people in town that I haven't made mad can be counted on one hand. But in the end we've always 'kissed and made up,' so to speak." Charley shook his head. "No, sir, I don't believe for a moment that any of our regular citizens would be evil enough to do something like this."

Ferrell stroked his chin for a moment. "The truth is, Charley, I'm inclined to agree with you. It probably was someone from the railroad. But we can't just go charging someone without some kind of proof."

"Yeah, I know."

"What are you going to do now?"

"I'm going to rebuild my newspaper office, that's what I'm going to do."

Marshal Ferrell nodded. "Yeah, I would have made book that that's what you intended to do."

Duff learned about the fire that afternoon when he came into town for the specially called meeting of the Cattlemen's Association of Laramie County that was to be held that night. He had planned to have dinner with Meagan before the meeting, and because her dress shop was on the same street as the newspaper, he learned of its destruction when he passed by the charred remains of the building.

Duff stopped to look it for a long moment. Sky, his horse, was made nervous by the burnt smell and became a little agitated. He made it known by tossing his head that he wanted to go on.

"All right, boy. We'll be for going on then," Duff said as he reached down to pat Sky's neck.

He was met with quite a different aroma, that of pan-fried steak, when he climbed the stairs to Meagan's apartment over the top of her dress shop. He tapped lightly on the door to announce his presence, then opened the door. "Meagan?"

"Come in, come in. I hope you're hungry." She greeted him with a quick kiss.

"Here now, lass, 'n would you be for tellin' me when I ever wasn't hungry?"

Meagan laughed, then the smile left her face. "You saw it? Charley's building?"

"Aye, I saw what was left of it, and 'tis a sad sight."

"Duff, people are saying that it was no accident. They're saying that it was arson."

"Given the current situation, 'tis possible that it could be."

"It's just that, well, I know almost everyone in town. And we may have a few cantankerous people, and there are a lot of people who have been upset with some of the things Charley has printed, but I just can't believe that any local citizen would do such a thing."

"People from Walbach, Uva, 'n even Fort Laramie are also upset. It could have been one of them," Duff suggested.

"Yes, that is a possibility."

Chapter Fifteen

The meeting was scheduled for seven p.m., and the sun was a large orange disk hanging just over the Laramie Mountains as the county residents began arriving by horseback, buggy, surrey, buckboard, and wagon.

The residents of the town watched the ranchers and farmers arrive, most with a sense of curiosity as to what they might decide, but some with a barely subdued animosity. Nearly everyone in town wanted the railroad, and they were resentful of anything, or anyone, that might prevent it. They were afraid that the planned meeting might have just that purpose in mind.

For the children of the ranchers and farmers, it was an exciting adventure, and even the rural women enjoyed the opportunity it would give them to visit. Such opportunities were rare because they lived so far apart. As the men went into the Cattlemen's Hall on the corner of Swan and Third Street, the women and children scattered throughout the town.

After dinner with Meagan, Duff had joined Elmer

at Fiddler's Green Saloon while waiting for the meeting to begin.

"Will Meagan be comin' to the meetin'?" Elmer asked. The meeting was closed to anyone who wasn't a member, or who had not received a specific invitation to attend, but, like Elmer, Meagan was a partner in Sky Meadow and because of that, a member of the Association.

"I asked her if she wanted to come and she said she dinnae think she would."

"I wonder if Charley Blanton will show up?"

"I expect he will, 'twas his article in the newspaper that got everyone all fired up."

"Yeah, and speakin' o' fired up it also more 'n likely got his newspaper office burnt down," Elmer said.

"Aye, that is probably true."

Biff Johnson had been standing at the door looking out over the batwings down toward Cattlemen's Hall. He went back to Duff and Elmer's table. "If you two are going, I should tell you that quite a few of 'em are gathered down at the hall now," he said.

"Then 'tis best we go," Duff replied. "I would nae want Webb to get all nervous worrying about us."

Webb Dakota, owner of Sundown Ranch, was the president of the Cattlemen's Association, and he had already asked Duff at least three times if he would be there.

"You may have a bit of trouble tonight," Biff suggested.

"What kind of trouble?" Elmer asked.

"Elmer, I don't have to tell you that there are a whole lot of people in town who want the railroad to come through, and they're looking at this meeting of the cattlemen as an obstacle that might prevent it."

"Aye, like they looked at the newspaper as an obstacle to prevent it," Duff said.

"No, I don't think so," Biff said, shaking his head. "At least, not the same people. Charley has spent quite a bit of time in here today. I mean, without the newspaper, where else would he go? Anyway, Charley isn't blaming anyone in town for it. He thinks it was the railroad people themselves who burned down his paper."

"It could be, I suppose," Duff agreed. "But we've nae way of proving it."

"Yeah, that's just what Marshal Ferrell is saying," Biff replied.

Roy Streeter and Hank Mitchell were in the little building next door to Martin Gilmore's Law office, the building that the town had provided for the railroad.

"It worked out just like you thought it would," Streeter said to the man sitting behind the desk. "Half the people think it was someone in town that burnt down the newspaper office, 'n most o' the others think it was maybe somebody from Walbach or Uva."

"Good. We no longer have the newspaper to worry about, and as long as we have everyone at each other's throats, then nobody will be paying that much attention to us, which means we can keep on with our plan."

"Yes, well, the people in the towns might be for us, but the ranchers are something else," Streeter said. "They've got a big meetin' goin' on down at the Cattlemen's Association building right now, 'n I'm tellin' you, boss, this could wind up bein' trouble for us."

"If they do try and cause any trouble we have enough men to resist, and we can resist with force. Remember, we have the law on our side."

Hank Mitchell chuckled. "Yeah, we're railroad police. I never thought I would be a badge packer, but here I am, a-wearin' one."

By the time Duff and Elmer stepped into the Association Hall, every rancher and farmer from the valley was there, and the two had to look around for a seat. When everyone was gathered and seated, Webb Dakota picked up his gavel and called the meeting to attention.

"Gentlemen, I don't expect I'll have to give you a reason why we're having this meeting. This railroad business is getting out of hand. First, we have seen thousands of acres of free range gobbled up." He held up his hand. "Yes, I know that the free rangeland is government property, but our cattle have grazed on it for as long as we have had cattle here. And losing that grazing land is workin' a hardship on all of us. But it didn't stop there. A few days ago we saw our first example of what they are calling eminent domain. Jonas, I'm going to let you tell the others what happened."

Jonas Perkins came to the front and looked out over his fellow ranchers. "Well, by now, I reckon you have all heard that Poindexter and some of his men from the railroad come to see me the other day. And the visit warn't nothin' you could say was a sociable call, neither. 'Cause what they done was, they bought up all my land that was watered by Bear Creek."

"They bought it, you say?" Dale Allen asked. "Well, that's somethin' isn't it? I mean at least they didn't just take the land like they been doin' with the free-range acreage."

"Yes, they bought it. They give me sixteen hundred dollars for eight hundred acres, and told me it belonged to the C and FL Railroad now."

"What? Are you actually saying that all they give you for that land was *sixteen hundred dollars*? Are you *serious*?" David Lewis said, literally shouting the last word.

"Sixteen hundred dollars," Perkins repeated.

"Why, that's only two dollars an acre, and that land is worth fifty dollars an acre, easy!"

"Yes, maybe even a little more because it's well watered. But I wasn't able to set the price. According to the railroad, it was the government that sets the price."

"And they dammed up Bear Creek too, which means I'm not gettin' any of the water, either, and that ain't right," Goodman added. "There ain't nothin' that's right about it."

"Tell them what happened this mornin', Jonas," Dakota said.

"Wait, don't tell me. They bought up some more of your land," Earl Davis, of the Davis Ranch said.

"No, this mornin' they came back to see me with a proposition," Perkins continued. "They offered to let me buy my land back."

"They offered to let you buy your land back? Well, that's good. It could be that some of our protestin' is gettin' through to 'em," Lewis said.

"Not quite. Remember, I told you that they bought it for two dollars an acre. Now they say I can buy it back from them for twenty-five dollars an acre," Perkins said bitterly. "Oh, they did point out that I would be getting the land for less than it is worth."

"I thought I was the only one they had done that to," Dale Allen said. "They took my free rangeland, then offered to sell it to me for forty dollars an acre, pointing out to me that it had never been my property in the first place."

"Gentlemen, none of this makes sense to me," Dempster said. Though Dempster was a banker and not a rancher or farmer, he did so much business with them that he was a member by default. This was the first time he had spoken since the meeting began.

"What do you mean, it doesn't make any sense to you?" Dakota asked.

"The C and FL is a subsidiary of the P R and M Corporation. The Poindexter Railroad and Maritime Corporation is one of the most highly respected companies in America, and they are known for their honest and decent business practices. That's why I say this makes no sense. I have certainly followed the founder of that company over the years, and he is the textbook example of the American entrepreneur who got where he is today by his own intelligence and industry.

"What do you mean?" Dakota asked.

"Well, for example, he wasn't born with a silver spoon in his mouth; he didn't inherit a railroad and a shipping company, he didn't even inherit any money. Why he was once an ordinary seaman himself, starting out on the very ships he now owns. And even there he prevailed because he went from ordinary seaman to ship's captain. No, sir, from everything I have read about Preston Poindexter, he is a man of honor and integrity.

"Who?" Elmer called out. "What was that name you just said?"

"Preston Poindexter," Dempster said. "He is the one who owns P R and M Corporation, and he's the father of Jake Poindexter, the man we're dealing with."

"Are you sure his name is Preston Poindexter 'n that he once commanded a ship?"

"Yes, I'm positive."

"Elmer, what is your interest in all this?" Dakota asked.

"Because if the Preston Poindexter that you're talkin' about is who I think it is, I know him. I know him real personal."

Chapter Sixteen

"I have a suggestion," Dale Allen said.

"The floor is open to any and all suggestions," Dakota replied.

"Duff MacCallister is the biggest rancher in the valley 'n probably is the best known and most respected. I think that we should ask him to go down to the C and FL office to have a visit with Poindexter, and find out just when this road is goin' to be built."

"Yeah, and ask him not to take no more land," Lewis said.

"Duff, would you be willing to do that?" Dakota asked.

"Aye, I'll do that, but seeing as Elmer may know Poindexter's father, I would like for him to go with me."

"Sure, I'll go," Elmer said.

"Gentlemen, I don't want to butt into what would be the business of the cattlemen, but since the C and FL is doing so much business with the bank, it might be helpful if I went with Duff and Elmer when they visit with Poindexter. That is, Duff, if you don't mind."

"I don't mind at all. I think it would be a good thing for you to come with us," Duff said.

"Good, then it's settled," Dakota said. "Is there any more business?"

"Yeah," Lewis said. "Jonas and Merlin, seein' as neither one of you can get to Bear Creek anymore, if you'd like, you two can bring your cows onto Trail Back to get to the water."

"Thank you, David," Jonas said. "I really appreciate that."

"Yeah, me too," Merlin added. "Thanks, David."

After the meeting was adjourned, Duff, Elmer, and Dempster walked down to the C&FL building, then stepped inside, where they were met by Streeter.

"What do you want?" Streeter asked gruffly.

"We would like to speak with Mr. Poindexter," Duff said.

"What for?"

"We'll be for taking that up with Mr. Poindexter," Duff said. "If he has nae objection to you bein' there when we talk, that's fine."

"Yeah, all right. Wait here for moment."

Streeter stepped into another office then a moment later came back out. "He'll see you."

When Duff, Elmer, and Dempster responded to the invitation, the man they had come to see was standing behind his desk. "Yes, what can I do for you gentlemen?" he said by way of greeting them.

"We've just come from a meeting of the ranchers, 'n we'll be for asking you a few questions, if you don't mind."

"Whether I mind or not depends on the questions."

"Then I'll ask the most difficult questions first. 'Tis the way you are taking the land that is causing the most concern."

"We haven't taken any of your land, so what is your interest in this?"

"I am a friend to those you have taken land from, and they 'n the Cattlemen's Association have asked that I"—Duff paused, then with a motion, took in Elmer and Dempster—"that *we* speak to you about the problem."

"Mr. MacCallister, as I have explained to everyone who has been affected by our land acquisition, this is a necessary step in building a railroad. Some may be hurt initially, but that is only temporary. In the end, most will benefit."

"Yes," Dempster said, speaking for the first time. "That is the way of progress. But as Mr. MacCallister has just pointed out to you, there seems to be no discernable pattern to your land acquisition. You've taken land parcels that are widely separated and inconsistent with what one would perceive to be the most logical route between Cheyenne and Fort Laramie."

"Yes, as the local newspaper pointed out before the tragic fire, we have not yet surveyed the route. And until the route is surveyed and agreed upon, we must consider all options, and that means acquiring land for several possible routes of the railroad."

"Is it true, Mr. Poindexter, that you have taken land, then attempted to sell it back to the very people you took it from?" Duff asked.

"Yes, that's true, but it is certainly within our right

to do that. You see, the Land Grant Act of 1864 isn't just to give us land over which to lay our track, it is also to provide us with real estate that we can sell in order to raise construction money.

"I'm told, Mr. MacCallister, that you are an immigrant, but recently arrived from Scotland. What you may not know is that this magnificent network of railroads that joins the Atlantic to the Pacific, and crisscrosses so much of America, was built by the same tactic we are employing here. We acquire land to sell, and in order for these land sales to be profitable, the land we acquire must be valuable."

"Even if it results in breaking the very people you are here to serve?" Duff asked.

"Our number one priority, Mr. MacCallister, is to make a profit. If, in making a profit, the people are served, then that is good. But you must understand that everything we have done, and will continue to do, is legal. And because the law is on our side, any resistance to our activity would be illegal, and we will act accordingly. That is why our railroad police also hold commissions as deputy United States Marshals. Now, gentlemen, will that be all?"

Duff and Dempster exchanged looks, but Elmer, as he had been doing from the moment they had entered the office, was staring at Poindexter. "You don't act nothin' at all like Pete. 'N you don't look like him, neither."

"Who is Pete, and why should I look like him?"

"It don't matter none."

"Gentlemen, I know that the ways of business and high finance may be a bit beyond your comprehension, so may I suggest you leave all the details to us? After all, we share the common goal of getting the railroad built, do we not?"

"Aye, 'tis our goal, all right."

"Then please allow the Poindexter Railroad and Maritime Corporation the opportunity to get the job done without all this troublesome opposition."

"Good day to you," Duff said as he led the other two men out of the C&FL headquarters.

"Good day, sir."

"Duff, if we're leavin' now, why don't we have us a drink a-fore we go back home?" Elmer asked, once they were out on the street.

"Aye, a wee bit of scotch would go down just fine, now. Mr. Dempster, would you be for joining us?"

"I'd better not. I told Julia I would come home immediately after the meeting," Dempster replied.

"Give the missus my regards."

Back in the C&FL building, Streeter stood watching at the window until he was sure they were actually leaving. Then he turned around to ask the question that had been bothering him for the last few minutes. "Who's Pete?"

"I don't have the slightest idea. But I feel that these men, at least MacCallister and this Elmer person, are going to cause us trouble."

"We can take care of that. All we have to do is kill all three of 'em."

"No."

"Why do you say no? Like you said, they're goin' to cause us trouble, and that means we're for sure goin' to have to get rid of 'em."

"When I say no, I mean don't do anything about Dempster as he is the banker and we are dependent upon him in order to keep our operation going. As for as the other two, MacCallister and Gleason, yes, I would like to see them, uh, eliminated. But I don't want any of our men to do it, because it would inevitably lead back to all of us. This is the West, some call it the Wild West. You certainly should be able to find someone who can handle the job for us."

"It's going to cost money."

"We've got money. We've got a lot of money and as long as everything continues to go our way, we'll have a lot more money. But to ensure that, it would be best if MacCallister and Gleason were, uh, no longer around to cause any trouble for us. I'll leave it up to you to make the arrangements.

Streeter smiled. "Yeah, I'd be happy to take care of it for you."

"Elmer, would you be for telling me who Pete is?" Duff picked up the shot glass and took a drink after he asked the question.

"That would be Preston Poindexter, the boy's daddy," Elmer answered. "He was my cap'n when I served as bosun on the *Appalachia.*"

"And you called your captain by his given name?"

"No, his given name was Preston. Pete was just what we called him, but we never even done that while we was still on the ship. We didn't start callin' him that until after the *Appalachia* went down 'n we was stranded on the island."

"Elmer, you mean to say that you were on a ship that sank, and you were stranded on an island?"

"Yeah, for more 'n three months we was stranded."

"Oh, do tell us about it," Kay asked enthusiastically. "Was your ship sunk by pirates?"

"Well, there warn't no pirates, but I'll tell you the story if you'd like."

Kay, Biff, and Webb Dakota and Jonas Perkins, who had come from the Cattlemen's Association meeting, as well as some of the other customers who were present in Fiddler's Green knew that Elmer was quite a raconteur. And upon learning that a story was about to be told, they all gathered around to hear the tale. Many of them moved chairs over from the other tables so that they became an audience to the drama as described by Elmer Gleason.

At sea, on board the S.S. Appalachia

The typhoon was unexpected, bowling down on them from out of the Western Pacific. Bound for Australia when the typhoon hit, they were in the central Pacific, just north of the equator, and some 1,700 miles southwest of the Hawaiian Islands.

The canvas was struck, and Captain Poindexter gave the order to bring the ship into the wind, but Elmer saw right away that they weren't going to be able to weather the storm. The foremast was whipping back and forth like a wand, and when Elmer heard a loud crack he was afraid it was going to come down.

"Cap'n, we need to take down the foremast before

it comes down on its own," Elmer said. "If we take it down, we can control it."

"Aye, Bosun, take it down," Preston Poindexter ordered.

"Lemon, Shuler, Bennet, you three go aloft and cut all stays and braces from the foremast then get some lines attached. Lamdin, when they're ready, you 'n Cook take axes to it. Bring it down to port," Elmer ordered, though the shrieking howl of the storm was so loud he had to cup his hands around his mouth and shout at the top of his voice.

Once the three men he had ordered aloft were in place, he could only watch. No way he could shout any instructions to them. He saw Shuler slip and thought he was going to fall, but somehow, he seemed to be hanging by his legs.

"Bosun, Shuler has got his leg stuck betwixt the t'gallant spar 'n the brace," Cook said.

"I see 'im!" Elmer said as he started up the mast.

"Bosun, you try 'n get Shuler loose 'n you'll both get killed," Lamdin shouted, but his warning was carried away by the wind.

The ship was rising and falling on the twenty-foot-high waves, as well as rolling at least forty-five degrees from side to side. Above Elmer, Shuler was hanging upside down by the leg that was jammed into the rigging, and his arms were stretched down toward the deck.

It took maximum effort, not just to climb, but also to hold on to the mast. Just before he reached the topgallant spar, there was another loud crack, and Elmer felt it even above the violent gyrations of the ship. Finally he reached the spar, then straddling it so he could hang on with his legs, he inched his way out to Shuler.

"Shuler, you still conscious?" he shouted.

"M' leg's hung up," Shuler called back.

"Yeah, well, you'd be dead iffen it wasn't," Elmer said. Reaching down, he was able to grab Shuler by his waistband, then, with a mighty heave, pulled him upright.

Once Shuler was upright, he was able to regain his purchase on the spar, and after a quick cut of two more braces, he was free and followed Elmer back down the mast.

"All right, Lamdin, you 'n Cook take your axes to it. The rest of you, bear a hand on the lines, pull it down to the port, then push it overboard."

It took less than a minute to bring the mast down and jettison it, so that there was no longer any danger of it falling into the other masts and rigging.

They fought the storm valiantly for twelve hours, but in the end, even though the winds and the sea had finally abated, they lost the battle. The storm had caused some severe damage below the waterline, damage that they didn't even know they had sustained, until someone went below and reported that water was pouring in. The water was rising faster than the bilge pumps could handle, and the ship began going down by the bow. Finally, when Preston Poindexter couldn't save her, he gave the order to abandon ship.

* * *

"Howland Island, it was," Elmer said. "We knowed where we was, 'cause Cap'n Poindexter was a good navigator. 'N when it come time to get into the lifeboats, well sir, Cap'n Poindexter had his map 'n a pocket compass, 'n he led us. We was in them three boats for ten days till we landed. We didn't lose a soul while we was at sea neither."

"What did you eat, Mr. Gleason?" Kay asked.

"We had birds, a lot of birds, 'n we done pretty well fishin' too, so they didn't none of us get too hungry."

"Was there fresh water?" Guthrie asked.

"No, there ain't no fresh water nowhere on Howland Island. We done what we could to catch 'n hold the rainwater, but the only problem is, it didn't rain that much. We wound up havin' to boil seawater so's that it evaporated, then catch the vapor 'n let it turn back into water so's that all the salt was gone. That kept us a-goin' in between the rainfalls."

"My goodness, how did you know how to do that?" Kay asked.

Elmer chuckled. "Darlin', I'm from Missouri 'n I didn't know no one that wasn't distillin' corn liquor. I figured if you could distill corn mash, you could distill salt water 'n turns out that we could."

"I'll bet all the others were glad you knew about distillin' whiskey," one of the customers said.

Elmer chuckled. "Yeah, some of 'em was wantin' me to make some whiskey, but it was hard enough to get fresh water from the salt water. Anyhow, Pete told me that what I done may have more 'n likely saved a mess of us from dyin' of thirst."

"Pete," Duff said. "Aye, you did say that he asked to be called Pete."

"Yeah, Cap'n Poindexter said that if we was to all think of ourselves as friends, rather than just sailors on a ship, that we have a better chance of survivin' 'cause we would do things for one another. It was his idea that we call each other by our first names, 'n that's when we found out that his family 'n friends all called him Pete, instead of Preston."

"How long were you all on that island, Mr. Gleason?" Kay asked.

"We was on it for three months, one week, 'n four days," Elmer said. "We was finally rescued by a British ship, the *Dauntless*, it was. They took us to Honolulu, 'n there we got an American ship to take us back home."

"Are you sure that this man you knew is the same Preston Poindexter who owns the Poindexter Railroad and Maritime Corporation?" Duff asked.

"No, now to be truthful, I ain't sure it's the same one. But if the feller that owns this company is the same one that I know, it just don't seem nothin' at all like him to be doin' things the way he is. And this feller Jake Poindexter don't look nothin' at all like Pete."

It was Meagan who came up with the idea. "If Preston Poindexter is the same man who is Elmer's friend, and if he really is the kind of man Elmer believes him to be, he might be willing to put a stop to what his son is doing out here. All you would have to do is go to New York to see him."

"Aye, I could see Elmer and me going to New York."

"I'm going with you."

"You don't need to, we can—"

"Do you think I'm going to miss out on the opportunity to go to New York?" Meagan asked. "No, sir, I'm going."

Chapter Seventeen

Streeter was in Fiddler's Green when he overheard the conversation of a couple of the customers at a nearby table.

"Yeah, Miss Parker is goin' with 'em," one of them was saying. "She, MacCallister 'n Gleason. It looks like all three of 'em is a-goin' to New York."

"What are they going to New York for?"

"Ha, get this. It turns out that Elmer Gleason knows Poindexter."

"What do you mean? We all know him. He's been all over town."

"No, I ain't talkin' 'bout that Poindexter. I'm talking 'bout the old man, Preston Poindexter. The man who owns the whole company."

"What's Gleason goin' to see him for?"

"I don't know if it's to stop the buildin' of the railroad, or just to stop 'em from takin' up all the land. Whatever it is, they're plannin' on leavin' come Monday, 'n will more 'n likely be there within a week."

"Why're they waitin' till Monday? That's six days from now. Seems to me like if they was really goin' to do it, they'd just do it, 'n not wait around none."

"Yeah, well it turns out that Miss Parker is needin' to finish a dress for Webb Dakota's daughter, Amanda. She's marryin' that army fella from Fort Laramie."

"Oh, yeah, that would be Lieutenant Kirby. He's a nice fella, I've met him."

Streeter listened to the conversation until it turned to a discussion of Amanda Dakota, and how lucky Lieutenant Kirby was to be marrying her. Not having any interest in the details of the upcoming wedding, Streeter left the saloon to report on what he had just heard.

"They're goin' to New York?"

"Yeah," Streeter said. "I heard some folks talkin' 'bout it down at Fiddler's Green. Seems like MacCallister 'n Gleason are plannin' on goin' to New York to talk to someone there about the railroad. They'll be leavin' come Monday."

"We can't let that happen. If they go to corporate headquarters with information about what we are doing here, it could not only stop the flow of income, it could put us in severe legal jeopardy. We have to stop them."

"There ain't no way of stoppin' 'em short of killin' 'em," Dixon said.

"I agree. I had hoped to avoid such a thing, but I'm afraid we are going to have to get someone to take care of that part of the job for us."

"Why do we have to get somebody else to do it?" Dixon asked. "I'll kill every last one of 'em. Hell, I'd love to do it."

"Yeah, especially that old fool Gleason. How hard could it be to kill him?" Caldwell asked.

"A lot harder 'n you might think," Streeter said. "You said it yourself, he's an old man. How do you think he got to be so old?"

"No, I don't want to risk anyone within our particular company. We can't take the chance of any of us getting caught. It would come back onto the rest of us. I will need somebody else, somebody that would be willing to kill them for money."

"How much money?" Dixon asked.

"Why do you ask? Do you have someone in mind?"

"Yeah, I have someone in mind."

"I would be willing to pay five hundred dollars to have the job done. That would be two hundred fifty dollars each for MacCallister and Gleason."

"I know somebody that'll do it for that much money." Clete Dixon chuckled. "Hell, he'd prob'ly even do it for less money, seein' as he's got him a reason for wantin' it to be done."

"Who is this person you are speaking of, and where can we find him?"

"His name is Grant Slocum, and his brother, Drury, was hung a few months ago on account of MacCallister found 'im, 'n brought 'im in. That mean's he's got it in for MacCallister."

"Wait a minute, I've heard of Grant Slocum," Streeter said. "Ain't he supposed to be some kind of a gunfighter or somethin'?"

"Yeah," Dixon said.

"Hell, somebody like that prob'ly won't come to a one-cow town like Chugwater, even for five hundred dollars," Hank Mitchell said.

"I can get im to come," Dixon said. "If MacCallister 'n Gleason ain't leavin' till next Monday that'll give 'im plenty of time to get here."

"Why are you so sure that you will be able to get 'im?" Mitchell asked.

"On account of 'cause me 'n him was cell mates for two years, 'n we got along real good."

"Where is he now?"

"Last I heard he was in North Platte, Nebraska."

"Wait, did you say he is in North Platte?"

"Yeah."

"Then that's perfect. You don't have to bring him here. The train to New York will be going through North Platte. He can do the job there. No way it could be connected to us or to anything that's going on here."

"How we goin' to do that?" Streeter asked. "We can't very well send 'im a telegram a-tellin' 'im we want 'im to kill MacCallister and Gleason."

"No, but there is plenty of time for Dixon to go to North Platte and get there before MacCallister does. I'll give the five hundred dollars to take with you."

"If I'm goin' to be there with 'im, I'll be takin' part in the killin'," Dixon said. "I know you said you didn't want none of us involved in it, but if the killin' happens there, they ain't likely to connect us with it, even if I am part of it."

"Yes, I see your point."

"So it ought to be worth a thousand dollars, don't you think? That way me 'n Slocum can split the money, five hundred dollars apiece."

"Why are you concerned about that? You are already making much more money than that, and by the time we are through with this job it will be worth thousands of dollars to everyone involved."

"You could say that it's a bonus."

"What about the rest of you? Do any of you have any objections to Dixon getting extra money for doing this job?"

"Hell, it's fine with me," Mitchell replied, being the only one to answer. "It's like you said, if we don't get MacCallister took care of, why he's likely to mess ever'thing up."

The others gave their assent by nods.

"All right. If you leave now you can be to Cheyenne in time to take the first eastbound train tomorrow."

"The money?"

"Come down to the bank with me, and I'll draw out the money. In fact I'll give you fifteen hundred dollars. The five hundred extra is for expenses."

"Hello, Mr. Poindexter," the bank teller said. "How can I help you?"

"Hello, Mr. Hirsh. I have to withdraw one thousand dollars from my account. Here is the draft."

"Yes sir," Hirsh said, examining the draft. "It will take just a moment. I don't keep that much cash in the drawer, and I will need Mr. Dempster's authorization to access the vault."

"We're in no hurry."

The two men watched as the teller approached Dempster with the draft. Dempster nodded, went to the vault, then came to the teller's window to personally hand over the money.

"Mr. Poindexter, speaking as a member of this

community, I can say that we are all looking forward to the arrival of the railroad. But our rural residents, our ranchers and farmers, are also valued members of our community. And if the railroad breaks them, what good will it do us?"

"I understand your concern, Mr. Dempster. I know that some of what we have been doing may have caused some difficulty but, unfortunately it had to be done."

"Perhaps, Mr. Poindexter, the C and FL can be more judicious in any future land acquisitions?" Dempster suggested.

"I shall take your concerns under advisement, Mr. Dempster."

It was just after dark the next day when Dixon stepped down from the train in North Platte. He had no address for Grant Slocum, but there were eight saloons in town, so he knew where to start.

He found him in the fifth saloon he checked. Slocum was standing at the far end of the bar staring into an almost empty mug of beer. Dixon stepped up to the opposite end of the bar.

"What'll you have?" asked the bartender, a thin man wearing a shirt with red and white vertical stripes. He had a small, well-trimmed moustache and dark, slicked-back hair.

"I'll have a beer, and I would like to buy a beer for the feller down there in the green shirt."

"You want to buy him a beer?" the bartender asked, surprised by the request.

"You have a problem with that?" Dixon asked, his voice a caustic challenge.

"No, no, I don't have any problem with it, mister. I was just wantin' to make sure I heard it right, as all."

"When you give him the beer, I want you to tell 'im who bought it for him."

"How can I do that when I don't even know your name?"

"He knows my name. You just point me out to him. Bring me my beer first."

A moment later, with his beer in front of him, Dixon watched as the bartender put the beer in front of Slocum and turned to point toward him. Slocum looked up in confusion at first, then, when he saw Dixon he smiled and held up his beer.

Dixon started toward an empty table, signaling for Slocum to join him.

"Clete Dixon," Slocum said as he sat at the table. "What brings you to North Platte?"

"You do. You bring me to North Platte. How would you like to make five hundred dollars?"

"Who do I have to kill?" It wasn't an offhand response. Slocum fully expected to have to kill someone to earn that kind of money.

"Two people, not just one. But I intend to help."

"You ain't told me who they are."

"Duff MacCallister and Elmer Gleason will be comin' through North Platte by train this Monday night. They are on their way to New York, but for reasons that I don't need to go into, some people don't want them to get to New York."

"Duff MacCallister? Wait a minute, you mean he ain't dead?"

"No, he ain't dead. What made you think that?"

Slocum thought of the gunfire he had heard on

the road just north of Cheyenne, which he assumed at the time had killed MacCallister. He took a swallow of his beer then looked at Dixon with a meditative stare. "You got the money with you?"

Dixon hesitated for a moment, then he nodded. "Yeah, I got it."

"Give it to me now. I plan to have a little fun between now and Monday."

"Grant, I hope you ain't plannin' on drinkin' from now to Monday. You're goin' to have to be sober to get the job done."

"Who said anythin' about drinkin' from now to Monday?"

"You did. You said you was plannin' on havin' fun between now 'n then."

"Yeah, well, Miss Maybelle's House of Elegant Ladies ain't exactly where you go just to drink."

Dixon smiled. "Well, yeah, I'll give you the money now, 'n maybe you can introduce me to some o' these elegant ladies."

Guthrie Lumber and Supply furnished the wood, paint, shingles, windows, nails, et cetera, and friends, neighbors, and other businessmen of the city pitched in to help rebuild the office for the *Chugwater Defender*. When it was rebuilt, Charley Blanton rented a wagon from the livery to go to Cheyenne to pick up a new press and type. Because he was going to pick it up on the same Monday as Duff, Elmer, and Meagan were to leave, they all went together, making the trip down on Sunday.

The four of them stayed in the Interocean Hotel

that night and ate supper together in the hotel dining room.

"Duff, when you get back home I'm going to want you to tell me everything you have learned," Charley said. "If Jake Poindexter is pulling a fast one on his father, I want to know all about it."

"If it really is Jake Poindexter," Elmer said.

"What do you mean, if it really is Jake Poindexter? Why wouldn't it be?" Charley asked. "And if it isn't him, who is it? And where is Jake Poindexter?"

"I don't know," Elmer said. "Dead, maybe. I may be wrong, but it's just hard for me to believe that a good man like Cap'n Poindexter could sire a son like that no-account skunk that's callin' hisself Jake Poindexter. Besides which, this feller that's callin' hisself Jake Poindexter don't look nothin' like his pa."

"If it isn't Jake Poindexter, how is it that he is getting so much support from the Poindexter Corporation? Dempster tells me there's a little over one hundred thousand dollars on deposit for Jake Poindexter in the Chugwater Bank. It seems very unlikely that some charlatan would have access to that much money," Charley said.

"It's like I said, I could be wrong. But I need to talk to Cap'n Poindexter to find out for sure. I'd be willin' to bet that he don't know ever'thing that's goin' on out here. Or if he does know, he don't know that it's causin' people to suffer. I'm tellin' you that Cap'n Poindexter just ain't that kind of person."

"I hope you are right, Elmer," Meagan said. "I'm like everyone else here. I want to see Chugwater get a railroad, but not if it is going to ruin the lives of so many of our people, so many of my friends."

"I promise you that having my newspaper office burned to the ground will not stop me from publishing as much information about the C and FL Railroad company as I am able to learn," Charley said. "That's why I want you to share with me what you may learn on your trip to New York. I am a firm believer that the more light you can shed on a subject, the better you will be able to deal with it."

"Will you have your paper up and running by the time we come back?" Duff asked.

"Are you kidding? I've come here to pick up a new press. I'll have my newspaper operating within a day after I return."

True to his promise, the very next day after Charley Blanton returned to Chugwater, he put out a special issue of his paper.

Chugwater Defender *Redux*

WHAT MAKES A PERSON GO INTO THE NEWSPAPER BUSINESS? Is it because of some inherent nosiness? Is it because someone is basically a gossip, and publishing the latest information in a newspaper that will exponentially spread the gossip satisfies that need?

Or is it, as I am prone to think, a basic love of people? This love of people drives one to share the latest news with everyone in order to make the lives of the readers fuller by providing them with a comprehensive understanding of what's going on around them.

I cannot remember when I didn't want to be a newspaperman and, as a child, even before I learned to write, I would scribble the news on scraps of paper, then distribute my newspaper to my mother, grandmother, aunts, anyone I could find. I was bound to be a newspaperman and so I have become one.

Now, however, I have learned something new. I have learned that there is a symbiotic relationship between the newspaper and its readers. When my office was destroyed by fire it was my friends, my readers, my partners in this news business who came to the fore and rebuilt the building. But, it wasn't just the lumber, paint, and nails they provided. They provided love, not just for the newspaper but for their fellow citizens, those who read the paper and thus share in each other's lives.

I am humbled and eternally grateful, and I pledge to you that the reborn DEFENDER will be even more a part of the spirit of Chugwater.

Chapter Eighteen

"Where are we going to do it?" Dixon asked.

Clete Dixon and Grant Slocum were waiting in the Union Pacific depot in North Platte for the eastbound train, the one on which they had been told that Duff MacCallister and Elmer Gleason were passengers. It was lacking fifteen minutes of three o'clock in the morning, and according to the dispatcher the train was due to arrive at three.

"It's more 'n likely they're sleepin' right now 'n cause they'll be in berths we won't know where they're at. But they'll be comin' to the dinin' car for breakfast in the mornin' 'n we'll be keepin' an eye open for 'em. Oncet we know just where it is that they're at, why, we'll be able to take care 'of em easy," Slocum said.

Using some of the expense money Dixon had brought with him, the two men had bought a round-trip ticket to New York. If the opportunity presented itself, they would take care of them before the train reached New York. But if they weren't able to do it on the train, Dixon had been given the name of someone in New York who would be able to help.

"Here comes the train!" someone shouted, and the departing passengers, as well as those who were meeting arriving passengers, stepped out onto the platform to watch the train arrive.

Meagan was sleeping in the bottom berth, and when the train stopped, the cessation of motion and the sound of wheels rolling on the track caused her to awaken. She pulled the curtain aside just far enough to look outside and saw the boarding passengers.

A couple of the passengers aroused her interest, and she pulled the curtain open a little more, but just as she did so, they stepped onto the car before she could get a closer look.

Very soon the train started moving again, and she lay there, staring up into the darkness of her berth, thinking about the two men she had just seen, or who she thought she may have seen. She couldn't put a name to either of the passengers, nor could she think of where she may have seen them before. But the more she thought about it, the less likely it seemed to her that they could possibly be anyone she knew. She had no idea where the train was right now, but she knew they were several hours east of Cheyenne, so what would be the likelihood of encountering anyone she knew this far from home?

Still, she couldn't get over the nagging feeling that she had seen at least one of the two men somewhere before.

She tried to concentrate on the faces of the boarding passengers, but it was dark on the boarding platform and her glimpse was too fleeting. Finally the motion of the train and sound of the steel wheels rolling on the steel track had a soothing effect and she drifted off to sleep again.

"I know it might sound silly," Meagan said at breakfast the next morning, "but I thought I saw someone that I knew getting on the train last night."

Meagan, Duff, and Elmer were having breakfast in the dining car as they were passing through eastern Nebraska at a rate of forty miles every hour.

"Who did you see?" Duff asked as he spread butter on his biscuit.

"That's just it. I don't know the person I think I saw."

"Meagan, pardon me for sayin' this, but that don't make no sense a-tall," Elmer said. "You think you saw someone you knew, but you don't know 'im?"

Meagan chuckled. "I said that it might sound silly. But last night, or maybe it was early in the morning, at one of the places where the train stopped, we took on some passengers. I just happened to look out the window and I saw him. Actually, there were two of them, but I only recognized one. Well, I didn't exactly recognize him. Like I say, it's just someone that I think I've seen before. And I may be totally wrong. After all, I just got a brief glimpse."

"Ships that pass in the night," Duff said.

"What are you talkin' about?" Elmer asked. "We ain't on no ship."

"It means a chance encounter without actually meeting," Duff explained. "It's from a poem by Longfellow.

*Ships that pass in the night, and speak each other in
    passing,*
*Only a signal shown and a distant voice in the
    darkness;*
*So on the ocean of life we pass and speak one
    another,*
*Only a look and a voice, then darkness again and a
    silence.*

"Oh, that's beautiful," Meagan said. "And yes, it was exactly like that."

"Well, if they got on the train you're more 'n likely to see 'em agin. 'N iffen you do see 'em maybe you can figure out who they are," Gleason proposed.

"I suppose so," Meagan said. "It's just that . . ." she left her sentence unfinished.

"What is it, lass? This is more than just trying to remember who they are, isn't it?" Duff asked.

"Yes. I can't explain it, Duff. But I have such a sense of foreboding about the two men. I know it makes no sense at all. But I just can't get rid of the feeling that, somehow, their presence represents danger to us."

"I'm nae one to discount feelings, for they have saved m' life more than once. If you see them again, you'll be for tellin' me, will you now lass?"

"Yes, of course."

"They're on the train, all right," Dixon said. "I peeked in through the door to the dining car, 'n I seen 'em. The onliest thing is, there's a woman with 'em."

"Yeah, well, that don't make no never mind,"

Slocum said. "She ain't goin' to be no trouble, 'n if she gets in the way, we'll kill her, too."

"Are you goin' to do it on the train?"

"If I see the chance to do it, I will, but more 'n likely I'll have to wait until I catch them off the train. We'll be changin' trains in Chicago 'n we'll be there for a couple of hours before the next train leaves for New York. I expect I'll get a chance to do it whilest we are in Chicago."

"All right. I expect we had better stay out of the way as much as we can whilest we're on the train. Iffen one of 'em was to see me, they'd for sure recognize me," Dixon said.

"It's more 'n likely that they won't none of 'em know me," Slocum said. "So I can keep an eye on 'em so's they don't get away from us."

It was late in the afternoon of the following day when the train pulled into Union Station in Chicago. Here, they would have several hours between trains, and Meagan suggested they should see some of the city while they were there.

After a short ride from the depot, they took a walk alongside the lake.

"Isn't it beautiful?" Meagan asked. "I wish we had water to look at back in Wyoming."

"Ha! I've seen enough water," Elmer said. "When I come back onto the beach the last time, I got a length of hawser 'n hung it over my shoulder, 'n started walkin' inland. Then when somebody seen it 'n ask me what it was, I figured I was far enough away from the ocean so as to be able to settle down."

Duff laughed. "Elmer, you have a bit of blarney about you. Are you for certain that you aren't a bit Irish?"

"What's a hawser?" Meagan asked innocently.

"Now, do you see what I'm talkin' about?" Elmer asked with a cackling laugh. "I'm far enough away from the sea."

"A hawser is a very thick rope for to moor or tow a ship," Duff explained.

Just as they were approaching a rather large hedge row, a man stepped out in front of them. He was holding a pistol pointed at Duff. "Hello, MacCallister," the man said in a low, mocking voice. "I'll bet you never thought you would see me here, did you?"

"I never expected to see you anywhere, as I've never seen you before. I don't know who you are," Duff said.

"Duff, this is one of the two men I was telling you about. One of the two men I saw getting on the train, back in North Platte."

"I know who the sidewinder is," Elmer said. "Miss Meagan, please excuse the language," he added.

"That's all right, Elmer. I have a feeling he *is* a son of a bitch."

"My name is Slocum. Grant Slocum. Does that mean anythin' to you?"

"Aye, the name Slocum is known to me. That is, if you are talkin' about the evil brigand who was hanged for murdering Mr. Gorman, his wife, 'n the wee ones. 'Tis a name of shame, 'n 'tis a wonder you would bandy it about so."

"Drury was my brother, and you kilt 'im," Slocum said angrily.

"Nae, I dinnae kill him. But I have no sorrow that he was made to pay for his crime."

"Well, you same as kilt 'im. You brought 'im in."

"Both of us brought 'im in, sonny," Elmer said, his voice dripping with anger and challenge.

"Yeah, 'n both of you are goin' to pay for it, too, seein' as I aim to kill both of you," Slocum insisted.

"What about me, Mr. Slocum?" Meagan asked. "Am I going to pay for it as well?"

"You didn't have nothin' to do with it like these here two did."

"But if you kill them, won't you have to kill me, as well? Surely you wouldn't expect me to keep quiet about it, would you?"

Slocum smiled, and the grotesque stretch of his mouth made his face look even more evil than before. "Well now, you're pretty smart, ain't you? You got it all figured out. Yeah, I reckon I will have to kill you too."

Elmer started drifting over to his left, opening up some distance between him and Duff and Meagan.

"Where are you going?" Slocum demanded.

"If you're goin' to commence a-shootin' them two, I'd just as soon be out of the way so's I don't get hit by any of the bullets," Elmer said.

"What are you talkin' about, you fool? I'm goin' to kill all three of you."

Elmer took another few steps to his left, opening up an even greater distance between them. Duff realized then what Elmer was doing, and while Slocum was paying attention to Elmer, Duff was able to inch just a little closer.

"Well, if you're plannin' on shootin' all of us, I'd

just as soon you shoot me first," Elmer said. "I wouldn't want to have to watch the lady gettin' shot."

"All right. If that's the way you want it, I'll be glad to oblige," Slocum said, and he raised the pistol, pointing it toward Elmer.

By now, though, Elmer had opened up enough distance so that the gun, being pointed at Elmer, was at an angle of at least sixty degrees from Duff. And that was all the advantage he needed.

"Get down, lass," Duff shouted loudly.

When Duff shouted, Slocum's reflexive action was to look back toward Duff. Unfortunately for Slocum his reflexive action was with his glance only, and not with the pistol. He was much slower in trying to bring the pistol to bear, and as it came around Duff grabbed Slocum's gun hand, twisting it back toward himself.

Slocum was already in the act of pulling the trigger, and the gun went off. The result of Duff's application of force was that Slocum shot himself in the chest. He made a grunting sound, then fell.

Meagan, who had dropped to the ground on Duff's orders, was helped up by Elmer, who had come back to her. Duff was leaning over, checking Slocum's condition.

"Is he—?" Meagan started

"Dead?" Duff asked before she could complete the question. "Aye, lass, he's dead."

"So, what do we do now?" she asked.

"I think we should go to the police," Duff replied.

"Why?" Elmer asked.

"Because 'tis the right thing to do."

"No, it ain't," Elmer said, shaking his head. "You

think the police would listen to our story then just let us go? No, they would keep us here while they investigated this 'n investigated that. We would miss our train today, 'n probably for the next two or three days. In the meantime, this Slocum feller would still be dead and the folks back home would still have to be dealin' with a railroad that ain't actually goin' nowhere."

"I think Elmer is right," Meagan said. "It isn't as if we are running away from anything. All three of us are totally innocent. I think we should go, now."

"Aye, 'tis thinkin' I am that the two of you are right. I think we have seen enough of the city, and should be getting back to the depot."

"You know, 'tis queer to think that Slocum would be for following me all the way to Chicago to avenge his brother," Duff said later that night as the train they were on headed for New York.

"I been thinkin' that same thing," Elmer said. "What was Slocum doin' in Chicago? 'N how is it that he just happened to know that you was here?"

"He didn't just happen to be here. He was sent here to kill us, and it didn't have anything to do with revenge for his brother," Meagan replied.

"What are you sayin', lass? Why do you think he was here?"

"I told you he was one of the two men I saw getting on the train?"

"Aye."

"I have remembered who the other man was. It was one of the C and FL railroad police, the one named Dixon."

"I'll be damned," Elmer said. "It wasn't just you they come after. They found out we was comin' to New York 'n they come after all of us to keep us from talkin' to Pete Poindexter."

"If Mr. Poindexter doesn't know what is going on back home, I can see why his son might go to great lengths to prevent it. Even if it means murder," Meagan said.

"Yeah, well, that's figurin' that the man we been callin' Jake Poindexter actually is Pete's son. I've been doubtin' that he is for some time, 'n now I'm near 'bout sure it ain't really him."

"If the person we have been calling Jake Poindexter isn't him, then where is Jake Poindexter?" Meagan asked.

"I'd say he's more 'n likely dead," Elmer said.

Clete Dixon saw MacCallister, Gleason, and the dress shop woman board the train to New York. He didn't see Slocum again, and that left only two possibilities. Slocum kept the money and ran away, or Slocum was discovered by MacCallister, and killed.

Either way, the problem remained. MacCallister was still alive, and Dixon had to keep him from seeing Preston Poindexter.

Chapter Nineteen

Chugwater

The Wild Hog had become the de facto head-quarters for the C&FL railroad police, and at the moment Pogue Flannigan and Roy Streeter were having a beer.

"You think they'll be able to take care of MacCallister 'n Gleason?" Flannigan asked.

"Yeah, I think so. MacCallister 'n Gleason won't be expectin' nothin', bein' as they're so far from home. Dixon 'n this feller Slocum who's with 'im will have the edge, 'n I figure they'll ambush 'em somewhere." Streeter chuckled. "Hell, I wish the boss woulda sent me instead of Dixon. I'd love to be the one that kills MacCallister."

"I don't think he's goin' to be all that easy to kill. They say he's just real good with a gun."

"Is he? Well, what difference does that make?"

"What do you mean, what difference does that make?" Flannigan replied, surprised by Streeter's comment. "If you face him down, you might not be the one left standin' when it's all over."

"Who said anythin' 'bout facin' MacCallister down?

If you shoot someone in the back, they're just as dead as iffen you shot 'em in the front. 'N I expect that's exactly how Dixon 'n Slocum plan to do it."

"Yeah, I guess you're right."

"You damn right, I'm right," Streeter said with a smug chuckle.

"But it ain't goin' to do us no good just to get rid of MacCallister 'n Gleason, you know," Flannigan said.

"Why not? You don't think any o' these other ranchers will be able to step up 'n take MacCallister's place, do you? 'N if none of the ranchers can do it, you know damn well there ain't no sodbuster who can."

"No, I'm talkin' about the Chinaman. We're goin' to get rid of the Chinaman, too."

"What Chinaman?" Streeter asked.

"The one that works for MacCallister. Wang Chow."

"Are you kiddin', Pogue? What kind o' trouble are you expectin' a Chinaman to give us?"

"This here ain't no ordinary slant eye. He's got some kind of special way o' fightin' that there ain't nobody never seen before. Why me 'n Clete had the drop on 'im, 'n the next thing you know, me 'n Clete was both down, 'n when we come to the guns was back in our holsters, only there didn't neither one of 'em have the cylinder in 'em. Somehow that Chinaman had took 'em out."

"Yeah, well, if we take care of MacCallister, there won't be anybody left to be givin' the Chinaman orders on what to do, so I wouldn't worry about it," Streeter said.

"That may be, but I'd still like to see the Chinaman took care of." Flannigan said.

"Why? I told you, he don't matter none."

"It's personal with me."

"How are you goin' to do it? You said yourself that he took care of you 'n Dixon all by his ownself. 'N the boss ain't goin' to let any of us take up any time just to deal with a celestial."

"I've got three men that ain't one of us, but they'll come with me to deal with the celestial if I give 'em a hunnert dollars apiece."

"You got three hunnert dollars?"

"No, but I thought maybe the boss would give it to me iffen he knew it was to take care of MacCallister's Chinaman."

"Who do you have?"

"Loomis, Pollard, 'n Muldoon."

"Muldoon? Ain't he a prizefighter?"

"He was, till he kilt a man in the ring. Now there won't nobody fight 'im no more, so lately, he's been makin' a livin' by beatin' up people for money."

"All right. Wait here. I'll get the money for you." Streeter chuckled. "I'd like to see Muldoon 'n that Chinaman fight. I think it would be real entertainin'."

"Where we goin' to find 'im?" Loomis asked after Dixon had gathered the men he needed for the job.

"It's noon, ain't it? Ever'day at noon, he's been comin' in to have his dinner at Lu Win's Restaurant," Dixon replied. "He's prob'ly there right now."

The noon traffic in the street and on the boardwalks was busy as the four men marched toward Lu Win's Restaurant. And march it was, rather than walk. The four men were moving as if unified by a common goal and a dedication of purpose.

"What is it you think them folks have in mind?" someone asked as the four men moved toward the Chinese restaurant with such resolution.

"I don't know, but I'd be willin' to bet they ain't goin' in there for any fish 'n rice."

Muldoon went in first, kicking the door open so their entrance was announced by a loud bang. Although some of the diners were Chinese, most of the restaurant customers were American. Startled by the abrupt entrance, they dropped their knives and forks—chopsticks for the more adventurous—and looked toward the door. What they saw was a big man with a bald head and no neck, wide shoulders, and powerful-looking arms.

"Which one of you Chinamen calls hisself Wang Chow?" the big man called out, his voice booming like thunder.

Wang Chow was sitting at a table in the middle of the room, and though he was facing the door, he didn't bother to look up. He continued to eat, deftly picking up a small piece of beef with his chopsticks.

"That's him right there," Flannigan said, pointing.

"Hey you, Chinaman. They say you are some kind of fancy fighter," Muldoon said. "Is that true?"

"Hell, let's don't mess around with 'im." Immediately after his comment, Pollard threw a knife.

The action was smooth and so swiftly done that nobody realized what was happening until the knife, one that was especially designed for throwing, was flying through the air toward Wang.

He had still not looked up, but at the last second, and to the shock of everyone in the dining room, Wang held up his chopsticks and with a quick scissors action, trapped the knife between them. With a flick of his wrist, and aided somewhat by the leverage action of the chopsticks, he sent the knife back from where it came.

The entire incident happened so quickly that some of those who were prepared to see Wang die by the knife didn't grasp the reversal of the situation until it was too late. Pollard let out a gasp as the knife stabbed, hilt deep, into his shoulder.

"What the? What the hell just happened? Where'd that knife come from?" Loomis asked.

"It come from the Chinaman hisself," Flannigan said.

"Don't nobody else try 'n do nothin' like that," Muldoon warned. "I'll take care of this puny little toad all by myself.

With Pollard groaning in pain behind him, Muldoon walked over to the table then stood there, looking down at Wang, who was still eating. "Hey, you, Chinaman. It ain't polite to eat whilest people is talkin' to you."

"A thousand pardons, *Xiānshēng*," Wang replied.

"What did you call me?" Muldoon bellowed angrily.

"Please, he didn't call you anything!" Lu Win called out. "It is a term of respect. He said sir."

Muldoon made a fist of his right hand and cocked his arm out. He held his left hand out, palm up, and began curling his fingers.

"They say you're quite the fighter. Stand up. I'd like to see just how good you are."

Wang stood up then approached Muldoon, standing within a couple feet of him.

"Yeah, that's a good boy," Muldoon mocked. At

almost the same time he sent a powerful right fist whistling toward Wang.

Wang leaned back, doing it so gradually that most hadn't even seen him move. They thought Muldoon had simply missed.

Muldoon had put so much power into the swing that it actually threw him off balance, and he had to take a couple of quick steps to remain standing. When he recovered, he tried a left jab, and Wang leaned to one side just far enough to let the fist slip by him.

With a cry of rage, Muldoon tried again and again to hit Wang. At that moment there could have been no greater picture of the two men than that which they were providing. Even though Muldoon was missing practically every blow, there was brute force and power in his movements and all could see that.

Wang, by contrast, could have been a *maître de ballet*, so graceful were his reactions that, with a minimum of movement, he avoided all of Muldoon's attempts to hit him.

The big man halted. Breathing hard from his unsuccessful attempts to hit Wang, he stared at the smaller man. "You think you're somethin', don't you? Well, dodge this." He grabbed a nearby table and swept it easily up over his head with the legs of the table pointing up.

"Dodge this one!" he shouted as he swung the table down toward Wang.

Too wide to allow Wang any room to maneuver, the table made a loud crashing sound as it joined Muldoon's shout of triumph. The others in the restaurant, nearly all of whom knew Wang, gasped in anxiety and concern.

To everyone's surprise, they saw that Muldoon had been left holding two halves of a table that had been literally split in two. The mystery of how it was done was quickly solved by the sight of Wang standing with his right hand held up, the knife-edge of the hand forward.

Muldoon looked at the two halves of the table as if trying to figure out what had just happened. Then, tossing one of the table halves aside, and with the bellow of a bull, he raised the other half over his head, intending to use it as a club. But he was never able to start the downward swing.

Wang shot the heel of his hand toward the big man, connecting with his forehead, and Muldoon went down.

"You can keep your one hunnert dollars. I'm gettin' the hell outta here!" Loomis shouted as he bolted toward the door.

Flannigan hadn't done a thing since the four of them came into the restaurant, but was the only one of the four left standing—Loomis and a wounded Pollard had run away, and Muldoon was lying on his backside on the floor of the restaurant with a broken table half lying on either side of him.

"Wang, is it all right if I pick up Muldoon and go?" Flannigan asked.

"You may go," Wang replied.

"Mister?" one of the other dining room patrons said to Flannigan. "You mighta noticed that Wang don't never wear no gun. But I do wear one. 'N if you stick your head back inside here in the next minute, I'll be a-shootin' at you."

"Yeah," one of the others said. "Me too."

"And me," said a third.

On the floor, Muldoon groaned and tried to move.

"Is he paralyzed?" Flannigan asked.

"He can walk," Wang replied.

Flannigan walked over to Muldoon, and with his help, Muldoon was able to get up.

"Come on. Let's go," Flannigan said.

As the two men left, Wang looked at the broken table, then toward Lu Win. "*Wǒ hěn bàoqiàn zhè zhāng zhuōzi. Wǒ huì fù qián de.*"

"Do not be sorry about the table, Master Wang," Lu Win said, responding in English to the apology Wang had given in Mandarin Chinese. "There is no need for you to pay for it."

"Hell, Lu Win, I'll pay for it myself," a customer said. This is the one who had cautioned Flannigan about coming back in. "It was well worth it to be able to see this."

The others in the restaurant applauded.

Chapter Twenty

Sky Meadow

Roy Streeter, Hank Mitchell, and Dusty Caldwell were on an exploratory scout for Collins.

"This here is part o' the Sky Meadow Ranch," Mitchell said. "Folks say that this is s'pose to be the most valuable land in the whole valley, with two creeks furnishin' the water."

"Look over there," Caldwell said, pointing to a gather. "Are them cows or buffalo? I ain't never seen me no cows that look like that, but they seem too little to be buffs."

"They're what's called Black Angus," Mitchell said. "They're 'bout the most expensive cows a feller can have."

"Wooee, there sure is a lot of 'em," Caldwell said. "This MacCallister feller must be rich."

"They say he is," Mitchell replied. "Wait a minute. Look over there. Ain't them celestials s'posed to be workin' for us? What are they doin' here, workin' for MacCallister?"

"Damn if I know," Streeter said. "Why don't we just ride down there 'n find out?"

* * *

Wang Chow was watching as Cong Sing and two more of his countrymen were stretching strands of barbed wire between two of the fence posts. Wang looked up as the three riders approached.

"Here, what are you heathens doin'?" one of the three asked.

"Can you not see? We are erecting a fence," Wang Chow replied.

"Well, seein' as we are about to take over this here part of the ranch, you ain't got no right to be a-doin' that, so I'm tellin' you now to stop it." As he made the demand, Streeter pulled his pistol. The two men with him pulled theirs as well.

Wang stepped up to the fence line and took one end of the strand of barbed wire from Cong Sing.

"*Xiansheng* MacCallister asked that this be done in his absence, and until he says otherwise, we will continue to do so." He held up the end of the wire to illustrate his point.

"Yeah? Well, how is it you're goin' to be able to do that with a bullet in your head?"

Without saying a word, Wang snapped the hand that was holding the end of the barbed wire back down quickly. The result was an arch that appeared in the strand then traveled down the wire so that it encountered all three men, striking each of them in the hand that held the pistols, causing all of them to drop their guns.

"What the hell!" Streeter shouted in surprise, alarm, and some pain, for the barbs of the wire had cut through the skin. He, Mitchell, and Caldwell were all three holding painful, bleeding wrists. Cong Sing moved quickly to recover the dropped weapons.

"Why, you little—" Streeter shouted in anger. He slid down from the saddle, pulled a large knife, and charged toward Wang.

Wang stepped to one side then brought the side of his hand crashing down on the back of Streeter's neck. Streeter went down like a poleaxed steer.

"Streeter!" Mitchell called. He glared at Wang. "Did you kill him?"

"He will live. But if you do not leave now, and take him with you, I will kill him." Wang spoke the words as if he were talking about the weather. "And then I will kill both of you," he added, the words calm but bloodcurdling.

"Let's get 'im up on his horse 'n get out of here," Mitchell said.

Mitchell and Caldwell got down and helped a groggy but conscious Streeter onto his horse.

Mitchell held his hand out toward Cong Sing. "Gimme our guns back."

"No," Wang said. "You may get your guns from the marshal's office."

Mitchell pointed his finger toward Wang. "Look here, you yellow-skinned creeper! One o' these days I'm goin' to catch you when you can't do none of them Chink tricks you been pullin' on us. 'N when I do, I plan to shoot your ass dead."

"Leave now, please," Wang ordered.

Mitchell continued to glare at Wang.

"We better go, Hank," Caldwell said. "Ole' Streeter here is barely able to stay in the saddle."

Mitchell glared at Wang a moment longer, growing

even more agitated by the fact that the expression on Wang's face remained totally calm. "Them guns better be at the marshal's office today," he said with a growl as he and the other two men rode away.

"I tell you, that Chinaman ain't quite human," Mitchell said after he and Caldwell had returned to the C&FL office in town. They had brought Streeter with them, and though he was able to walk on his own, he was sitting on a chair against a wall, greatly disoriented.

"Of course he is human," Collins said. "He is just skilled in the art of fisticuffs."

"Yeah, well it ain't exactly fisticuffs," Mitchell said. "I don't know what you call it, but it ain't fightin'. Leastwise, it ain't nothin' like no normal man does."

"I heard of another feller that can fight like that," Jalen Nichols said.

"Another Chinaman?"

"No, this is an American named Zack Clark. And from what I've heard, he learned how to fight like that while he was in China. I heard tell that oncet three men took 'im on at the same time, 'n he kilt all three of 'em with his bare hands."

"If he kilt three men, how come it is that he ain't in jail?" Mitchell asked.

"He ain't in jail 'cause the three men he kilt all had knives 'n, like I said, he had only his bare hands. 'N get this. They was all three Chinamen, 'n all three of 'em could fight like this Chinaman Wang Chow can."

"Do you know this man?" Collins asked.

"No, I don't know him, I ain't actually never even

see 'im, but I sure heard about 'im when I lived in San Francisco."

"Do you think you can find him?"

"I don't know. If he still lives in San Francisco, I reckon I could. Why are you askin'?"

"Come to the bank with me," Collins said. "I will give you travel expenses of two hundred dollars. It won't cost that much to bring him back, and I'll give you a thousand dollars to entice him to come. Tell him there will be more money when he gets here."

"How much more?"

"More," Collins said without being specific.

New York City

From the moment the *New York Flyer* crossed the Hudson River, Meagan had been looking at the city, enthralled by the tall buildings and the sheer number of people, carriages, trolley cars, and electric wires. "Oh, Duff, have you ever seen such a thing?" she asked with awe in her voice.

"Aye, lass, for when I first arrived in this country, I lived here for a time."

"Oh, yes, I had almost forgotten. You have some cousins who are famous actors here."

"Aye, Andrew and Rosanna MacCallister are my kinsmen."

For a while after arriving from Scotland, Duff had worked as stage manager in the theater where his cousins, the twins Andrew and Rosanna, starred in the Broadway production of *The Highlander.*

"Will we be seeing them while we are here?"

"Aye, lass, 'tis sure I am that we can work out a time to see them."

Reaching Grand Central Depot, the train stopped, then began backing up, and Megan turned her attention to the sights outside. They were on but one of a large network of railroad tracks, nearly every track occupied by a train. Opening the window and looking in the direction they were going, she saw a huge five-story building

The train backed into the station, then Meagan's view was blocked off by two trains that were already in place. This train and the one closest to it were separated by a long, narrow, brick path. They were under an overhead roof of some sort and, finally, they came to a complete stop.

"All right, folks, this is Grand Central Depot," the conductor said, coming through the car. "Please watch your step as you leave the train."

Duff, Meagan, and Elmer followed the other passengers through the aisle of the car, then down the steps, and onto the brick platform. There were other trains arriving and departing, and the roof, which was high overhead, seemed to capture the sounds of chugging engines, vented steam, rolling wheels, clattering connectors, squeaking breaks, clanging bells, and hundreds of voices, all united to cast a cacophonous clamor back down.

Dixon was still on the train, but he was in a car three cars farther toward the rear end of the train. He was looking through the window, studying the detraining passengers, and he saw MacCallister and the other two walk by.

Reaching into his pocket, Dixon withdrew a piece of paper with a telephone number on it. He'd been told to call the number if the issue hadn't been resolved by the time he arrived in New York, but not to call it unless all other avenues had been closed.

Well, as far as he was concerned, all other avenues had closed. He had no intention of taking them on by himself.

Unaware that they were being observed from the train, Meagan spoke within a few seconds after they passed the spying Dixon. "I'm sure it'll be a few minutes before we'll be able to claim our luggage, so I think we should get something to eat."

"Aye, it sounds like a good idea to me," Duff agreed.

They stepped into the Grand Central Diner, then were shown to a table and given a menu.

"Oh, Elmer, look at how beautiful these menus are. I wonder if we could keep one. We should show it to Vi. Maybe she could have Charley make one for her that is just as beautiful as this one is."

"Why?" Elmer replied. "It won't make her pies taste any better, will it?"

"No, I suppose you've got me there," Meagan replied with a chuckle.

Inside the depot an operator could be paid to make a telephone call. Clete Dixon paid the five-cent fare and gave the operator the number he wished to call and the name of the person with whom he wished to speak.

A moment later, the operator looked over at him. "I have your party on the line, sir."

"Uh, what am I s'posed to do? Do I come over there 'n speak through that thing you're talkin' into?"

"No, sir. If you pick up that phone, I will connect you."

Dixon picked up the phone, and no more than a couple of seconds later, he heard the operator's voice in the earpiece.

"Go ahead, Mr. Dixon."

"Hello?" Dixon said tentatively. "Do you hear me?"

"I hear you. What do you want, Dixon?"

"MacCallister 'n two others have come to New York. They plan to talk to Mr. Poindexter, 'n when they do, it's goin' to cause a lot of trouble for us."

"Meet me at the corner of Forty Second and Lexington."

"Where's that at?"

"It is nearby. I'm sure you will have no trouble finding it."

"Do you think—" Dixon was unable to finish his question. The other party had hung up.

After getting directions from someone, Dixon walked the short distance to the corner of 42nd and Lexington, then realized he had no idea who to look for. He stood there for about ten minutes, then someone stepped up to him.

"Are you Dixon?"

"Yeah, I am, but how did you know?"

"You are the only one wearing boots, denim trousers, a plaid shirt, and a Stetson hat."

Dixon glanced around at the others, and chuckled. "Yeah, I reckon I am, ain't I?"

"Where are these three people now?"

"Last I seen of 'em, they was eatin' dinner back there in the depot."

"You haven't seen them since last night?"

"No, I seen 'em just a little while ago. I told you I seen 'em eatin' dinner."

"Oh, you mean lunch. Well, if they are still at lunch, then we will have time to make arrangements for them."

With baggage in hand, Duff, Meagan, and Elmer took a cab to the Fifth Avenue Hotel. Once there Duff called the Poindexter Railroad and Maritime Corporation.

"P R and M," a woman's voice said.

"I would like to speak with Mr. Poindexter, please," Duff said.

"May I inquire as to the nature of the call, sir?"

"I would nae be for wanting to discuss it with anyone but himself."

"Sir, Mr. Poindexter is a very busy man. You must understand that I can't just let anyone call and speak to him."

"Aye, I can see the limitations that are put upon you, lass, but would there be another I could speak with who perhaps has more authority to decide?"

"I can let you speak with Mr. Norman Jamison, sir. He is the executive secretary, but I'm sure he will tell you the same thing."

"Then, if you will, lass, please let me speak with Mr. Jamison."

"Very well, sir, please hold the line for a moment."

Duff waited for a moment, then he heard a man's voice.

"This is Norman Jamison, executive secretary to Mr. Poindexter. Miss Margrabe said that you would not tell her the reason for your call."

"I will tell Mr. Poindexter why I'm calling."

"He isn't here, right now, but as I said, I am his executive secretary, which means that whatever you are asking him for will have to come through me anyway. So you may as well tell me what it this is about."

"I will tell you that 'tis about the C and FL Railroad being built in Wyoming between Cheyenne and Fort Laramie. 'N I will also tell you that I will nae be asking for anything but want only to give him some information."

"Tell me again your name?"

"M' name is Duff MacCallister 'n there are two others with me, being Miss Meagan Parker 'n Mr. Elmer Gleason. 'Tis representing the citizens of Chugwater, we are."

There was pause before Jamison spoke again. "Very well, Mr. MacCallister. If you, and your friends, would present yourself at the office of the corporate headquarters by nine o'clock tomorrow morning, I will arrange a visit with Mr. Poindexter for you."

"'N would you be for tellin' me the address?"

"Where are you staying?" Jamison asked.

"We are in the Fifth Avenue Hotel."

"Well, then, you are within easy walking distance. It's at the corner of Fifth Avenue and Fifty-third Street. The building is clearly marked. You can't miss it."

"'Tis thanking you I am, Mr. Jamison, 'n we'll see you tomorrow morning."

"We're not going to be able to see him until tomorrow?" Meagan asked after Duff hung up the phone.

"Aye, we can nae see him until tomorrow."

"Good!" Meagan said with a happy smile. "That means we can do something fun tonight."

"'N would you be for tellin' me lass, what would you like to do?"

Meagan held up a copy of the newspaper. "I picked this up at the front desk. Did you know that Andrew and Rosanne MacCallister are doing another play?"

"What is the play?"

"*The Way Home.* It has gotten very good reviews."

"And may I take it that you would be for wanting to see the play?"

"Oh, yes, very much. That is, if we can get tickets. The newspaper article says it is sold out."

"Let me call m' kinsmen 'n see if they can help."

Chapter Twenty-one

Duff called a number he remembered, and he recognized Andrew's voice when the call was answered. "Andrew, m' kinsman."

"Duff MacCallister? This is you? Are you in New York?" Andrew replied happily.

"Aye, 'tis here I am."

"Well, that is wonderful! Rosanne and I will be very happy to see you."

"Andrew, 'tis a favor I shall be asking of you. Would it be possible for me 'n two of my friends to get tickets to the play you 'n Rosanne are doing?"

"Yes, yes of course. I will have them waiting for you at the Will Call box office. And after the play we must have a late dinner. I am so looking forward to seeing you again."

"As am I, cousin. And 'tis thankin' you I am for making available the tickets."

When Duff, Meagan and Elmer showed up at the box office of the Rex Theater on West 48th Street at Broadway that evening, the ticket clerk looked at the three of them with total disdain. "There are no seats available. You should have checked before you made the trip here."

"I'm told that there will be three tickets at the box office," Duff said.

"Is that so? Who told you?"

"'Twas my cousin, Andrew, who told me."

"Andrew? Andrew who?"

"Andrew MacCallister," a third voice said. "I have their tickets. Hello, Mr. MacCallister. It's been a long time since you were stage manager here. It's good to see you again."

"Jared Simmons. You still work here. That's good to see," Duff said with a wide smile.

"I'm the head usher now," Simmons said proudly. "Come, I'll personally escort you to your private box."

"I'm sorry, Mr. Simmons, I didn't know," the ticket agent said.

"It's not me you should be apologizing to," Simmons said.

"Mr. MacCallister, please forgive me."

"Och, 'tis nae a thing to forgive, lad. You were just doing your job."

"Oh," Meagan said as Jared led them into the theater. "This is even more beautiful than the Cheyenne Opera House." She started toward the mezzanine.

"No, miss, this way," Simmons said.

"The balcony? Oh, I thought . . . never mind," Meagan said. "It was rude of me to comment."

"I think you will be pleased, miss."

Simmons led them upstairs but instead of going through a door and into the balcony he led them down the corridor to a series of doors, then stopped at the last door and opened it. "You will be sitting here," he said with a wide grin.

The door led to a private box, but not just any box. It was the closest box to the stage, affording its occupants the best view and the best acoustics of anyone in the theater.

"Oh, my," Meagan said, her voice reflecting her awe. "I have never had such a seat."

"I will return after the play," Simmons said. "Mr. and Miss MacCallister want me to take you backstage so you can visit."

"Thank you, Jared," Duff said.

"No, thank you, sir. Even though I was but an apprentice usher when you worked here, you always treated me well. I'm glad for the opportunity to pay you back."

As they waited for the curtain to rise, Megan reached across to take Duff's hand in her own. "Oh, it must have been wonderful for you to have worked here."

"Aye, 'twas a pleasant experience. But 'tis nae a thing I would want to go back to."

The lights in the theater dimmed, and the buzz of conversation halted. Then, as the curtain opened and the stage was well lit by footlights, a spotlight found Andrew MacCallister standing center stage.

ANDREW (in the role of Benjamin Quarrels, *looking stage right*): Here, the battle was fought, and here, so many were lost.

* * *

For three acts, the play continued with drama and scenery changes to depict the trials and tribulations of a family torn by war. Then came the last scene.

ANDREW: Think not of all the trouble and despair we have seen. That is behind us now, and we have prevailed.

ROSANNE (portraying Laura Fontaine): Survive we have, but only because of you, Benjamin. It was your valor and tenacity that pulled us through all the travails and hardship.

ANDREW: I cannot accept such laurels without acknowledging your own courage and spirit.

ROSANNE: And, what path shall we take now?

ANDREW: What path now? Now we shall take the way home.

The curtain falls.

"Oh, it was such a wonderful play," Meagan said. "I could feel every scene as if I were actually living through it myself."

Shortly after the curtain fell, Jared Simmons, as promised, appeared at the door of the VIP box.

"Come with me. I'll take you backstage." Simmons chuckled. "Though you, of course, don't need to be guided, do you, Mr. MacCallister?"

"Nae, but 'tis good to be guided by an old friend," Duff said.

Andrew and Rosanne, with makeup and costumes removed, were waiting in the greenroom.

"Duff, it is wonderful to see you again!" Andrew said, shaking his hand.

Rosanne gave him a hug.

Duff introduced Meagan and Elmer.

"I have called ahead and reserved us a table at Delmonico's," Andrew said. "And we've a carriage waiting. What do you say to a late dinner?"

"I say 'tis a fine idea," Duff said.

During the dinner Meagan spoke glowingly and knowledgably about the play she had just seen.

"You have a marvelous insight, my dear. How would you like a job as drama critic for the *New York Times*?" Andrew asked. "I think they could use a columnist who has such a keen eye for talent."

Rosanne laughed. "Oh, hush, Andrew. The critics have always been fair."

"You don't understand, sister. I don't want fair. I want adoration."

Everyone at the table laughed, catching the attention of the other diners.

"Duff, I don't flatter myself to think that you came to New York just to watch Rosanne and me perform. What has brought you to the city?"

"We've come to meet with Preston Poindexter," Duff replied.

"Oh, he is a very good man," Andrew said.

"Why do you say that?"

"Recently an orphanage was about to close for lack of funds. Forty children between the ages of four and twelve, difficult ages to place in a family, were living there. They were going to be separated and sent to other orphanages. Do you understand what this means? The only family those children had, were each other."

"But Mr. Poindexter stepped up and gave the orphanage one million dollars," Rosanne said. "Isn't that wonderful?"

"Aye, 'tis a fine deed," Duff said.

"Why have you come to see him? Do you want him to donate to some charity?"

"'Tis nae a charity, but a railroad."

"Then you'll be talking to the right person, because he has built many of them."

"Yeah, well, this one we want him to stop," Elmer said.

"Why would you be against a railroad?" Andrew asked, confused by Elmer's response.

Over the next several minutes, with Duff, Elmer, and Meagan all adding to the story, Andrew and Rosanne were told of the difficulties the ranchers and farmers in Chugwater Valley were having with the indiscriminate acquisition of land and the disastrous results.

Andrew shook his head. "That doesn't sound like Preston Poindexter. He has built several connector railroads and in every case the result has been very positive for all the residents. And as I said earlier, he has always been there for anyone who needs help."

"That's what I've been tellin' ever'one," Elmer said. "This sure don't sound like Pete."

"Pete?" Andrew asked.

"Aye, Pete," Duff said. "As it turns out, Elmer knows Preston Poindexter personally."

At the urging of Duff and Meagan, Elmer told

the story of his service aboard, and the sinking of, the *Appalachia*.

"He was the best cap'n, 'n as fine a man as I ever knowed," Elmer concluded.

"Then I'm certain you will get a satisfactory response to your problem," Andrew suggested.

"Aye, that is our hope," Duff said.

"How are you goin' to do it?" Dixon asked. "You can't just go into Delmonico's 'n shoot 'em. And there's too many people out on the street, so you can't do it here, either."

"That ain't your problem," Al Todaro replied.

"Maybe how you handle 'em ain't my problem, but stoppin' 'em a-fore they get a chance to talk to Poindexter is."

"It'll be took care of," Todaro promised.

It was just after one o'clock in the morning when Todaro entered the lobby of the Fifth Avenue Hotel. It was illuminated by electric lamps, but only three were on. Despite the dim lighting, he could see that none of the sofas or chairs were occupied. When he stepped up to the front desk, the night clerk had his chair tipped back against the wall, and he was snoring loudly.

Todaro examined the guest book and, locating the room for Duff MacCallister, took the 502 spare key from the board. He started toward the elevator then

198 *William W. Johnstone*

stopped. Because of what he intended to do, it would be best if nobody saw him. He took the stairs.

On the fifth floor he walked down the dimly lit hall, checking the room numbers. When he reached room 502, he let himself in with the key he had taken and closed the door behind him. With knife in hand, he started toward the bed. In the darkness, he stumbled against a chair and it made a sound as it scooted no more than an inch or two across the floor.

Grabbing the chair quickly to prevent it from falling over, he stood there for a long moment to ascertain whether or not MacCallister had heard him.

There was no response from the bed, and Todaro breathed a sigh of relief. He had not been heard.

When Duff had checked into the hotel earlier in the day, he had booked three adjacent rooms. Connected by a door, two of the rooms were to be occupied by Duff and Meagan. However, booking three rooms was only for propriety's sake. In actuality, Duff was spending the night in room 504 with Meagan, and that left 502 empty.

At the moment Duff was sound asleep, but Meagan was not. The Fifth Avenue Hotel had all the modern conveniences, including, for the higher-priced rooms, bathrooms. And it was to take advantage of this facility that caused Meagan to be awake, out of bed, and adjacent to the wall that separated 504 from 502.

She heard a thump and a scrape.

She hurried back to the bed and shaking Duff awake, whispered to him. "Duff! Duff! Someone is in your room!"

He got out of bed. Though he had not been carrying a pistol while in New York, he had brought one with him. Reaching for it he walked over to the door that separated the two rooms, opened it quietly, and flipped on the light switch just beside the door.

A man was standing over the bed with a raised knife.

"No, no, don't shoot!" the man called in alarm, dropping the knife.

Chapter Twenty-two

Corporate headquarters of P R and M

"So you turned the robber over to the police, did you?" Norman Jamison asked later that morning when Duff, Meagan, and Elmer arrived in his office.

"Aye, but I'm nae so sure that the brigand was a thief. 'Tis more likely he was in my room for to kill me."

"Why on earth would he do that? Last night was your first night in New York, wasn't it?"

"Aye."

"Did he know you?"

"I cannae say that he did. I dinnae know him."

"Then why do you think he wanted to kill you?"

"He had a knife."

"And sometimes robbers have guns. I'm sure he meant to use it into frightening you so you would give him the money."

"Aye, that could be. But 'tis all water under the bridge now. When can we be for seeing Mr. Poindexter?"

"I'm afraid he isn't in today, he—"

At that moment the door to Poindexter's office opened, and he stepped out into the reception area.

"Norman, have we received a reply from Jake for the telegram I sent yesterday? We should have—" Poindexter stopped in midsentence and looked at Elmer.

"Do I know you, sir?"

Elmer smiled. "Yeah, Cap'n, you know me."

"Bosun Gleason?"

"That's me."

With a huge smile, Poindexter stuck out his hand and grabbed Elmer's hand. "What are you doing in New York, Elmer? Have you come to look for a job? If that's why you are here, I'll be more than happy to hire you. Why, I'll even give you your own ship to command."

"I appreciate that, Cap'n, but that ain't why I'm here. Me 'n my friends have been tryin' to get in to see you for the past two days, but this feller keeps tellin' us you ain't here. Only, it turns out that you are."

"Norman?" Poindexter asked with a questioning expression on his face.

"I confess, Mr. Poindexter, I did tell them you weren't here, but I did it to protect you. I do it quite often, actually. You don't have any idea how many people want to get in to see you, either to beg money from you, or to try and get you to invest in some ridiculous scheme they have planned."

"Yes, yes, I'm sure that is true, and I appreciate your efforts in protecting my time. But in this case I know this gentleman, and I will always find the time for him."

"I'm sorry, sir, but he said nothing about knowing you, and of course, I had no way of knowing."

"Come into my office, Elmer, and bring your friends with you. All of you, come in. Norman, please have Barkley bring coffee for us."

"Yes, sir," Jamison said.

Poindexter's rather commodious office was decorated with model ships, both wind and steam, as well as several intricately scale-modeled trains. The reception area was large enough to give everyone a seat without feeling crowded.

"I don't know if this man has ever spoken of it," Poindexter said once all were seated, "but he saved my life, and not my life alone, but the entire crew of the *Appalachia*. We were stranded on a waterless, deserted island, and many, if not all of us, would have died if Elmer hadn't designed a still to produce not whiskey, but clear drinking water."

"I tell you the truth, Cap'n, if we had been there for another month I think maybe I woulda found me a way to make some actual whiskey."

Poindexter laughed. "I've no doubt but that you would have, and I would have imbibed right along with the men. Now, if you didn't come seeking employment, what does bring you here?"

"I'm goin' to let Duff tell you, seein' as how he's a lot more smarter than I am, 'n he can talk a lot better, even if he is a foreigner 'n talks with one o' them foreign accents."

"Duff . . . ?" Poindexter phrased the word so that it was a question, asking that the last name be supplied.

"The name is MacCallister, Captain Poindexter. Duff MacCallister. 'N this fair lass is Miss Meagan

Parker. The three of us live in Chugwater, Wyoming. Does that name mean anything to you?"

"Chugwater? Oh, indeed it does," Poindexter replied with a proud smile. "My son Jake is there now and he's building a railroad, but of course if you live there you know that. Tell me, how is he doing?"

"He's the reason we are here, sir," Duff said. "That is, he and the railroad. We want it stopped."

"What?" Poindexter was so surprised by Duff's request for the building to be stopped that the word literally exploded from his mouth. "My word, I have communities all over America begging me to build a railroad for them, and never has any community been sorry for having made the request. Why would you not want the railroad?"

"The price is too high."

"I don't know what you mean. You aren't being charged for the railroad, so how can the price be so high?"

"Duff, let me tell him," Meagan said. At Duff's nod, she turned toward Poindexter. "Mr. Poindexter, I own a business in town, and nearly every business owner and resident of the town is for the railroad. I, myself, want the railroad. But Mr. MacCallister and Mr. Gleason are ranchers, and nearly every rancher and farmer is opposed to the railroad. No, let me change that. They aren't opposed to the arrival of the railroad but they, and many of the citizens of the town are opposed to the tactics being used to deprive the ranchers of their grassland and water."

"I know that can sometimes work a temporary

hardship, but it is necessary to obtain land to build the railroad."

"Yes, sir, I understand that. But in this case the land is being taken, either by government grant or eminent domain, then it is immediately offered for sale back to the person from which it was taken. And the asking price is quite exorbitant."

"Wait a minute. We would never sell land that we acquired back to the original owner like that. If, as the building progresses, we see that we don't need the land we have acquired, we would return it for the same price we paid for it."

"Yeah, knowin' you, I wouldn't think you would do such a thing," Elmer said. "That's why we come here to see you, to tell you about what's goin' on."

"Elmer, Mr. MacCallister, Miss Parker, I assure you I will look into this and I will return any land that we have acquired in such a way, and aren't using. But as to stopping the building of the railroad, it's a little late for that, isn't it? It has already been built beyond Chugwater."

Duff and the other two looked at each other.

"Mr. Poindexter, are you for thinking that the railroad has reached Chugwater?" Duff asked.

"Yes, and beyond, according to the latest report we have received."

"Cap'n, there ain't been so much as one mile of track that's been laid yet," Elmer said.

"What?" Poindexter's response was so quiet as to barely be heard. He looked up at two portraits that were on the wall, one of him, and the other of a young man. "But this is impossible. I just can't believe that

Jake would tell me the railroad had advanced that far if it had not."

"Is that a portrait of Jake?" Meagan asked.

"Yes, by the artist William Merritt Chase. Chase is a most accomplished artist, and this is a very good likeness. He's quite the handsome young man, isn't he?" Poindexter asked proudly.

Elmer shook his head. "That ain't him."

"What do you mean, that isn't him?"

"What he means is, the man who has come to Chugwater and is passing himself off as Jake Poindexter is someone other than the man in this picture," Meagan added.

"My God!" Poindexter said in a tone of voice that reflected fear and uncertainty. "If the man claiming to be my son isn't Jake, where is Jake?"

"We don't know," Elmer said. "And to tell you the truth, I ain't, for some time, thought the feller out there was the actual Jake. I mean, he don't look nothin' like you, 'n he sure as hell don't act like you."

"What are you goin' to do now?" Poindexter asked.

"Now that we know that the man claiming to be your son is nae your son, we also know that the buildin' o' the railroad is nae real," Duff said. "Whoever is passing himself off as your son is robbing you and us. So when we get back to Chugwater, I intend to confront that bogus gentlemen with the truth."

Poindexter moved quickly to the door of his office and jerked it open. "Norman!" he called. "Norman!"

"Yes, Mr. Poindexter?"

"How much money have we transferred to the C and FL operation?"

"To date we have transferred one hundred and ten thousand dollars, but that doesn't count the twenty-five thousand dollars that we previously transferred for Jake."

"How much of the railroad has been built?"

"Jake's last report was that fifty-three miles have been constructed, and that puts it just beyond Chugwater."

"These people say that not one mile has been built."

"Oh, Mr. Poindexter, that can't possibly be true!" Jamison said. "The construction reports have been submitted daily and are quite detailed."

"Whoever is making out those reports is lying to you," Elmer said. "We just come from there, 'n I'm tellin' you, there ain't been so much as a hunnert yards that's been built."

"Oh, my, I'm afraid I don't quite know what to say," Jamison replied.

"Norman, make arrangements for my private car to be attached to the next available train going toward Wyoming. I am going to Chugwater to personally check on this."

"Oh, Mr. Poindexter, do you think that's wise? I mean if there is some chicanery going on out there, it might be better for me to check on it."

"Bosun Gleason, Mr. MacCallister, and Miss Parker have just informed me that the man who is passing himself off as my son isn't Jake," Poindexter said resolutely. "I am going."

"Yes, sir, I'll call the railroad and make arrangements for your passage," Jamison said.

San Francisco

As soon as Jalen Nichols arrived in San Francisco, he began his search for Zack Clark. Because of Clark's reputation, it wasn't that hard to find him. He found him in the Bilge Water Saloon, an establishment that catered primarily to sailors and dockworkers.

"Yeah, that's him down there," the bartender said. "What do you want with 'im?"

"It ain't none of your business what I want with 'im," Nichols said.

"I reckon you're right about that," the bartender agreed. "But I wouldn't go pickin' no fights with 'im, iffen I was you."

Nichols walked down to the far end of the bar where Clark stood, staring into his glass."

"Clark?" Nichols said.

Clark neither responded, nor looked up at him.

"Are you Mr. Clark?"

Clark looked at him and the expression of total disdain in his eyes frightened Nichols to the degree that, for a moment, he considered just walking away.

"I am Clark. Who are you?"

"My name is Nichols. Are you the same man who they say can fight so good?"

"I am skilled in the Chinese martial art form of *Wushu.*"

"*Wushu?* Does that mean you can fight good?"

"*Shi,*" Clark replied. When he saw that Nichols was totally confused, he translated. "Yes."

"Mr. Clark, my boss sent me to find you. He wants to pay you a lot of money to do a job for us."

"How much money is a lot of money?" Zack Clark asked.

Nichols showed him a bound bundle of twenty-dollar bills. "There's a thousand dollars here, and much more if you will come with me to meet my boss."

"I do not fight for the enjoyment of others," Clark said.

Nichols chuckled. "Believe me, the only enjoyin' will be when Wang Chow is took care of."

The expression of boredom on Clark's face was suddenly transformed into one of intense interest. "Wang Chow, did you say?"

"Yeah, he's a Chinaman that lives there in Chugwater, 'n he's been givin' us some trouble. So we was wonderin' if—"

Before Nichols could finish his explanation, Clark reached for the bound packet of twenty-dollar bills. "I will come with you."

Chapter Twenty-three

New York City

"It'll be as easy as takin' candy from a baby," Dixon explained. "The private car is the last car on the train. As soon as it is separated they'll be all alone in the car, and the car will be out on the track, a long way from ever'one else. That's when we'll do it."

"Where's it goin' to be separated?" Kluge asked.

He, O'Malley, and Quinn were the three men who had been provided to Clete Dixon to "take care" of the problem with MacCallister, Gleason, and Meagan Parker.

"We'll be stopping for water halfway between White Horse Station and Lebanon. It'll be good 'n dark then, 'n that's where the four of us will get off. When the train leaves, it'll leave Poindexter's private car behind."

"How's that goin' to happen?" O'Malley asked.

"One of the porters is bein' paid fifty dollars to disconnect it," Dixon said with a grin.

The four men were standing on the depot platform waiting for the departure of the Cannon Ball Express.

The train had been delayed by a few minutes to connect Preston Poindexter's private car.

"Oh my," Meagan said as she examined the private car they would be traveling in. The name of the private car—*Emma Marie*—was painted in red script and outlined in gold right by the front door. Poindexter had named his private car after his wife.

At the moment, the car was parked on a side track under the great cover of the Grand Central Depot and, as before, the complex resonated with sounds of trains rolling in and out.

"The attachment orders say that we will be connected at fifteen minutes until nine," Poindexter said. "So we may as well board now, so I can give you a quick tour."

Duff, Meagan, Elmer, and Poindexter boarded the car, and as they waited for the connection, Poindexter was pointing out all the features of the private car.

"There are four bedrooms, as you can see. There is a galley and a dining area, as well as a sofa and two overstuffed chairs. There is also a 'necessary,' and it is back there, out of the way and allowing for total privacy. Uh, if you have to use it, don't use it while the train is standing in a station."

"How far will it be to the dining car?" Elmer asked.

Poindexter chuckled. "I don't know, and it won't matter."

"What do you mean, it won't matter?"

"I have arranged for a porter to serve us our meals and clean up afterward. He will also make our beds in the morning, so that our trip should be quite pleasant."

"My oh my, Mr. Poindexter, you seem to have thought of everything," Meagan said.

"Please, call me Pete. All of you."

"Cap'n comes a little easier to me," Elmer said.

Pete chuckled. "That's all right, Elmer. I haven't been called Captain in a long time, and to tell the truth, sometimes I miss it. So you can call me Captain if you wish."

"Meagan, you said a moment ago that I have thought of everything. But there is one thought I wish I could get rid of. The thought of what we might find when we get there bothers me. I'm very worried about Jake. I just hope that he . . . that they . . ." Pete was unable to complete his sentence.

"Pete, if it's of any comfort to you, I have a feeling that the lad is still alive," Duff said. "I've nae evidence of that, but the feeling is quite strong."

"Oh, I pray that you are right."

"I've been around Duff for a long time, Cap'n, 'n whenever he gets one o' them feelin's, why, it most generally is right. If he says your boy is still alive, I'd be willin' to bet a lot of money that he is."

"I learned to put my trust in you a long time ago, Bosun, so I have no compunctions about doing so now. I'm going to assume that Jake is still alive somewhere. To assume otherwise is too terrible to contemplate."

"'Tis my thinking, Pete, they must keep your son alive so that they can continue to have a way to get the money from you," Duff said.

"Yes, that would be true, wouldn't it? I shall cling to that thought," Pete replied.

There was a rap at the door and when Elmer opened it, one of the yard workers was standing on the platform.

"Excuse me, sir, but you folks might want to brace yourselves. We're about to make the connection."

Elmer stepped out onto the platform and watched the train approach, holding on to the rail when contact was made. Working quickly, the yardman who had given the notice connected the coupler, the airbrake hose, and the wire to provide electricity to the car. That done he stepped out to give a signal, and the train started forward.

Chugwater

"Hey, Collins, we got a telegram from Dixon," Streeter said.

"I've told you a hundred times to call me Mr. Poindexter," Collins replied. "As long as we can keep these yokels thinking I'm Jake Poindexter, we can continue to take their land and Poindexter's money. Let me see the telegram."

MACCALLISTER BRINGING SOMEONE
TO CHUGWATER FOR OBSERVATION
STOP WILL REASON WITH HIM AND
OTHERS STOP
DIXON

"Someone coming here for observation," Dusty Caldwell said. "What do you think that means?"

"I think it means that he is bringing Poindexter to Chugwater."

"What do you mean? Poindexter is already here. We got him locked up out at the line cabin."

"I'm talking about the senior Poindexter."

"Oh! That ain't good, is it? What will we do about it?" Caldwell asked.

Collins pointed to the telegram. "Hopefully, we won't have to do anything about it. The issue will be resolved before the train gets here. Dixon will take care of it."

"You mean reason with him? What makes Dixon think that the old man will reason with him?"

Collins chuckled. "Tell me, Dusty, suppose Dixon sent a telegram that read 'I will kill MacCallister, Poindexter, and the others.' That telegram would have to go through several terminals before getting here. How do you think the telegraphers would have handled it?"

"I expect they would have told the law."

"So, Dixon used the word *reason* instead."

"Oh, yeah, I see that now," Caldwell replied with a broad smile. "That's pretty smart of you to figure somethin' like that out."

"Thank you for your vote of confidence."

"What are we goin' to do with Jake Poindexter?" Streeter asked.

"Who is with him now?"

"Bo Hawken is with him right now. Butrum was, but him 'n Hawken have been tradin' off, night 'n day, so that one person won't neve have to be there for the whole twenty-four hours."

"Yes, that's a good idea," Collins replied.

"If you ask me, I think we should just kill 'im, 'n be done with it."

"But I haven't asked you, have I? I think it best serves our purpose to keep him alive. There may well come the time when would need to use him as a bargaining chip," Collins said.

"A bargaining chip for what?"

"For our lives," Collins said simply.

It had once been a line cabin on the Trail Back Ranch. At least six miles from the main house, it was perfect for their use. David Lewis, owner of Trail Back, had abandoned it even before the C&FL railroad had confiscated the land as part of the land grant procedure. It had been long empty when Collins's men discovered it, and it was there they had taken unsuspecting Jake Poindexter as their prisoner.

Jake had come west because he wanted adventure. Well, he was getting a lot more adventure than he ever wanted or had even imagined.

He was aware that Ed Collins was behind it. Collins had seemed like such a nice guy on the train. Jake had told him who he was and why he was coming west. He had even harbored the idea of offering Collins a job, and not just any job, but a job as second in command. He had it in mind that Collins could be his second in command and in fact, could even take over as supervisor of the C&FL once the railroad was completed.

But Collins had other ideas.

As Jake thought about it, he was certain that meeting Collins on the train had not been a chance encounter. Collins knew who he was, and not just because they had played football on opposing teams. He didn't know how, but Collins had prior knowledge that Jake was on his way to Chugwater to build a railroad. Jake was certain that Collins had arranged the meeting and, somehow, was taking advantage of the situation. But why had he done it? Was Collins building his own railroad? How could that be? Jake knew for a fact that the fees had already been paid and exclusive connection rights to the Union Pacific Railroad were already granted to the P R and M Corporation, by way of the C&FL Railroad. Without that connection, what good would it do Collins to build his own railroad?

Jake, who was used to living in a huge house, had been a prisoner in the shack for over four weeks, guarded night and day. Less than half the size of his room at his father's house, it had neither electricity nor running water. The bed was an uncomfortable tick mattress with no sheets and only one blanket. Although the days were quite warm, uncomfortably so, the nights were quite cool, and the one blanket did little to push away the cold.

"Hey, you, Poindexter," Hawken said.

"What do you want, Hawken?"

"Fry us up some bacon, 'n warm up some o' them beans."

"Bacon and beans," Jake said. "We have had the same thing to eat every meal since I have been here. Wouldn't you like to have something else?"

Hawken chuckled. "You may o' noticed that me 'n Butrum has been takin' turns guardin' you, 'n when I ain't the one that's here a-lookin' out over you, I do get me somethin' else to eat."

Jake walked over to the wood-burning stove and started to build a fire. Before he had been captured he had never before cooked, nor had he ever even built a fire. He chuckled as he thought about it. If he managed to get out of this situation alive, he would have accumulated a lot of new skills.

"How long are you people planning on keeping me here?" he asked.

"That's up to Collins. I ain't got no say in it."

"Why are you taking orders from Collins?"

"'Cause he's the boss, that's why."

Jake flipped over the four strips of bacon. "Here's what I don't understand. If you are going to be an outlaw and whatever it is you are engaged in now is certainly against the law, then why not work for yourself? What is the advantage to being an outlaw if you have to follow orders from someone else?"

"I, uh, why don't you just shut up 'n pay attention to your cookin'?" Hawken said.

Jake chuckled. "I've made you think, haven't I? At least to the degree you are capable of doing so. However, it is quite likely that cerebration may be beyond your capability."

"I don't know what you're talking about. How much longer on the bacon? I'm gettin' hungry."

"It's just about done," Jake said.

"Yeah, well, you just do your cookin' 'n shut up, unless you're tired of livin'."

Jake laid the bacon on two plates, then spooned out the beans. "I have no fear of your threats, Hawken. If Collins wanted me dead, I would already be dead.

He wants me alive for some reason, and as you said earlier, you are taking orders from him. Now, I shall ask you again. Do you want a biscuit?"

"Yeah."

Jake took the two plates over to the small table, then sat down across from Hawken. He bowed his head.

"What is it you're doin'?"

"I'm saying a blessing for my food."

"How come you ain't sayin' it out loud, so's it can go for both of us?" Hawken asked.

"Why should I do that, Hawken? I don't give a damn about your soul. I expect God has already consigned you to hell. Why should I do anything to stop it?"

Chapter Twenty-four

Back in Chugwater, Collins was at Fiddler's Green sharing a table with Streeter, Nichols, and Butrum.

"Whose turn is it that's supposed to be on watch tomorrow?" Nichols asked.

"I'll have him tomorrow, " Butrum said. "Damn, it's all I can do to spend one day in that line shack. I don't know how he's been able to stay there this long without goin' crazy."

"You talk too much, Butrum," Collins chastised. "If this thing is going to work out for us, we have to watch what we're saying."

"Yeah, I know. I won't say nothin' like that again."

"See that you don't. And make sure you are there by seven in the morning."

"It's damn near an hour's ride, which means I'll have to get up really early. Hell, who would put a line cabin at the foot of the damn cliff anyway?"

"When your watch is up, you'll want to be relived on time, won't you?" Collins challenged.

"Yeah, I will."

"Then don't you think Hawken would want that as well? You will be on time tomorrow."

"Oh, yeah, I'll be there. I always have been. I was just talkin' some, is all."

"Sometimes you talk too much."

Kay Greenly was sitting at a nearby table, having been invited to share a drink with Mutt Malloy and Irv Calhoun, cowboys who rode for the Trail Back brand. In between her "professional flirtations" with Mutt and Irv, she had been listening to the conversation between Collins, who she still thought of as Poindexter, and the railroad police who worked for him.

What did Butrum mean when he said that it was his time to keep an eye on him? Who was *him*, and why were they keeping an eye on him? she wondered.

". . . purtiest girl in town, 'n that's a fact," Mutt was saying.

Kay had not caught the first part of his comment, but she had heard enough to respond. Mutt was smiling and holding his beer mug out toward her, obviously having just proposed a toast.

"Why, Mutt, you don't expect me to drink a toast to myself, do you? That would be very inappropriate."

Mutt laughed. "All I said was, here's to the purtiest girl in town. What makes you think I was talking about you?"

Kay flashed a big, coquettish smile, then lay her finger along the dimple that had appeared in her cheek. "Why, Mutt, if you don't think I'm the prettiest girl in town, why aren't you sitting with the one you think is?"

"Haw!" Irv said. "I reckon she got you there,

Mutt. 'N Miss Kay, I do think you're the purtiest girl in town."

"Me too," Mutt said quickly. "I was just funnin' her, that's all."

Kay listened to as much of the conversation of the railroad people at the next table as she could, all the while making herself good company for Mutt and Irv. Then, after Collins, Streeter and Nichols left, leaving only Butrum behind, she asked Mutt and Irv the question that had been bothering her.

"Do either one of you know anything about a deserted cabin that's, oh, say about four or five miles from town?"

"Five miles from town?" Mutt replied. "What are you lookin' for a cabin that far from town for? 'N what would you do iffen you was to live there? You wouldn't be able to come into town ever' day to work here, that's for sure."

Out of the corner of her eye she saw Butrum react to her question, and she knew she may have made a mistake in asking it.

"Why, Mutt, if I had my own place somewhere, I believe I could make a really good living."

"You ain't talkin' farmin' or ranchin', are you?"

Kay reached across the table to touch Mutt's cheek and smiled. "There are other ways for a girl to make a living."

"I tell you what, missy," Butrum called over from his table. "If you go into business for yourself, I want to know about it. I might come visit you my ownself."

"It won't be cheap," Kay replied.

"That don't matter none. I got money," Butrum said.

Kay breathed a sigh of relief when she realized that Butrum's interest in her question about a deserted cabin was prurient. But she still wondered who they were watching over, and why and where they were doing it.

Chapter Twenty-five

It had been a little over two hours since they left Grand Central Depot, and though it was dark outside, the interior of the *Emma Marie* was brightly illuminated, not only by the sconce lamps on the walls, but by the electric chandelier suspended from an oak-paneled ceiling to light the seating area.

"This is the most glamorous trip I have ever taken." Meagan was sitting on one end of the sofa with her legs drawn up under her.

Duff was sitting on the other end of the same sofa and Elmer and Poindexter were sitting in chairs, facing them.

Pete had just uncorked a bottle of wine, and he held it out for their inspection. "*Penfolds Magill Estate Shiraz Adelaide Hills, 1850,*" he said. "It's an Australian wine that I discovered while I was still at sea, and I've come to appreciate it." He poured some of it into a glass, swirled it around to test its nose, then took a swallow. "Ah, yes. Excellent. I'm sure you will enjoy it."

He poured for Meagan first, and the red wine in her

glass caught a beam of light from the nearby sconce lamp then sent out a flash of fire.

When all were served, he raised his glass. "To a successful resolution of the difficulties in Chugwater."

Duff thought to add *and to the rescue of Jake,* but Poindexter was already convinced that Jake was still alive, and Duff decided that was best.

"Did you and Elmer ever serve together on any ship, other than the *Appalachia?*" Meagan asked.

"No, ma'am, but were together on that ship for four months, then an additional three months on Howland Island," Pete replied.

"'N we were a crew, even if we were on an island," Elmer added. "Oh, 'n Cap'n, here's somethin' you may not know. Duff has also been a sailor."

"Aye, but not like you two. 'Twas only one voyage I made. I stowed away on a ship in Scotland, 'n when I offered to pay my passage, the ship's captain said I should work my way across. So, my sailing days are for one crossing only."

"That wouldn't have been the *Hiawatha,* would it?" Pete asked.

"Aye, the *Hiawatha* it was," Duff said, surprised by the comment. "'N would you be for tellin' me how it is that you know such a thing?"

"Captain Powell told me the story of a Scotsman who sneaked aboard his ship at the Firth of Clyde. Would that be you?"

"Aye, for that was the captain, 'n that was where I boarded ship."

"Gabe Powell said that he was prepared for you to

be a dullard, but that you turned out to be the best sailor on the voyage."

"'Twas kind of the captain to say such a thing. I did as well as I could, but I would nae be for saying that I was the best."

"I own the *Hiawatha* now," Pete said. "And Gabe Powell is commodore of the P R and M's entire fleet."

"I wish I had known he was in New York, 'twould have been good to see him again."

"Oh," Meagan said. "We're slowing down." She looked through the window, but because it was dark outside and brightly lit inside, she saw nothing but their reflections.

"We'll be coming to a stop in a moment. We're halfway between White Horse Station and Lebanon, and here we'll take on water," Pete explained.

"You know where we are even though it's dark outside and you can't see?" Meagan asked.

"It isn't necessary to see, my dear. It's a matter of time and distance," Pete said.

Elmer chuckled. "I told you, the cap'n is a jim-dandy of a navigator."

Three cars ahead, Dixon was also looking through the window. The closeness and the ambient light enabled him to see the water tower. "This is where we get off," he said as soon as the train stopped.

He, Kluge, O'Malley, and Quinn stepped out onto the platform between the cars and jumped down. Though none of the men were wearing holsters, all four pulled out pistols as they moved quickly through the darkness, back to where Poindexter's brightly lit private car sat attached to the rear of the train.

"You sure that car's goin' to be left when the train pulls out?" Kluge asked. "'Cause if it ain't there, we're goin' to look pretty foolish bein' left behind with the car 'n the whole train gone."

"There he is," Dixon said, pointing to a shadowy figure between the front of the private car and the back of the train.

The man leaned over the couplings for a moment, then he hurried up alongside the train and climbed back on board.

"All right, boys, it looks to me like it's been done. All we have to do is get ready."

"Wait a minute," Quinn said. "If it's all disconnected like you say it is, how come all the lights is still on?"

"He left the electric connections so nobody in the car would suspect nothin' till the train pulls away."

"But don't that mean the car's still connected?" O'Malley asked.

"You think them little electric wires can pull that heavy car?" Dixon asked.

"Oh, no, I reckon not."

The engineer blew two short blasts of the whistle.

"Get ready, the train's about to leave," Dixon ordered, and he and the other three cocked their pistols.

"It would appear that we're about to get underway again," Pete said, but no sooner were the words out of his mouth than the car went black.

"What happened?" Meagan asked.

"There must have been a loose connection in the electric wires," Elmer said. "The train hasn't left yet. If we can stop it before it leaves, we can reconnect it. I'll go ahead and get the conductor to—"

"Elmer, there is something queer about this," Duff said. "The train has gone on and we're—"

Suddenly they heard the sound of gunfire from outside and several bullets crashed through the windows.

"Get down!" Duff shouted, grabbing Meagan and pulling her down.

"Is anyone hit?" Elmer asked.

"I wasn't hit," Pete said.

Duff and Meagan also reported that they were unharmed.

After it was determined that nobody had been hit, Pete suggested they would be safer in one of the bedrooms on the opposite side of the car from where the shooting had come from.

"The bullets would have three walls to come through," he pointed out.

"Aye, 'tis a good idea. Meagan, you 'n Pete get in there, but crawl."

Even as Duff was sending Meagan and Pete to safety, more bullets came crashing through the windows.

"Where will you be?" Meaghan asked.

"Me 'n Duff's are goin' to go outside 'n kill them rats that's tryin' to kill us," Elmer said.

"Are you ready?" Duff asked, his gun in hand.

"Yeah, I'm ready. Let's go get 'em."

Reaching the back of the car, first Duff, then Elmer, got down on their stomachs and slithered through the door and across the rear deck. While still on their stomachs, they rolled off the deck and onto the track berm, where Duff waited for Elmer.

When Elmer raised his pistol to fire back at the flame patterns, Duff reached out to stop him. "Nae, we should be for drawing the shooting away from the car."

"Yeah, I shoulda thought o' that," Elmer agreed.

"Elmer, you go about twenty yards that way," Duff said, pointing toward the front of the car. "I'll go to the back. Here, take this."

Duff gave Elmer his pistol.

"Why are you a-givin' me your gun?"

"I want you to hold your hands out like this," Duff said, spreading his arms wide. "Shoot both of the guns so that they'll think we are together over there. That way I'll be able to sneak up on them."

"'N just what is it you're a-plannin' on doin' when you get there, seein' as you won't have a gun with you?"

"I have this," Duff said, holding up the *sgian dubh*, the ceremonial knife that, when he was wearing the uniform of a Captain of the Black Watch, was kept tucked into the right kilt stocking.

"I've seen you use that thing before, so I ain't goin' to try 'n stop you," Elmer said.

The gunfire continued from the other side of the track, and Duff could hear the bullets hitting the side of the car. He prayed that Poindexter was right—that the three walls would stop the bullets.

He started to the left, while Elmer went right. Both had the advantage of darkness, as well as the elevated railroad berm to conceal their movements. Shortly after Duff got into position, he heard Elmer begin firing and, as Duff had instructed, he saw that Elmer was holding the pistols widely separated.

"Damn!" a voice said. "They's two of 'em that's got outta the car."

"It has to be MacCallister 'n Gleason," another voice said. "If we can take care o' them, the woman 'n Poindexter will be easy."

The attackers began shooting toward where they had seen Elmer shoot, and Duff was able to figure out that there were four of them,

He crossed the tracks, his movement unnoticed by any of the four trading gunfire with Elmer. Duff moved quickly through a drainage ditch adjacent to the track until he reached the first man.

Concentrating so intently on Elmer, the shooter neither heard nor saw Duff until Duff was on him.

"What the hell?" the shooter said, startled by Duff's unexpected appearance.

Duff held out his hand. "I'll be takin' your gun."

The shooter raised his gun but before he could pull the trigger, Duff made a sweep with his knife, opening up the man's stomach. As he went down, Duff grabbed his gun.

"Quinn, what the hell's goin' on over there? Who are you talkin' to?" asked the next man over.

"That would be me," Duff replied from about ten feet away from the man who had called out to Quinn. Too far to use his knife, but Duff had Quinn's pistol, and he fired just before his would-be assailant did. His assailant went down.

"Dixon, they got O'Malley and Quinn!"

"Kluge, you dumb peckerwood! Why did you call out my name?"

Dixon fired, but not at Duff. He shot Kluge in the back, then he turned and ran off into the dark.

"Duff?" Elmer called. "Duff, are you all right?"

"Aye, all is finished here."

Pete found a kerosene lantern which he lit, not only to provide illumination for them, but also to mark the car in the hope that an approaching train would see them before colliding with them.

"I heard Dixon's name called," Duff said.

"Clete Dixon is one of the railroad police with the C and FL," Meagan said.

"Railroad police? I don't have any railroad police," Pete said.

"You don't, but whoever is passing himself off as your son does," Meagan said.

"What I don't understand is how the imposter knows so much of the operation," Pete said. "And how was he able to convince Mr. Jamison to send so much money without arousing any suspicion? And why didn't Jamison share those requests with me?"

"Have you considered that it might nae be suspicious to Mr. Jamison?" Duff asked.

"What in heaven's name do you mean? Surely you don't suspect that Norman Jamison is involved in this, do you? Why he has been a loyal and valued employee for some years now."

"As I am nae familiar with the gentlemen, I can nae make such a judgment. 'Tis only a question I ask."

"Something is coming up the track!" Meagan said in alarm and the others looked in the direction she pointed. Some distance away they saw not one huge light as would be on the train but two lights, much lower and dimmer.

"That ain't no train," Elmer said.

"It's a handcar," Pete said in relief. "It's track checkers, inspecting the rails. And, they will have a telegraph key. They can send word back that we're stranded out here. Miss Parker, Mr. MacCallister, Bosun, we'll be reconnected and back on our way before you can say Jack Robinson."

Chapter Twenty-six

Charley Blanton was in his new building with a spanking-new printing press, platen, and a large gathering of type in various sizes and fonts. Though he had put out a special edition the day after he returned with the new press, he was about to put out the first scheduled issue of his paper when the jingle of a bell announced that someone had opened the front door. The notification bell was also a new edition.

Looking toward the front, he was surprised to see Kay Greenly coming in.

"Well now, Miss Kay, fancy seeing you here," Charley said with a welcome smile. "Have you come to see my new facilities?"

"Oh, your new building and facilities are quite lovely. I'm so glad you were able to get everything put together again. A town needs a newspaper."

"It does indeed. I'm glad you see that."

"Mr. Blanton, as you are a newspaperman I would imagine that you are aware of just about everything that goes on around here," Kay said.

"Well, I do try and keep abreast of things, though I

must admit that I don't quite understand everything that's going on with this . . . this *C and FL* business." He stressed the words, using a tone of voice that indicated his contempt for them. "But, I digress, my dear. You have a question, do you?"

"Yes. Do you know anything about a line cabin that's about an hour's ride from here? It may be at the foot of a mountain."

Charley chuckled. "I must confess that I hadn't anticipated such a question. About an hour from here, you say? Well, there's one like that on Trail Back. It sits at the foot of Tomahawk Mountain. Of course it's not Trail Back land anymore. It's now part of the land grant that the railroad has grabbed up, but even before that, David had abandoned the shack a long time ago. I'm not even sure it's still standing. Why are you asking about it?"

"Oh it's just something I heard that made me curious about it, is all," Kay said without being more specific.

"Yes, old abandoned buildings can be interesting, especially if there are several of them. In that case they become a ghost town. Which is what we might become if we don't get that railroad," Blanton said.

"Do you think we won't get the railroad?"

"Frankly, my dear, I do have my doubts."

"The people who have come to build the railroad, they . . ." Kay halted in midsentence.

"They what?"

"They aren't very nice people."

"You have struck the nail right on the head. You're right. They aren't very nice people."

"I read all of your stories about the railroad. You

were one of the first to realize it. Mr. Blanton, do you think the railroad people may have had something to do with the fire you had?"

"Oh, I don't just think, I know," Blanton replied. "Of course, as I have no proof other than an inherent knowledge of the fact, there's nothing I can do about it, other than be more careful."

"Are you saying that you mean be more careful about the articles you write?"

"No, my dear, I have no intention of being more careful with my articles. Nothing will infringe upon the freedom of the press, and I shall exercise that right as granted me by the First Amendment to the U.S. Constitution."

Kay smiled. "I am pleased to see that the Fourth Estate is in good hands."

"Fourth Estate? Miss Kay, you are not only beautiful, you are a most intriguing young woman."

Chapter Twenty-seven

From the *Chugwater Defender:*

An Honest Appraisal of the Company Who Would Give Us the Railroad

EDITORIAL COMMENT
by Charles Blanton

My earlier articles calling attention to the misdeeds of the C&FL Railroad company resulted in the loss, by arson, of my newspaper office, printing press, and associated equipment. And though it is my personal belief that the miscreants who pass themselves off as railroad police are the same ones who set fire to my property, I have no proof and thus am unable to make an official charge to that effect. Thus, you may regard my comment as opinion only, not substantiated by indisputable fact.

Despite the penalty I paid for my earlier articles, I will not be dissuaded from continuing to publish the truth as I see it as I am guaranteed the right to do so by the U.S. Constitution.

I have long expressed the opinion that there
is something nefarious about this man who
says he is Jake Poindexter and especially
those who claim to be railroad police. They
are not building a railroad. Proof of that is that
not one mile of track has been put down. The
C&FL are using our desire for a railroad as
cover for their misdeeds. It is precisely
because of these misdeeds that Messrs. Duff
MacCallister and Elmer Gleason, as well as
Miss Meagan Parker, have gone to New York
to plead our case with Preston Poindexter, the
president of the P R and M Corporation. P R
and M, Preston Rail and Maritime
Corporation owns the Cheyenne and Fort
Laramie Railroad, the company who is
supposedly laying tracks from Cheyenne to
Fort Laramie.

Mr. Gleason is an old acquaintance of Mr.
Poindexter, and it is Gleason's contention that
the elder Poindexter is a man of honor and
integrity who knows nothing of the chicanery
being pulled by the C&FL. This newspaper,
and all the residents of the Chugwater Valley,
indeed all of the residents who occupy the
towns, ranches, and farms between Cheyenne
and Fort Laramie hold on to the hope that our
little delegation to New York is successful in
bringing about a positive resolution to what is
going on here.

Collins had just finished reading Blanton's editorial
when the Western Union delivery boy showed up at
his office.

"Mr. Poindexter? This is for you, sir."

Collins took the telegram without comment.

NEGOTIATION WITH PARTIES
UNSUCCESSFUL STOP TRAIN CONTINUES
TO CHEYENNE WITHOUT ME STOP
FURTHER ATTEMPTS IMPOSSIBLE

Collins read the telegram growing angrier with each word. Then, with a growl of frustration, he ripped the little yellow sheet of paper into shreds and dropped it into the trash can. "Damn!" he said aloud.

"Will there be anything else, Mr. Poindexter?" the young Western Union boy asked.

"No, get out of here. I don't need you hanging around!"

"Yes, sir," the boy said, hurt by the harshness of the response even more than he was by the lack of the customary tip.

"What is it?" Streeter asked after the boy left.

"Dixon failed. MacCallister and the others are still alive and coming back this way. Dixon isn't even on the train anymore."

"Do you reckon they might have learned that you ain't the real Jake Poindexter?"

"I don't know. But I think it would be very much to our advantage if they don't make it back to Chugwater."

"How are we going to manage that? Like you said, Dixon ain't even on the train no more."

"You've spent some time in Cheyenne, haven't you, Streeter?"

"Yeah, I've spent quite a bit of time in Cheyenne."

"Do you think you could round up five men who would be capable of stopping MacCallister and the others from returning to Chugwater?"

"Yeah, if I could offer them enough money."

"I'll give you seven hundred dollars. That's one hundred apiece for each of the men you employ, and two hundred for you. You work out the details."

Streeter smiled. "MacCallister will never make it to Chugwater. 'N if you had sent me instead of Dixon, he wouldn't have even made it to New York."

"I have no confidence in your boasting about what you are going to do. Come back and brag about what you have *done*."

"Oh, yeah," Streeter replied. "You can count on that."

With the *Emma Marie* once more attached to a through train, Duff and the others continued their luxurious trip, passing through Pennsylvania, Ohio, and Indiana.

When they reached Chicago, a boy wearing a Western Union cap knocked on the door of the car while the train was stopped. "Are you Mr. Poindexter?" he asked.

"I am."

"I have a telegram for you."

"Thank you," Pete said, handing the boy a quarter.

"Thank you, sir," the boy replied with a proud smile.

Pete read the telegram, then, with a curious expression on his face, looked toward Duff and the others.

"What is it?" Duff asked.

Pete read the telegram aloud. "'Information has reached me that casts doubt upon the motives of MacCallister and Gleason. You may be in danger, and as your longtime assistant, I recommend you separate yourself from them at soonest opportunity.' It's from Jamison."

"Do you feel you're in danger?" Duff asked.

"Yes, after what we have just come through, I do feel that I'm in some danger, but not from you. I wonder where Jamison got his information."

"A better question to ask would be where are the blackhearts who are attacking us getting their information," Duff replied.

"Yes," Pete said. "That is a good question. I may just ask Mr. Jamison that self-same question."

"Nae," Duff said, holding out his hand. "'Twould be best nae to raise any suspicion."

"Then you think I shouldn't respond to his telegram?"

"I have a suggestion," Meagan said. "Why don't you thank him for the warning and say you plan to stay in Chicago for a while?"

"That won't work," Elmer said. "If there's someone spyin' on us, this here private car o' his sticks out like a sore thumb 'n they'll see it when we leave."

"I hate to say this, because I've never been on anything as lovely as this car," Meagan said. "But if we leave the car here and go the rest of the way as regular passengers, we might be able to sneak Mr. Poindexter into Chugwater before anyone figures out what's going on."

"Aye, 'tis a fine point, lass."

"I'll send the telegram telling him that I am taking his warning under advisement," Pete said.

HAVE TAKEN WARNING TO HEART STOP
SEPARATED FROM FELLOW TRAVELERS
AND REMAIN CHICAGO LOOKING AFTER
BUSINESS

A short time later Duff, Meagan, Elmer, and Pete Poindexter were passengers on the Wagner Parlor car as the train continued west.

"There it is," Meagan said, pointing as they passed the *Emma Marie* parked on a sidetrack. "Oh, what a lovely ride it was."

"Yeah, but you was right," Elmer said. "If we leave the car here, why we'll more 'n likely be able to sneak back home without nobody knowin' nothin' about it."

Corporate headquarters of P R and M

"Will there be a return telegram, sir?" The Western Union delivery boy asked.

"Yes." Jamison wrote a message on a piece of paper.

To Jake Poindexter, C&FL Railroad Office, Chugwater, Wyoming. Jake, your father had intended to visit you there but he stopped in Chicago and will not be continuing his trip. MacCallister, Gleason, and Miss Meagan are continuing the trip. New money transfer to follow. NJ

"Have the telegrapher send this. Apply it to our bill."
Jamison gave the boy a dollar bill.

"Thank you, sir!"

Chugwater

"Gentlemen," Collins said after he read the latest
telegram. "It would appear that we have successfully
avoided what could have been a serious problem."

"What do you mean?" Caldwell asked.

"Apparently Poindexter was coming here with
MacCallister, but he has changed his mind."

"You sent Streeter out to kill MacCallister 'n Gleason. If Poindexter was with 'em, it wouldn'ta been
that big a problem. All we woulda had to do is kill
Poindexter, too," Caldwell said.

"No, we couldn't do that," Collins said.

"Why not?"

"Have you never heard the term *Kill the goose that
lays the golden eggs*? If we kill Poindexter, our money
will be cut off."

"Oh, yeah," Caldwell said. "I see what you mean."

After a little more investigation, Kay Greenly
became convinced that the line shack that she had
heard the railroad police talking about a few days ago
was the same one Blanton had told her was on what
had been part of the Trail Back rangeland. And the
more she thought about it, the more curious she
became about who was being held there, and why.
She knew that the railroad police were also deputy
U.S. Marshals, which meant they had the authority to
arrest someone and bring them in. Why, if they had

found it necessary to arrest someone, was he not in the Chugwater jail?

She asked Marshal Ferrell that question.

"You're saying that the C and FL railroad police have arrested someone?"

"Apparently they have."

Ferrell shook his head. "Are you certain? I mean they do have the authority to arrest someone, and if they did, they would more than likely put them in my jail. But they would need a legitimate reason for making the arrest."

"What would be a legitimate reason?" Kay asked.

"Well, I don't know for certain. Perhaps it was someone who was sabotaging the construction of the railroad." Ferrell paused for a moment. "Except that no building is actually going on now. Are you sure you overheard them talking about a prisoner they were holding somewhere?"

"Well, they didn't actually say he was a prisoner, but I certainly got the impression that he was. All I actually heard them say was that it was someone they were keeping a watch on." Even as she was explaining the situation to Marshal Ferrell, Kay realized that she may be overreacting.

"Well, that could mean just about anything," Ferrell said. "It could be one of their own men who they think isn't earning his pay."

"Yes, I suppose it could," Kay admitted.

"Where are they holding this person?"

"I don't know," Kay replied, although she had a very good idea where the mysterious person was being held. Figuring she had already made a big enough fool of herself, she didn't share the information with

Ferrell. "I'm sorry I bothered you, Marshal. I really had no business coming to you like this."

"Now, don't you worry about that, Miss Greenly. You were right to express your concern. Ninety percent of a lawman's success comes from information provided by civilians."

Chapter Twenty-eight

Nichols and Clark came by train to Cheyenne, and by stagecoach from Cheyenne to Chugwater. Once they reached Chugwater, Nichols took Clark to the office the C&FL was using. Caldwell was in the office talking to Collins. Both of them looked up when Nichols and Clark stepped inside.

"I got 'im," Nichols said. "This here is Clark, the man I told you about."

"Thank you for coming, Mr. Clark," Collins said.

"Nichols said there would be more money."

"Yes, after you do the job."

"What's your name?" Clark asked.

"You will call me Poindexter."

"What do you mean, I'll call you Poindexter? Is that your name?"

"It is, as far as you are concerned."

"Yes, well, your name doesn't matter, anyway. The only name that matters is Wang Chow. You are certain that it is Wang Chow?"

"Wang Chow, yes. Mr. Clark, you seem to have a particular interest in his name. May I ask why?"

"If he is the one I'm looking for, and I will know

this as soon as I see him, then he is a man with great skill in the art of *Wushu*. He is a priest of the Shaolin Temple of Changlin."

"A priest?" Caldwell laughed. "Well, hell, if he's a priest, you shouldn't have no problem with him."

"Tell that to the *Taiyang*, or the *Yuequi*."

"The what?" Collins asked.

"They were warrior groups with every member a skilled fighter."

"And Wang Chow was a member of one of these . . . what did you call them? Warrior groups?" Collins asked.

"No, they were his enemies."

"What about them?"

"He killed them. All of them," Clark said.

"So, iffen he kilt all of his enemies, what I want to know is, how did the egg-sucker wind up in here in America?" Caldwell asked.

"He had no choice. He had to leave China," Clark replied. "After hearing about all the men he killed, the Dowager Ci'an issued a decree ordering his death, so he left China and came to America."

"How do you know all this?" Collins asked.

"I was there when it happened, and like Wang Chow, I am a priest of the Changlin Temple. In fact, I have been personally charged by Master Tse to find him and kill him in order that the disgrace he brought to the temple may be erased." Clark smiled. "I have been unable to find him until now, and thanks to the information you have provided, I shall fulfill my mission."

"Well, if you have come here to kill Wang Chow anyway, you don't need any more money, do you?"

Collins asked. "Wouldn't you say that we have done you a favor by telling you where he is?"

"You have promised more money," Clark said. "I don't think you want to go back on that promise." The implied threat wasn't that veiled.

"No, no, I'll give you the rest of the money." Collins gave a weak laugh. "I was just teasing you a bit."

"How much?"

"You have already been given a thousand dollars. I will give you one thousand more after the job is done."

"Where will I find Wang Chow?" Clark asked.

"There is a Chinese restaurant in town called Lu Win's. Apparently Wang Chow is attracted to Lu Win's daughter, Mae, so much so that he is a habitué of that establishment. If you spend some time there, you will most definitely encounter him."

"I will do so."

"Nichols told me that you killed three Chinamen. Is that true?" Collins asked.

"That is true."

"Well then, haven't you also disgraced this temple you're talking about?" Collins asked.

"I suppose I have. *Dàn sìmiào zhǐlìng shāsǐ Wang Chow réngrán zhànlì.*"

"What the hell? Is that Chinese?" Caldwell asked.

"Yes, of course it is Chinese. You can't live in China and be a disciple of Changlin without speaking the language."

"What did you say?"

"I said that the temple directive to kill Wang Chow still stands. And if I fulfill that order, I will be back in good graces with the Changlin Temple."

"Tell me, Clark, if you and Wang were both at this temple you are talking about, did you actually know him?"

Clark was silent for a long moment before he answered.

"Yes, I knew him. He was my best friend."

As Ed Collins and his men were holding their discussion with Clark, Kay Greenly was just stepping into the office of Mathers' Livery Stable.

"Yes, miss, can I help you?" asked Ken Kern, the stableman.

"Yes. I shall require a gentle horse," Kay replied.

"Yes, ma'am, I can give you Rhoda. She's 'bout the most gentle horse we got. Where is it you are a-goin?"

"Nowhere in particular," Kay replied. "I just felt as if I would like to go for a ride."

"Well, you sure got a purty day for it. You can just wait here in the office so as to stay out of the sun whilest I get Rhoda saddled up for you."

A few minutes later, Kern stepped back into the office. "Rhoda's waitin' out front for you."

"Thank you, Mr. Kern."

When Kay approached the horse she saw that Kern had put on a sidesaddle. "Sidesaddle?" she asked, the tone of her voice showing her disappointment.

"Yes, ma'am. Ladies like you shouldn't ought to ride astride. It just ain't fittin'. And Rhoda has been rode with a sidesaddle so many times that I'm not sure how she would act if someone was actually to ride her a-straddle."

"Ladies like me, huh?" Kay chuckled. "All right. Sidesaddle it shall be."

Within fifteen minutes, Kay was a little over a mile out of town heading west toward Tomahawk Mountain, which was a dark blue slab directly ahead of her. She had no idea why she was doing this, though the compulsion to do so was greater than her caution.

After about an hour's ride, the little cabin came into view. She stopped for a moment to have a look around, but a perusal of the approach to the cabin was across open range and offered no concealment, which meant that if she went any farther, she would be exposed.

"Rhoda, what in the world am I doing here?" she asked the question of the horse. Somehow, talking to the horse made it seem less like she was talking to herself. After a brief pause, she decided to chance it. Slapping her legs against Rhoda's sides, she continued on toward the deserted cabin.

She didn't discover that it *wasn't* deserted until she reached the cabin and dismounted.

The door opened and a man she recognized as one of the railroad police stepped outside. He had a pistol in his hand and he was pointing it at her. "You're one o' the whores that works at the Wild Hog, ain't you?"

"I do not work at the Wild Hog."

"Then maybe it's Fiddler's Green. Come to visit me, did you?"

"No, I don't know who you are. I was just out for a ride and I saw the cabin. I thought perhaps if someone lived here, I could get a drink of water."

"The name is Hawken. So, now that you know who I am, why don't you come inside 'n get real good look?"

"I thank you for the invitation, Mr. Hawken. But I've rented this horse and need to get it back to Mr. Mathers."

"You ain't understandin' me," Hawken replied. "I wasn't exactly *invitin'* you to come inside. What I was doin' was *tellin'* you to come inside. I mean, didn't you say you wanted a drink of water?" Hawken cocked the pistol. "Now you can either come inside, or you can die right here. It's your choice."

"Very well, Mr. Hawken, if you are that insistent on my company, perhaps I will accept your invitation. Now that I think about it, I believe I would like to have a look around."

As soon as Kay stepped into the little cabin, she saw a man sitting on a cot. He looked tired and haggard, and she saw that his legs were shackled together by a relatively short chain and ankle cuffs.

"Who are you?" she asked in a strained voice.

"I'm Jake Poindexter. Who are you?"

"You? You are Jake Poindexter? Then who is the man—?"

"I'm sure you are asking about the gentleman who is portraying me," Jake interrupted her in midquestion, providing immediately the answer she sought. "That would be Ed Collins. And excuse me for using the term *gentleman*, for he is certainly no gentleman."

"I knew it was something like this. It had to be."

"Well, little lady, it's too bad you seen Poindexter, 'n it's too bad you know about our little scheme,"

Hawken said. "On account of all that, you're goin' to have to stay here."

"Are you saying you are going to keep me here?" Kay asked, her words dripping with trepidation.

Hawken flashed an evil smile at Kay. "Yeah, I'm goin' to keep you here. I'm sorry I don't have no leg irons for you, but I'm either in here or right out front. 'N as you can see, they's only one door to this place, so I don't reckon you'll be a-goin' nowhere."

"I'm sorry, miss," Jake said after Hawken stepped back outside.

"There is no need for you be sorry. I got myself into it," Kay replied. "So, the editorials Mr. Blanton has been printing are true. The claim that we are getting a railroad is totally false."

"No, ma'am. There is nothing false about the railroad itself. What *is* false is Ed Collins. He and his henchman are engaged in some vile scheme to cheat my father."

"And the people of Chugwater," Kay added

"Indubitably."

"How did you wind up here, in this place?" Kay asked.

"I was met by a group of men at the depot when the train arrived in Cheyenne," Jake said. "I was told the men had been provided by Mr. Jamison, who is my father's executive assistant. They brought me here, saying this is where our headquarters would be. I was suspicious as soon as I saw the place, and my suspicions were quickly confirmed. Once here, they took me prisoner, and Ed Collins, who had befriended me on the train, showed his true colors."

"Oh, how horrible it must be for you to be here all this time."

"Yes, well the being here itself hasn't been all that bad. It's the idea of what lies before me that's disturbing. For some reason that I can't fathom, it must, temporarily at least, be to Collins's advantage to keep me alive, but I don't expect that to last. After they get as much money as they can, I will become a liability and they will be forced to kill me."

"And me," Kay added.

Jake nodded. "I didn't want to say that. I didn't want to distress you. But unfortunately you are right. They can't let you live if they kill me."

"They say curiosity once killed a cat," she said. "I suspect we shall see if curiosity kills a Kay."

Inexplicably, Jake chuckled. "I just met you and already, I like you. Who are you, anyway? Are you married? What brings you out here?"

"I told you, my name is Kay Greenly. I'm originally from Jackson, Mississippi, but now I live in Chugwater, where I'm a saloon hostess at Fiddler's Green."

"A saloon hostess? I'm not familiar with the term."

This time it was Kay who laughed. "You've never heard of a saloon hostess?"

Jake shook his head. "We don't have them in New York, or if we do, I've never encountered one. We have some saloons, of course, as well as bars, taverns, and clubs. Many of the private clubs have ladies who work there in one capacity or another, but they aren't called hostesses. What does a hostess do?"

"Well, it depends on the saloon," Kay said. "In many saloons, *hostess* is just another term for soiled dove. But that isn't so in Fiddler's Green."

"Soiled dove?"

"You really are naïve, aren't you? Yes, soiled dove. Prostitute."

"Oh, I've never heard the term. Prostitute, yes I've heard of that, but never the term *soiled dove*."

"As I said, the girls who work for Mr. Johnson are hostesses, not prostitutes. All we do is serve our clients and from time to time have a drink with them." She smiled. "I'll share a secret with you. When I share a drink, I drink tea. We all do. Heavens, if we actually drank that much whiskey, we would all be drunken sots."

Jake laughed out loud. "Yes, I think drinking tea is probably a smart thing to do. You say you are from Mississippi? What brings you to a place like Chugwater?"

"I came to marry an army officer who is stationed at Fort Laramie. Only, when I arrived, I discovered that the man who had professed his love to me all the time he was at West Point had married the colonel's daughter shortly after he arrived at Fort Laramie. And though he had earlier ask me to join him as soon as he was settled so we could be married, he neglected to tell me of the change of his plans. I was too embarrassed to go back home, so I stayed."

"Do your parents think you are married?"

"Both of my parents are deceased. There is only my older brother and his wife, and to tell the truth, I think they are glad to be rid of me."

"I find it interesting that you would wind up in Chugwater. This all started because I happened to see Chugwater on a map and found its name and location intriguing," Jake said. "Building a railroad here was actually my father's idea. My initial thought was to come to Chugwater just for the adventure."

"Some adventure this has turned out to be for you. I'm sure your wife and family are quite concerned about you."

"Fortunately, I have no wife to worry about me. I wouldn't be surprised if Ed Collins, the man who is portraying me, has been sending mail, telegrams, and reports back home convincing my parents that all is well. I do wish I had some way of notifying my father that all isn't as it seems."

Kay smiled. "Maybe he has been notified."

"What? How?"

Kay told Jake about the trip to New York taken by Duff, Elmer, and Meagan.

"It turns out that Elmer Gleason knows your father and—"

"The bosun!" Jake said. "Yes, he does know my father! And though I've never met him, I know all about him. My father has spoken of him."

"Then I have no doubt but that your father has learned of your status here," Kay said. "And Duff MacCallister, the man who went with Mr. Gleason, is a man of remarkable skills. I don't know him that well as I have only recently met him, but Mr. Johnson, the man for whom I work, has nothing but high praise and admiration for him."

Jake chuckled again.

"What is it? What's funny?"

"I'm sorry. It's the way you talk. You have a *lingua elegans* that one wouldn't expect from a lady who works as a saloon hostess."

"I have a what?" Kay replied, her tone of voice reflecting some irritation from the remark.

"I'm sorry. Please, I meant the comment to be a compliment. I was referring to the sophistication of your language."

Smiling, Kay affected a heavy Southern accent. "Well, honey, just 'cause I'm a Southern girl from Jackson doesn't mean I don't know a subject from a verb." Dropping the accent, she continued. "I attended the University of Mississippi for two years, dropping out to come marry Lieutenant Andrew Knox. You know the rest of the story."

"Yes, ma'am, I do. Kay . . . may I call you Kay?"

"Of course you may."

"Kay, I'm sorry you have put yourself in danger, but I'm glad that you came. From what you have just told me, I feel much more confident about my future, which, under the circumstances, will also be your future."

"I'm glad you feel so confident about it. Your confidence makes me somewhat less afraid."

Jake reached out to take her hand. "And I don't mind telling you, I appreciate the company."

"All right," Kay said with a chuckle. "But when we get back to Chugwater, you owe me a drink of tea."

"Which I will gladly buy," Jake said, sharing the laugh.

Chapter Twenty-nine

"What do you mean one of the saloon whores is out at the cabin? How did she turn up there?" Collins asked.

"According to what she said when she rode up, she was just out ridin' 'n seen the cabin 'n got curious," Hawken said.

"Is she still there?"

"Yeah, I mean, she's seen the real Poindexter, so it ain't like we could let her go. Butrum's watchin' her now. Hell, he's watchin' both of 'em there at the line shack."

"That's true. As long as she's alive, she is a threat to us all."

"You said as long as she's alive. What if she ain't alive?" Hawken asked.

"Yes, if she . . . no, wait. She may be a threat to us, but she might also offer an opportunity. We'll keep watch on both of them." Collins cackled a ribald laugh. "A man and a woman put together in drastic circumstances, who knows what will happen?"

Cheyenne

It had taken two days for Roy Streeter to find men to do his job. He was in the Bella Union Saloon with the three men he had picked. As they were sharing a beer, he compiled a mental resume for each of them.

Simon Newcomb got his nose bitten off in a fight with another inmate while was incarcerated in the Arizona Territorial Prison. Because of that, his nose was little more than two holes just above his lips. The result was one of the ugliest man Streeter had ever seen. A few years ago he had seen Newcomb shoot and kill Orson Dumas, who was himself a deadly shot. Streeter didn't know how many men Newcomb had killed, but he was sure it was more than one.

Clarence Rand, the second of the three, had dark brown eyes, black hair, and a beard. Rand had served ten years in prison for bank robbery. He was tried at the same time for the murder of a deputy sheriff, but because there were no witnesses to the killing and only circumstantial evidence, a slick lawyer got him off the murder charge.

The third man, Doc Wilson, was clearly the most dangerous of the three, but he had never served a day in prison. It was said of him that he had killed twelve men, and Streeter was personally aware of at least three of Doc Wilson's victims. Though he was called "Doc," Wilson was neither a physician nor a dentist, but got the name because he had almost surgically dissected the body of more than one of the men he had killed.

"When's this here train sposed to get to Cheyenne?" Rand asked.

"Tomorrow."

"Where's the money?" Doc Wilson asked.

"I don't have all of the money with me," Streeter replied.

"Why not? Didn't you say we would get a hunnert dollars apiece for the job?"

"Yes, and you will, after the job is done. I'll give each of you fifty dollars now, 'n you'll have to trust me for the rest."

Doc Wilson chuckled a low, growling type of chuckle. "You don't understand, do you, Streeter? It ain't that I have to trust you. You're goin' to have to trust *me*."

"What do you mean?" Streeter was made somewhat uncomfortable by Doc Wilson's comment.

"'Cause after we kill these two fellers you're a-wantin' us to kill, if you don't give us the rest of the money, I'll kill you. 'N you can count on that."

"No, you won't kill 'm," Newcomb said.

For a moment Streeter thought he had an ally.

"Iffen he don't give us the money he owes us, *we'll* kill 'im," Newcomb added as a humorless smile spread across his lips.

"I don't know what you men are a-gettin' all hepped up about," Streeter said, trying to reassert some control over the situation. "It's a simple enough job. We'll pick us a good place on the road between here 'n Chugwater 'n when we get the chance, we'll shoot 'em down. After we've kilt both of 'em, I'll take the three of you to the place where I've put the money, 'n I'll give each of you the rest of the hunnert dollars."

"Sounds like a simple enough job to me. 'N an easy

enough way to make a hunnert dollars." Rand smiled. "'N I got plans for that money."

"Plannin' on spendin' it all on whores, are you?" Newcomb asked with a laugh.

"You got any better ideas on how to spend it?" Rand replied.

The other three men laughed, though Streeter's laughter was more from relief that they were no longer talking about killing him.

On board the Union Pacific "California Special"

The conductor came walking through the Pullman car. "Folks," he called out. "It's seven o'clock. We'll be arriving in Cheyenne at eight o'clock. If any of you are plannin' on eatin' breakfast in the dining car, now would be the time to do so."

Traveling through the car, he repeated his call three more times before he exited through the back door.

Although they had abandoned the private car in Chicago, Duff, Meagan, and Elmer were still traveling first class thanks to Preston Poindexter's largesse.

Meagan heard a tap on the door of her roomette.

"Meagan?" It was Duff's voice.

"Go away. I'm still sleeping."

"Lass, you've not long left before—"

Meagan, who was fully dressed, jerked the door open and laughed.

"I thought you said—"

"I'm a fast dresser. I'm also hungry."

"I'll gather the other two," Duff offered.

As it turned out, Elmer and Pete, like Meagan, were

already up and dressed so the four walked through the intermediate cars that separated them from the diner. Luckily they were among the earliest diners and were able to find a table they could share. Duff and Meagan sat on one side, and Elmer and Pete sat on the other.

"We left our horses in Cheyenne, but we'll have to buy or rent one for you," Duff said.

"I would prefer to buy a horse."

"Can you ride, Cap'n?" Elmer asked. "Or maybe you'd rather rent a buggy."

"I'm not what you call an accomplished rider, but I am certainly capable of staying in the saddle. I have no wish to rent a buggy."

Elmer chuckled. "Well, all you have to do is stay in the saddle long enough 'n you'll get where you're going."

Their breakfast was delivered then and for the next several minutes their conversation was subdued as they ate.

Cheyenne Depot

Streeter, Newcomb, Rand, and Doc Wilson waited at the depot but not in the waiting room, or even on the platform. Waiting there would put them in plain view of the arriving passengers. They were actually just outside the freight office, from which position they would be able to see the detraining passengers without exposing themselves.

"You're sure they'll be on this train?" Doc Wilson asked.

"Yeah, I'm sure. The information I got was that Poindexter left the train in Chicago, 'n MacCallister 'n Gleason come on by their ownselves. Well, not quite by their ownselves, seein' as I reckon the woman is still with 'em. So they'll be here unless they decided to get off the train somewhere between here 'n Chicago, which ain't very likely."

"Will you recognize 'em?" Rand asked.

"Oh yeah. I've seen 'em both a bunch o' times, comin' into town like they was kings or somethin'," Streeter said. "I've seen the woman too, so they ain't likely to get by without—" He for a moment, then he continued. "There! There them sons of the devil is."

"Which ones?"

"Them two right there with that woman."

"She bein' there don't matter none," Doc Wilson said. "We can kill her as easy as we can MacCallister 'n Gleason."

"You won't go cuttin' her up though, will you, Doc?" Newcomb asked. "Leastwise not right away."

"Who's that other man with 'em?" Rand asked.

"I don't have no idea. More 'n likely it's just someone they met on the train. He ain't our problem."

"What if he's with 'em?" Newcomb asked. "What I mean is, what if he's also goin' to Chugwater 'n decides to go along with 'em?"

"Then we'll kill him, too."

"I've been thinking about it," Duff said to Pete. "'N 'tis thinking I am that we should be for taking you to my ranch before we go into town. You'll be safer there."

"Yes, I think that's probably a pretty good idea," Meagan said.

"Safe? Why should my safety be an issue? I'm in no danger. My son is the one who is in danger."

"May I remind you that your son was not on the train coming from New York, and yet we were fired upon? Someone tried to kill you," Meagan pointed out.

"Yes, I guess that is true, isn't it?" Pete replied. He turned toward Duff. "All right. I hereby place myself under your command until all this is over, and as such, I will follow all your instructions."

Elmer chuckled. "Hell, Cap'n, you sorta been under his command ever since we left New York."

Pete laughed as well.

"Right here," Streeter said. "I picked this place out when I come up to Cheyenne yesterday. Doc, you 'n Newcomb get over on the other side of the road behind them rocks. That way they won't nobody that's a-comin' up from the south that'll be able to see you." He pointed to the opposite side of the road. "Me 'n Rand will be over here." He figured Rand was less frightening.

"Iffen you seen this place yesterday 'n figured out this is where we was goin' to wait to kill 'em then I reckon this is where you got the rest of the money hid, ain't it?" Doc Wilson asked before anyone got into position.

"No, it ain't here, but I got it somewhere safe," Streeter said.

"Is it easy to get to?" Newcomb asked. "Reason I asked is, after we get the job done we ain't a-goin' to be wantin' to wait around for a long time a-fore we get the rest of what's comin' to us."

"It's close by." Streeter pointed across the road. "Now go on over there 'n get in position. They only got eight miles to come 'n we prob'ly didn't get that much of a head start on 'em. I don't reckon it'll be that long before we see 'em comin' down the road."

Duff and Elmer were riding in front while Meagan and Pete were bringing up the rear.

"Duff, stop," she called.

The little group of riders came to a halt.

"What is it, lass? Why do you wish to stop?"

"This is where it happened before."

"Where what happened before?" Elmer asked.

"This is where I got shot."

"Aye, 'twas here that Creech 'n the brigand with him ambushed us."

Meagan frowned. "I've got a feeling, Duff. Something isn't right."

"It's prob'ly just cause you was shot here is all," Elmer said.

Duff stood in his stirrups and looked down the road. He hadn't experienced any apprehension before, but now that Meagan had brought it up, he too was feeling a bit disquieted.

Elmer noticed Duff's reaction. "You think maybe there's somethin' to it, Duff?"

"Aye, there could be. Meagan, you and Pete get off the road 'n wait in the same ditch you and I did the last time we were here. Elmer 'n I will ride on through. If we are nae fired on, I'll call you on through. If we are attacked, the two of you wait here."

"Mr. Poindexter can wait here, but I'm also armed,"

she said. "And if shooting starts and you are greatly outnumbered, you'll need my gun."

"Nae, lass," Duff said authoritatively. "Your job will be to get Pete to safety."

"Duff's right, Meagan," Elmer added.

Reluctantly, Meagan turned and started toward the ditch that paralleled the road. "Come along, Mr. Poindexter."

Pete followed her lead without protest.

"What the hell?" Rand said when he saw Meagan and the older man pull away from the others. "What's goin' on? Why are they doin' that?"

Streeter had seen the same thing. Cupping his hands around his mouth, he called across the road, modulating his volume so that he hoped only Doc Wilson and Newcomb would be able to hear him. "Doc, somethin's gone wrong. We need to call this off."

"I ain't walkin' away from this," Wilson called back, making no attempt to modulate his volume.

Immediately following his shout, he and Newcomb stepped out into the road and started shooting.

"That's a dumb thing for them to do!" Streeter said. "I'm getting the hell out of here!"

"Me too!" Rand said as he and Streeter scrambled to their horses.

"Duff!" Elmer shouted as the two men appeared in the road in front of them, blazing away.

Duff wasn't hit, but he could hear pops of the bullets as they passed by.

Although Wilson and Newcomb shot first, they didn't shoot accurately. Duff did shoot accurately and it required only two shots to bring the attackers down.

As the echo of the last gunshot faded away, Duff and Elmer sat quietly on their horses, holding guns at the ready.

Meagan came riding up behind them.

"Meagan, go back. Wait until 'tis all clear," Duff ordered.

"It's clear. There were two more, but I saw them riding away, fast."

Duff, Elmer, and Meagan approached the two men who lay on the road about thirty yards in front of them. Elmer dismounted, then turned both of them over with his foot."

"This one is Simon Newcomb," Elmer said. "I know for sure who that ugly demon is, seein' as his nose was bit off 'n I've seen him before. I don't know this other 'n though."

"Hmm. Neither of them are with the C and FL," Duff said. "I wonder why they attacked us."

"None of the people who attacked while we were on the train were with the C and FL either," Meagan said. "But there's no doubt that they were doing it for the C and FL."

Duff nodded. "Aye, lass, I see your point. These two were probably sent by the C and FL to do what the other attackers weren't successful in doing."

"What are we gonna do with Newcomb 'n this other feller?" Elmer asked.

"We'll pull them off the road, then tell Marshal Coats about them when we get to Walbach," Duff said.

"Meagan, if you would be for bringing Pete up, we'll resume our journey."

"All right," Meagan said.

As she rode back to get Poindexter, Duff dismounted to pull one of the bodies off the road. Elmer took care of the other one.

Chapter Thirty

They reached Sky Meadow in the early afternoon and were welcomed by Wang Chow. He told them of the visit they had from some of the railroad police. "They said they were looking at land that they would soon take," Wang said.

"I don't know who those men are, but they are not railroad police for the C and FL," Pete said. "I never use railroad police to enforce any land acquisitions. I have always done it by negotiation until we reach a mutually agreed-upon settlement. And I have authorized no one to act as railroad police for the C and FL."

"I didn't think you would," Elmer said. "That's what made me think there was somethin' fishy 'bout this whole thing, 'n that's why we come to New York to talk to you in the first place."

Cong Sing came up to where Duff and the others were and, putting his hands together prayerlike, he made a slight dip of his head. "It is good to see that you have safely returned, *Xiangshen* MacCallister."

"Thank you, Cong Sing."

Duff introduced Pete to Cong Sing, telling Cong

Sing that Pete was the father of Jake Poindexter. Then he told him that he was certain the man who was passing himself off as Jake was an imposter.

"I'm not quite sure what is happening out here," Pete said, "but I intend to get to the bottom of it, put a stop to it, then build a railroad that everyone here, whether urban or rural will be well served and happy with the result."

"*Wǒ rènwéi tā kěnéng shìgè hǎorén,*" Cong Sing said to Wang Chow.

"Thank you for saying I am a good man," Pete said. "I will try to live up to your expectations."

"You speak our language," Cong Sing said, surprised by the fact.

Pete smiled. "*Wǒ zài hǎishàng de shíhòu, Wǒ duō cì fǎngwèn Zhōngguó*

"What did you just tell them?" Meagan asked.

"I told Mr. Cong that when I was at sea, I visited China many times."

"I'm quite impressed," she said. "Duff, I thank you for taking me to New York with you. I feel privileged to have met Mr. Poindexter. I loved visiting the city and I loved seeing your cousins Andrew and Roseanne star in the play, *The Way Home.* Every moment of the trip was very exciting, though I must confess that I could have done without *some* of the excitement." She smiled at her comment.

"Miss Parker, the privilege of meeting you is all mine," Pete said with a slight nod of his head.

"Thank you, Mr. Poindexter, but now I feel that I must get back to town and check on my dress shop."

"Wang, would you be for going with her?" Duff

asked. "The way things have been going, I would feel better if the lass didn't have to go alone."

"*Shi*, I will go."

"It isn't necessary"—she smiled at Wang Chow—"but I would enjoy the company."

"We'll rest today and go into town tomorrow," Duff said. "Tomorrow we'll be for seeing the man who calls himself Jake Poindexter. We may as well start at the top."

"Yes," Pete said. "I would much like to meet the man who is passing himself off as my son."

The line cabin

It had been three days since Kay arrived at the line cabin. She had met both men who were taking turns guarding Jake and her. Butrum, on guard duty at the moment, was outside. She was inside with Jake, cooking for the three of them.

"I have to confess that in addition to enjoying your company, I'm also glad that the task of cooking has fallen upon your shoulders," he said. "I had absolutely no experience in the kitchen before winding up in this regrettable situation."

"It is only right that I do the cooking. After all, I am getting more rest than you. You've given me the cot and you're sleeping on the floor."

Jake chuckled. "Believe me, Kay, having now slept on the cot and the floor, there is very little difference."

"Perhaps that is so." she laughed. "I must say, Jake, that after all you have gone through, you are some kind of a man to still able to laugh at things."

"Oh? Look at you. You are still laughing at things."

"I've only been here three days. You've been here for four *weeks.*"

"I wish you hadn't come at all," Jake said. "Oh, don't get me wrong, I love having you here. To be honest, until you showed up I had about given up on everything. My life had no meaning at all. It's amazing what a transformation in my life you have brought about in just three days. But it is for your sake that I wish you hadn't come."

"I know this may sound very dumb, Jake, but given all the difficulties and the uncertain future, I'm glad I'm here. I would not have met you otherwise."

"I wonder if you know exactly who it is that you have met. This time last year I was a, well, there's no other way of putting it, but I was a rake and a wastrel. I am the only son of one of the richest men in America, and I rarely thought beyond the next day. And only the connection with my father kept me from being thrown out of a dozen or more clubs." Jake chuckled. "Despite that, I was thrown out of the Union Club."

"Why?"

"Oh, I think it would embarrass me too much to tell you why. But what I'm trying to say is, the man you have met is not the same man I was then. I've grown, and in the last three days since you have been here, I like to think that I have also gained a new perspective in personal relationships."

"Jake, before you get too, uh, introspective, I think you should remember who I am."

"I know who you are. You are Kay Greenly from Jackson, Mississippi, you attended college at the University of Mississippi, and though it may not be Oxford College, it is at least in Oxford, Mississippi," he teased.

"And," he added, "you are one of the most beautiful women I have ever met."

"I'm also a bar girl. We are trained to make men attracted to us. And you must admit, Jake, this"—she took in the little cabin in with a wave of her hand—"is not the way a man and woman would normally meet."

"I don't care how it is that we met. And I know that you are a bar girl, but—"

"Jake, stop!" Kay said with a sob, holding out her hand. "You don't know everything!"

"I don't care what I don't know."

"Maybe you don't, but your family and your friends would care. When I got to Fort Laramie and learned that my . . . fiancé . . . had married another without even having the decency to tell me about it before I left Mississippi, I sort of had a rebellious breakdown. I couldn't go back home to face my brother and sister-in-law or my friends, and tell them that the young man with whom I had exchanged letters of encouragement and support for the whole time he was in West Point, had betrayed me.

"Unwilling to go back home, I went to Cheyenne, where I worked in a saloon and there"—Kay was quiet for a long moment—"there, I . . . I was more than just a hostess." She hung her head in shame.

"But you left," Jake said.

Kay nodded. "I left, but it was too late. I was already a fallen woman."

"You are certainly not a fallen woman. Why, I've never known anyone who could stand as high and hold their head as erect as you. Kay, in the last three days I have seen you under stress that only one in a thousand could handle without breaking. You are not only the most beautiful woman I have ever known; you are also the bravest and the most resourceful."

Her eyes brimming with tears, Kay reached out to lay her hand on Jake's arm. "And you are the most foolish man I have ever me. The kindest, the smartest, and the bravest, but also the most foolish." She smiled through her tears. "And despite the predicament I find myself in, I am glad I came out here."

"I'm glad, too. But tell me, Kay, how in world did you find this place?"

"I overheard some of the railroad police talking about keeping someone confined in a cabin. I got curious as to who it was, and why they were keeping someone a prisoner. I asked Mr. Blanton about the cabin, and he told me where it might be. I didn't tell him why I was looking for it, but now I think that was a mistake. I probably should have told him. If I had told him, he might have passed the word on to others so there might be someone looking for us. As it is, no one knows that I am here."

"Who is Mr. Blanton?"

"He's the newspaper editor. He's a really brave man, too. He has often printed stories against Jake Poindexter and way the railroad police are acting."

"He prints stories against me?"

Kay laughed. "No, not against you, silly. He doesn't know about you. Nobody in town knows about you. Mr. Blanton prints stories about the man who is passing himself off as you."

"Ed Collins," Jake said.

"Yes, against Ed Collins, the man everyone thinks is you. By the way, they burned Mr. Blanton's newspaper office down."

"Who burned it down?"

"Nobody knows for sure, but nearly everyone thinks that it was the railroad people who did it."

"Lord almighty," Jake said, putting his hands to his forehead. "The railroad that I came here to build . . . that is, the legitimate railroad . . . will never be able to climb out of this mess. They will only remember those imposters."

"That isn't necessarily so," Kay replied. "There are some good people in Chugwater, Jake, and once they know the truth, they'll support you. And that is also true of the ranchers and farmers in the valley who have suffered the most. Once they know the truth, they, too, will support you."

"Perhaps so, but the operative terms there are *once they know the truth.*"

"They will know the truth and they'll hear it from you. I know they will."

"How are they going to hear it from me since I am a prisoner?"

"Because I believe we'll come up with a way to escape."

"Escape, yes. If you get the opportunity to escape, Kay, I want you to take it." He reached down to rub his ankles beneath the leg irons. "There's no way I can escape, not with these things on. I can't ride a horse. I can't even walk. But you, on the other hand, could get away. Then you could tell someone where I am."

"Yes. Yes, I could tell someone about you if I could get away, couldn't I?"

"It will be dangerous for you. So you mustn't try until the opportunity is just right."

"Wait, that will do no good. What if I did escape

and told the marshal about you? Why, they would just move you, or maybe even worse."

"But you have to try. Promise me, you will try."

"I'll try," Kay promised.

Morris Butrum came back inside then. "Hey, bar girl. How much longer till you got somethin' fixed to eat?"

"It will be ready soon," Kay said.

"I tell you the truth, I'm glad you come out here. Before you come, Poindexter was doin' all the cookin' 'n he can't cook worth a damn." Butrum looked over toward Jake, who was tenderly rubbing the red rawness under his shackles. "Them leg irons hurt, don't they?"

"They are quite uncomfortable," Jake admitted.

"Yeah, I know they are. I've had to wear 'em myself a few times. When a sheriff or a U.S. Marshal moves you around, they like to put them things on you."

"You've had to wear them? Why Mr. Butrum, here I thought you were a law officer," Kay said, her voice dripping with sarcasm.

Butrum laughed out loud. "Yeah, that's a good one, ain't it? Me bein' a law officer, I mean. You know what else about them leg irons that I find funny?"

"No, but please tell me what you think is funny about these leg irons. I'm afraid I can find no humor in them, at all," Jake replied.

"Well, that's 'cause you ain't thinkin' about it. I mean here you are, spending these last three days with a whore, only seein' as how you're all trussed up like that, they ain't a damn thing you can do about it." Butrum cackled loudly and slapped his hand on his knee. "No sir, you can't do nothin' a-tall about it. I can't do nothin' about it neither, at least not now, but soon as Collins tells me it's all right, well, me 'n the whore there will have us a little party, 'n we'll let you watch."

Kay cringed as Butrum laughed again.

Chapter Thirty-one

Chugwater

When Wang Chow stepped into Lu Win's Restaurant, he saw many more *Měiguó rén* than *Zhōngwén*. It was very popular with Americans so there were always more Americans than Chinese.

Mae Win was taking an order from a man who was sitting alone at a table. Although the man had his back to Wang, there was something familiar about him, a familiarity from Wang's past.

Having taken his order, Mae Win turned to go the kitchen, then she saw Wang and smiled broadly. "Wang, how happy I am to see you."

The man who had just given the order turned when she spoke and looked directly at Wang.

Wang gasped in surprise. *"Lǎohǔ!"* The word was almost an expulsion of his breath.

"I am no longer the Tiger. Here, I go by my *Měiguó* name. I am Zack Clark."

"I did not know that you had left China." Wang smiled. "I will eat with you, and it will be as it was when we were novitiates together at the temple.

"Huānyíng nǐ, wǒ de péngyǒu," Wang added.

"Thank you, but here, I speak only English," Clark replied just as Mae Win returned, carrying his order.

She had heard Wang say *welcome my friend*. "You are friends?"

"Mae, this is Zack Clark. I met him at the Shaolin Temple of Changlin. There he was called *Lǎohǔ*. We called him the Tiger because of his fierce fighting ability."

"Is he as good as you?" Mae asked.

"We fought many matches in training," Wang said. "It shames me to say that I never bested him."

Impressed by Wang's words, she said to Clark, "Oh, you must be very good."

"I am humbled by your praise," Clark said, putting his hands together and making a slight bow of his head.

"How is it that you know our ways so well?" Mae asked.

"I was born in China and I lived there for many years."

"You were born in China?" Mae was surprised by the revelation.

"My parents were missionaries. They were killed when I was but six years old. I was taken in by a Chinese woman until I became of age to enter the temple."

"It is there that we met," Wang said, picking up the story. "We were both boys then, but we became good friends and remained so until I left."

"*Shi.* You left because the Empress Dowager Ci'an issued a decree ordering your death."

"You know of this?" Wang asked.

"*Shi.* Everyone knows of this."

"It shames me that I brought dishonor to the

Shaolin Temple of Changlin," Wang said, his voice
showing his contrition.

Clark smiled. "But we will not speak of this now.
Now, we will speak as we did when we were very good
friends."

The line cabin

Butrum had had no intention of eating supper
with Kay and Jake. "Ain't no need for me to eat beans
'n bacon here when I can get me a good steak 'n some
taters in town, which is what I'm a-goin' to do soon as
Hawken gets here. Onliest thing is, the needle-brain
is pert' near always late, 'n there ain't no doubt in my
mind but what he'll be late again tonight."

Because the time finally lacked but an hour of
sunset, Butrum was standing out on the front porch,
looking for Hawken.

"I think this might be the best time to escape," Kay
said, speaking quietly enough so not to be overheard
by Butrum.

"Yes, I can help you crawl through the back window
and if you run you can get into the trees," Jake
replied, just as quietly. "Butrum's standing out front
looking for Hawken, so he won't see you, and you
won't even be missed until Hawken gets here. And
like Butrum says, Hawken is always late. You would
have at least an hour, maybe even longer of a head
start."

"You mean *we'll* have a head start."

Jake shook his head. "Kay, you know I can't go with
you. I would slow you down too much. Why, I can
barely walk in these things, let alone run."

"You won't have to run, or even walk. There are two

horses here—the one I came on and Butrum's horse. We'll ride out of here."

"How am I going to ride? With these leg irons, there's no way I can straddle a horse."

Kay smiled. "How are you at riding sidesaddle?"

"Sidesaddle?"

"You do know what a sidesaddle is, don't you? They are designed so you don't have to straddle a horse. It isn't considered proper for a woman to ride astride. And it just so happens that the horse I rode out here on has a sidesaddle. If we can get you up on it, those leg irons won't matter. Then, after we get those cuffs off, we'll switch horses."

"Yes!" Jake said enthusiastically, breaking into a broad smile. Just as quickly, the smile disappeared. "It'll never work. Even if we could sneak out, these things are so awkward that Butrum would be on us before we can even saddle the horses."

"Oh, you of little faith," Kay said.

Over the next few minutes Kay outlined her plan. At first, Jake was opposed to it, suggesting that it might be too dangerous for her.

"Jake, you said yourself that when this was over, they would probably kill us, didn't you?"

Jake nodded. "Yes, I believe they will."

"Even a mewing kitten will fight if it is backed into a corner. We have been backed into a corner, Jake. And I would rather be killed trying to escape than to let them murder me."

Jake nodded. "All right."

"It'll take us a minute to get ready."

No more than a minute later, Kay opened the door.

"Mr. Butrum?" she called in the same sultry voice she had developed as a hostess.

"Yeah, whatta ya want?"

"I want to know if you were serious when you said that you and I could have a little party?"

"What?" Butrum asked, turning to look at her for the first time.

She was holding the door open, and she was totally nude.

"What the hell?" The exclamation burst out in total shock.

"Come on in, and let's party," Kay invited. She laughed, a sexy, trilling little laugh.

Butrum stepped inside. "What . . . what about him?" he asked, nodding his head toward Jake.

"I want to watch," Jake said.

"Can you believe it? He said he would give me one hundred dollars if he could watch. I've had men pay to watch me before, but nobody has ever paid me that much. So, what do you say? You want to help me earn a hundred dollars?"

"Yeah, hell yeah!" Butrum said with an enthusiastic smile.

"Well, honey, you can't do it with your clothes on."

Excitedly, Butrum started to undress. Just as both arms were temporarily caught up in the sleeves, Jake stepped up behind him and hit Butrum over the head with a piece of firewood. He went down like a poleaxed steer.

"Is he dead?" Jake asked.

Kay knelt down and put her ear over his nose and

mouth. "He's just knocked out. He's still breathing. Get his pistol while I get dressed."

"His pistol, yes." Just as Jake was pulling the pistol from its holster, Butrum regained consciousness.

"You bottom-feeder, you hit me!" Butrum shouted and even as he was getting to his feet, he put both hands around Jake's neck and began squeezing. The pistol fell to the floor.

"I don't care what Collins says, I'm goin' to kill you, you bastard!" Butrum didn't notice Kay pick up the gun.

The two men went down to the floor with Butrum on top, his hands still wrapped around Jake's neck. Jake was making strange gurgling noises. Seeing his face turning blue, Kay pointed the pistol toward Butrum's head and at point-blank range, pulled the trigger.

Without a word Butrum fell with a little pool of blood and brain detritus spreading under his head.

Still struggling to breathe, Jake put his hands to his neck. Quickly, Kay moved over to kneel beside him, and she put her hand on his shoulder. "Jake! Jake! Are you all right?"

Jake coughed once, then he sat up and took a few deep breaths. "Yes. Yes, I'm all right."

In a spontaneous action that shocked her as much as it did him, Kay put both arms around his neck and kissed him deeply, on the mouth. The kiss lasted several dizzying seconds before she realized what she was doing, With a little cry of alarm she pulled away from him. "Oh, I'm sorry! I'm so sorry!"

Jake smiled at her. "Sorry as in you think it may

have offended me? Or sorry as in you wish you hadn't done it at all."

Kay returned the smile. "Come to think of it, I'm not sorry. Come on. We need to get the horses saddled and get out of here before Hawken comes."

"Don't you think you should get dressed first?"

"Oh!" Kay gasped as if just realizing she was naked.

Just over fifteen minutes later, with only a dim glow over Tomahawk Mountain in the west, both horses were saddled.

"Tell me how to ride on this thing," Jake said.

"You see this little stub coming up from the saddle here? That's how you hold yourself on to the horse . . . by hooking your knee around it. You can get your legs open far enough to do that, can't you?"

"Yes, I can bend and open my knees all right. But the question is, how am I going to get in the saddle?"

"You grab hold of that stub and pull yourself up. I'll wrap my arms around your legs and lift at the same time."

Following Kay's instructions, and with her help, Jake managed to pull himself into the saddle. Kay mounted Butrum's horse a few seconds later.

"Which way now?" Jake asked.

Kay pointed. "This way, away from town. I don't want to take a chance of running into Hawken."

"Butrum!" Hawken called when he reached the line cabin about half an hour later. "Butrum, as you can see I'm here on time, so don't you be late in the morning!" He dismounted and tied his horse off at the porch rail. "How come you ain't got your horse out here 'n ready?" He stepped up onto the porch. "Hell, I figured you'd be ready to go by now."

When Hawken went inside, he gasped. Butrum was lying on the floor, his head in a puddle of blood.

"Damn, what happened to you?"

Chapter Thirty-two

Jake and Kay had ridden for at least two hours.

"Let's spend the night here," Kay said.

"I'm sorry. I'll bet you are tired. Of course we'll spend the night here if you want to."

"It's not just that I'm tired. It's also that I don't know exactly where we are, and I don't want to wander around in the dark getting us even more lost.

Jake chuckled. "That sounds like a good idea."

"You need help getting down?" Kay asked as she dismounted.

"Not too much help, but I would feel better if you stand there and sort of guide me down."

"All right."

Jake slid down without any difficulty, then they tethered their mounts where the horses would have access to some grass. That done, they found a tree with a rather large trunk and sat down, using the tree trunk as a backrest.

"Ahh, this feels good," Jake said.

"Damn," Kay said. "We were so anxious to get out of there that we made a huge, stupid, mistake."

"What mistake?"

"We should have grabbed the bacon and beans."

"To tell the truth, I'm damn sick of the bacon and beans. I do wish we had brought some of the coffee, though."

"We'll look for some chicory tomorrow," Kay said.

"Chicory?"

"During the war, the Yankee navy blockaded all the Southern ports so that we couldn't get any coffee. I don't remember because I was too young, but mama said that everyone in the South began drinking chicory instead of coffee, and some of the folks developed such a taste for it that they still drink it. I've drunk it, and it does taste a lot like coffee, though it is a little bitterer. If we find any tomorrow, I'll brew us some chicory coffee. That is, if you're willing to try it."

"Oh, I'm willing all right." Jake slapped at a mosquito.

The night was filled with noise from the chirping sounds of crickets, to the hooting of owls, to the howling of coyotes.

"Is that a wolf?" Jake asked apprehensively, when he heard the first howl.

Kay laughed. "No, it's just a little old coyote. And they're too afraid of humans to come around us. The biggest thing we'll have to worry about tonight is mosquitoes.

As if on cue, another one bit Jake. He slapped it and at yet another mosquito. "I see what you mean about the mosquitoes. They don't seem to be bothering you as much."

"That's because they know you are new out here and they want some new blood," Kay teased.

"I'm sure that's right," he said with a little laugh. "Kay, may I ask you a question?"

"Sure, ask me anything you want. I have no secrets from you." She laughed sheepishly. "Boy, is that an understatement. I *really* have no secrets from you."

"Don't worry. I kept my eyes closed the whole time."

"Sure you did," Kay replied, and they both laughed. "What is your question?"

"Where did you learn to shoot a gun?"

"Why, from the same place any Southern girl learns. My daddy was a colonel in the Twelfth Mississippi Cavalry. He was teaching me to shoot almost as soon as I could walk."

"I couldn't have done what you did back at the cabin."

"I'm sure, if you were put in position to save your own life, or that of another, you would be able to kill someone," Kay replied defensively.

"No, no, don't get me wrong," Jake said, reaching out to put his hand on her shoulder. "I'm not talking about killing him. I certainly would have killed him in self-defense or to protect you. But I would have had to bash the snake's head in with that piece of firewood or something. When I said I couldn't have done what you did, what I meant was, I couldn't have done it because I don't know how to shoot a gun."

Kay smiled in relief that Jake wasn't condemning her for killing Butrum, but also out of amusement to think he didn't know how to shoot a gun. "Jake Poindexter, have you never shot a gun in your life?"

"I've never had any call to."

"Butrum had two boxes of cartridges in his saddlebags, so if nothing else comes from this, I at least intend to teach you how to shoot a gun. There is also a rifle in his saddle holster, so part of teaching you to shoot will have a more practical application. We will shoot some game. And I assure you that any game we kill will be better than bacon and beans."

Jake began rubbing the redness under his leg irons.

"I wish we could get those things off of you," Kay said. "But Butrum didn't have a key."

"I doubt Hawken would have had a key, either. I'm quite sure that the key is in Collins's hands."

"We'll find a blacksmith somewhere. He'll be able to get that off."

C&FL office, Chugwater

"Gone?" Collins shouted explosively. "What do you mean they're gone?"

"I mean they ain't there, neither one of 'em. Poindexter's gone 'n so is the girl," Hawken said, clarifying his statement.

"Why didn't you stop them?"

"I couldn'ta stopped 'em on account of I warn't there yet when it happened."

"That means they got away while Butrum was watching them. Where is Butrum? He has some explaining to do."

"Butrum won't be explaining nothin' on account of Butrum is dead. He's lyin' out there in the line shack now, deader 'n a doornail."

"Damn!" Collins said. "Am I surrounded by incompetents? I sent Streeter out to take care of MacCallister, Gleason, and that woman, and he failed. And now you tell me Butrum got himself killed by a bar girl and a man in leg irons."

"You want me to go see if I can find Poindexter 'n the whore?" Hawken asked.

"They won't be able to get far in the dark, and you wouldn't be able to find them. You can go in the morning. I'll send Flannigan with you."

"All right. We'll find 'em."

Just down the street from the C&FL office, Biff Johnson was visiting with Marshal Bill Ferrell. He was sharing his concern over Kay's extended absence. "Sometimes the girls will take a day or two off. I don't ever say anything about it because I like to give them free rein. But this will be the fourth night Kay hasn't shown up, and to be honest, I'm getting a little worried about her. I asked the other girls, and she didn't say anything to them about taking off."

"Four nights you say. That would be Tuesday?"

"Yes. Well, Tuesday night. She was in earlier Tuesday."

"That's the day she came to see me. But to be honest with you, I didn't really give it any further thought. I should have."

"Kay came to see you? What about? Was she in danger?"

"No, at least she didn't say or act in any way that would make me think she was in danger."

"Well, what did she come to see you about?"

"She said she overheard some of the C and FL men talking about keeping a watch on someone, but as we talked we decided it might be one of the railroad men who was being held for some internal disciplinary problem. Since she had no specifics as to who was being held, or even where they might be holding him, there wasn't much I could do about it."

"Bill, would you do me a favor and sort of ask around? Kay isn't like most of the girls I get. She's smart, and though she's never said anything about it, I get the feeling that she has a better-than-average education. I'm worried about her, and the other girls are worried, as well."

"You know that I have no authority outside the city limits, but I'll check around town and see if anyone knows anything."

"Thanks. I'd feel a lot better about this if you would."

The prairie chicken raised its head and looked around.

"He feels that we are here," Kay said quietly. "If you want breakfast, don't miss. Now, line up the rifle this way. Look through this rear sight at the front sight, and put the front sight on the chicken. Tell me when you have that done."

Jake raised the rifle to his shoulder and lined up the sights just as Kay had explained. "I've got it all lined up."

"All right. Now, take the slack out of the trigger, but don't pull it all the way back yet. Hold your breath, and sort of squeeze, rather than pull, the trigger."

Jake squeezed off the shot. The chicken fell over and went into a death-convulsion flapping of its wings.

"You did it!" Kay said with a happy smile.

"I hate to be negative, but how are we going to cook him?" Jake asked. "We don't have a skillet or anything."

Kay chuckled. "We don't need a skillet. All we need is a fire and a green twig. And thanks to Butrum's saddlebags, we have matches to start a fire."

An hour later, Jake sucked the last piece of meat off a bone. "I've eaten at Empire House and Del Monaco's, but I've never enjoyed a meal more." He reached down to massage his ankles.

"Let me do it," Kay said, and taking off his shoes, she sat with Jake's feet in her lap, gently, very gently, rubbing the rawness caused by the ankle cuffs.

"That feels good," Jake said.

"We've got to get these things off of you. We need to find a blacksmith."

"Do you have any idea where we are?"

"I know we're west of Chugwater," Kay said. "But I'm a little frightened to go back that way. I'm sure that Collins's men will be out looking for us. We should be fairly close to Bordeaux."

"Bordeaux?"

"Yes, I've heard some of the men talk about it, but I've never been there. I know they said that it's slightly northwest of Chugwater."

"Well, then we shall ride northwest," Jake said.

"I'm not sure where northwest is."

Jake smiled. "Your father taught you how to shoot. My father taught me how to navigate. We don't have a compass, but we do have the sun."

Jake stood up and nodded toward the sun, which was halfway up in its morning transit. He turned his back to the sun and with his right hand, pointed straight ahead.

"That is west." He moved his right hand to a position forty-five degrees to the right of his right hand. "Therefore, this is north." He moved his hand to an angle about forty-five degrees to the left.

"And that, my dear lady, would be northwest, or a heading of about three hundred and fifteen degrees. Now, you said slightly northwest, so we'll split the difference between three hundred and sixty degrees, and two hundred and seventy degrees, which would be three hundred fifteen degrees, or, this way," he said with a final point.

"Oh, my, I am impressed!" Kay said.

"Well, I didn't want to be someone wearing leg irons who was doing nothing more than tagging along for the company." Jake smiled. "Though, I must say that I am finding the company most agreeable."

"I think we should be going," Kay suggested.

"You'll have to help me get mounted."

After both horses were saddled, Jake stood beside his mount as Kay approached to help him into the saddle.

"Are you ready?" Kay asked.

"Not quite."

"What do you need?"

"This," Jake said, putting his arms around Kay and pulling her to him. He kissed her, not hard and demanding, but as soft as the brush of a butterfly's wing. It was but a brief moment, then he pulled away continuing to stare at her.

She could feel the heat of them burning on her skin.

Kay was surprised by the kiss, but she was even more shocked by her own reaction to it. She felt a tingling in her lips that spread throughout her body and warmed her blood. Reaching up, she touched her lips and held her fingers there for a long moment.

"I'm sorry," Jake said. "I didn't mean to presume."

"I don't consider it a presumption," she said with a smile. "But, if we are going to get those leg irons off, we're going to have to find a blacksmith, so we need to get going."

As before, Kay wrapped her arms around Jake's legs as he grabbed the stub on the saddle to pull himself up.

"You'd better let me set the heading," Jake said, once they were both mounted.

"I'd better let you do what?"

"Let me lead," Jake said.

"Oh, yes, I think that would be a good idea."

Chapter Thirty-three

Chugwater in the morning was alive with activity. Conveyances of every kind, from personal buggies to large freight wagons, rolled up and down the street. Businesses were beginning to open for the day's business, and the boardwalks were filling with pedestrians.

Bo Hawken and Pogue Flannigan were in the C&FL office, talking with Ed Collins.

"Do you think you can find them?" Collins asked.

"Hell yes, I can find them," Hawken said. "I mean, how hard can it be, what with him a-wearin' them leg irons? They sure as hell can't have gotten far last night. 'N seein' as they didn't come back to town, that means they're still wanderin' around somewhere between here 'n Tomahawk Mountain. I figure we can find 'em before this day is over."

"All right. Find them," Collins ordered.

"You'd better give us the key to Poindexter's leg irons," Hawken said.

"Why should I do that?"

"Well, think about it, Collins," Flannigan said. "If

he's in leg irons, how are we supposed to get him back to the cabin? He can't ride, 'n he can barely walk."

"You won't be bringing him back," Collins said. "You won't be bringing either one of them back. I want you to kill them."

"What do we do with 'em after we kill 'em?"

"No need to worry about that. Wolves and buzzards will take care of them."

"Hey, Collins," Flannigan said with an evil smiled. "What about the woman. Is it all right if we . . . uh . . ."

"Do anything you want with her, before or after you kill her. All I care about is that both of them are dead."

"Ha! I been waitin' for this," Hawken said. "Come on, Pogue, let's go find 'em."

Shortly after Hawken and Flannigan left, Collins walked from his office down to the Western Union office.

"Good morning, Mr. Poindexter," Hodge Deckert said with a warm greeting. "Another telegram?"

"Yes."

"I must say you have certainly given me a lot of business since you arrived. Another one to New York?"

"Yes. May I have the pad and pencil, please?"

Deckert provided the items, and Collins began to write. *Our guest is gone. I have made plans to avoid an unexpected visit from him, but I feel it best to relocate C&FL.*

Collins handed his message to Deckert. "Please send this right away and notify me the moment I receive a reply."

Deckert read the message. "Oh, my, you are leaving Chugwater?"

"Just send the message," Collins said. "Same address as before."

When Collins returned to his office, he saw the banker, Bob Dempster, waiting for him. "Mr. Dempster, can I help you?"

"Mr. Poindexter, I have just been informed that a rather substantial amount of money is being transferred to your account."

"How much is a substantial amount?"

"It is one hundred thousand dollars."

"Yes, I've been expecting it," Collins replied in a calm voice. "How soon will the money get here?"

"Well, the total amount won't get here, of course. Only about twenty-five thousand dollars in actual cash will be transferred," Dempster said. "For a transfer that large, it is actually all paperwork and calculations. You see, what we do is credit your account with the sum without actually having to make an actual cash transfer. You may withdraw it as you need it, and we'll make adjustments to the balance."

"Where is the actual cash now?"

"That's what I'm trying to explain to you. There is no cash now. There is only a telegraphic accounting of the money. The cash, of course, is still in the bank of origin, which, if the last transfers are indicative, would be the New York Bank for Savings."

"I know that some cash has been transferred here from the earlier transactions."

"Well yes, of course, a rather significant amount of cash has actually been transferred. But more than half of the earlier transactions are still a matter of accounting between the four banks involved, the New York Bank for Saving, Wells Fargo in Denver, the Cheyenne Bank and Trust, and of course, this bank."

"How much do I have?"

"At the moment you have just $97,000 credited to your account, but I would have to check to give you the exact figure."

"All right. Suppose I walk down to the bank with you and we check."

"Of course," Dempster said, making an effort not to show that he was a little annoyed by his client's attitude that seemed to border on mistrust.

"Your account is currently credited with ninety-seven thousand, six hundred and fifty dollars. Of course, as soon as we get the wire transfer confirmation from First Bank and Trust in Cheyenne recording the latest transfer, that amount will significantly increase," Dempster said.

"I don't want it to come here."

"I beg your pardon?"

"I want the credit of that one hundred thousand to remain in the First Bank and Trust in Cheyenne. Now, if you would, please tell me how much actual cash I have available for immediate withdrawal."

"At the moment you have forty thousand dollars in actual cash."

"Is the money bound?"

"Yes, it is just as we received it from Wells Fargo in Denver, twenty-dollar bills bound in bundles of one hundred."

"That would be"—Collins paused for a moment to do some figuring—"twenty bundles. I wish to withdraw it all."

"You . . . you are taking all your available cash from our bank?" Dempster asked, the tone of his voice indicating his disappointment over losing such a large account.

"Yes, I shall want all the cash that is available, and please transfer the remaining funds on credit to the account in Cheyenne."

"Why would you do this?"

"I fear that the cost of doing business has become too dear in Chugwater. There are too many people who are opposed to the railroad. I'm sure I will be able to find a more friendly welcome somewhere else."

"I understand that you have met with some opposition here, but there are just as many, or perhaps even more, who have been supportive. However, if you wish to leave, I'm sure I will be unable to change your mind. But I really wouldn't recommend you traveling with that much cash on hand. If you wish, I can make a wire transfer of these funds to your new location."

"No, I'll be back for the cash."

"Very good, sir."

"Let's stop here for a moment," Jake said.

"Oh, are we lost?" Kay asked.

"No, I have another reason for stopping. Kay, would you help me get down, please?"

Kay dismounted, then walked up to Jake's horse. She smiled at him. "If you have to find a place to, uh, have a little privacy, why didn't you say so? I'll stay with the horses while you go, then you can come back and stay with the horses while I go."

"Sounds like a workable plan to me," Jake said. "But I'd rather not do it from up here. I do believe it will work better if I can get down from the horse," he teased.

"Oh, sorry 'bout that," Kay said, stepping up to help him dismount.

Once down from the horse Jake pulled the pistol from his waistband and started to give it to Kay. Earlier they had divided Butrum's two weapons, Kay keeping the rifle, and Jake taking the pistol.

"No, you may as well keep it," Kay said. "You never know, you might see a rattlesnake," she added with a chuckle.

"Oh, Lord, I hope not. But to tell the truth, I don't even know what one looks like."

"Don't worry. If you see one, he will introduce himself to you."

"What?"

Kay chuckled. "Why do you think they call them *rattle*snakes?"

"Oh, yes, I suppose you're right." Jake walked into a copse of trees. "Mr. Snake, let's be friends. I'll only be a minute."

Kay laughed as she saw him disappear behind the trees. She had never met anyone like him, and yes, she had only known him for a few days, but already she knew that she was in love with him.

How dumb of me! she scolded herself. *I am a bar girl, and he is one of the wealthiest men in America. Oh, Jake, why couldn't you be a poor cowboy?*

* * *

"There they are," Hawken said quietly as he pointed.

"I only see the woman," Flannigan replied. "Where's Poindexter?"

"I figure he couldn't keep up, what with being in leg irons, so she probably left 'im somewhere 'n is goin' for help."

"Yeah, but Collins wants both of 'em kilt."

"We'll find out from the whore where he is," Hawken said.

"You been a bad girl, ain't you? Last time I seen you, you was in the cabin."

"Hawken!" Kay gasped, spinning around to see the two men approaching her. "What are you doing here?"

"I'm lookin' for you," Hawken said. "You the one that kilt Butrum? I figure it has to have been you, 'cause I don't figure that eastern dude Poindexter coulda done it. Hell, he'd probably pee in his pants if he had to shoot a gun."

"No, I just peed on a tree," Jake said, his words startling Hawken and Flannigan. Jake was holding a pistol.

"What the hell?" Hawken shouted. He already had his gun in his hand and he swung it around to aim at Jake but he was too late. Jake pulled the trigger and Hawken went down. Flannigan's pistol was still in the holster and he made a grab for it, but Jake shot again and, like Hawken before him, Flannigan went down.

"Kay, are you all right?" Jake asked, the smoking gun still in his hand.

"Yes, I am," Kay said in an awestruck voice. "Jake, you were wonderful! Absolutely wonderful!"

Jake held the pistol out and looked at it. "Yeah," he said with a laugh. "I did pretty well at that, didn't I?"

After learning from Charley Blanton that Kay had asked about the old Trail Back line cabin, Biff Johnson also found out that Kay had rented a horse from Mather's Livery Stable.

"Yes, sir," Ken Kern said. "She took Rhoda four days ago. She said she was goin' for a ride."

"Four days ago, and you haven't reported it?" Biff asked, the tone of his voice displaying his anger and concern.

"I didn't want to get her in trouble," Kern said. "I wanted to give her a chancet to bring the horse back on her own."

"She went to that cabin," Biff said to Charley.

"Yes, I think so, as well."

"I'm going out there to check it out."

"I'm going with you," Charley said.

As the two men dismounted in front of the cabin, they could smell the fetid odor of decomposition.

"Damn!" Biff said. "Only one thing can make a smell like that."

"Oh Lord, Biff, you don't think it's the girl, do you?"

"I pray that it isn't Kay, but we have to check it out." Holding a handkerchief to his nose, Biff approached the cabin. As he got closer, he could hear the buzz of thousands of flies. He pushed the door open.

"Is it—" Charley started, but he didn't finish his question before Biff answered.

"It's one of the railroad policemen," Biff said. "I'm not sure which one it is, but I think it might be Butrum."

Chapter Thirty-four

Cheyenne

With four men riding with him, Collins had no fear of anyone robbing him. And, because none of the four were aware that he had so much cash with them, he wasn't afraid of them robbing him, either.

When they rode into town, they dismounted in front of the Bella Union Saloon.

"Well, look over there standin' at the bar," Caldwell said.

"Dixon, what are you doin' here?" Streeter asked.

"I just come in on the train this mornin'. I thought I'd have a drink before I went back to Chugwater."

"There's no need in going back yet," Collins said. "We're all here."

"What do you mean, we're all here? Where's Hawken, Butrum, and Flannigan?" Dixon asked.

"Butrum got hisself kilt," Nichols said.

"And Hawken and Flannigan are taking care of a little job for me."

"Little job? It ain't all that little," Mitchell said. "Them two kilt Butrum before they escaped."

"What two are you talkin' about?" Dixon asked.

"Some whore that works at Fiddler's Green, the one called Kay, found out, somehow, that we was holdin' the real Jake Poindexter as prisoner, 'n she found 'im, then somehow they managed to kill Butrum 'n escape."

"'N now Hawken 'n Flannigan is out lookin' for 'em," Streeter said.

"You know what? Here we are in a saloon 'n we ain't got hardly no money to spend," Caldwell said.

"If you gentlemen will just wait here, I'll take care of that," Collins said. "I have an account here. I'll go to the bank and get some money."

"Yes, sir, how may I help you?" the teller asked as Collins stepped up to the window a few minutes later.

"My name is Jake Poindexter, and I have an account here."

The teller examined a ledger book, then looked up at Collins with an obsequious expression on his face. "Yes, sir, I see that you do have an account with us. A rather substantial account."

Collins put his carpet bag on the lip of the counter, then began withdrawing the bound bundles of cash.

"I wish to make a deposit."

"Yes, sir! How much?"

"All but this," he said, withholding one bundle and taking five hundred from one of the others.

Once the deposit was made, Collins walked back to

the Bella Union, where he saw his five men sitting at a table. He joined them.

"Did you get any money?" Streeter asked.

Collins smiled, and put some money on the table. "There's twenty-five hundred dollars there, five hundred apiece. That ought to hold you for a while."

"I thought there was a lot more money than that," Streeter said.

"There soon will be." Collins didn't mention the sizeable amount of cash that he had just deposited. "Also, I will soon be getting another wire transfer of money, but in order to make certain we can get it, we are going to have get rid of Jake Poindexter. Otherwise he could stop it."

"We had him for five weeks," Mitchell said. "Why didn't we just kill the yellow dog while we had him?"

"At the time I didn't think that it would be the best thing to do, but the situation has changed. Now he and the girl have become a liability, and both of them need to be killed."

"Hell, what do we have to worry about Jake Poindexter for? Ain't Hawken 'n Flannigan chasin' them down?" Streeter asked.

"They are, and I have every confidence that they will find them."

"What about his papa, the old man, what's his name? Preston?" Dixon asked.

"Preston Poindexter is no problem. I've received word that he's still in Chicago," Collins said

"No, he ain't in Chicago," Dixon said.

"What do you mean he isn't in Chicago? I have word from my source in New York that he is."

"Well, your feller in New York don't know nothin',

'cause when I come through Chicago I seen that
private car him the other 'uns was a-ridin' in, 'n there
warn't nobody in it. So I asked some folks, 'n they said
that all four of the ones that was in the car come on to
Cheyenne."

"Damn, that could be trouble," Collins said.

"No more trouble than Jake Poindexter. Him 'n
that woman bein' free like that is worrisome," Caldwell said.

"I'm not too worried about Jake Poindexter," Collins
said. "When he escaped he was in leg irons and I don't
think he'll be able to get very far with such an imped-
iment."

"You reckon he's still got 'em on?" Streeter asked.

"I'm quite sure that he does, as Butrum didn't have
a key," Collins replied.

"Where are we going to go after this?" Mitchell
asked.

Collins smiled. "After we divide the money, I shall
be returning to New York. Where you gentlemen go
will be entirely up to you."

"When are we goin' to divide up the money?"
Streeter asked.

"As soon as the account is transferred to the bank,
I shall put in a demand on the actual cash. We will
have to wait until the cash comes from Denver, but
that shouldn't take more than a few days, a week at
the most."

Sky Meadow

After breakfast Duff, Elmer, and Pete rode into
Chugwater, Wang having ridden in a short while earlier.

As the three men rode into town, there were a few curious glances toward Pete. He was someone none of the townspeople had ever seen before. But he was with Duff and Elmer, both of whom were very familiar figures in town, so the expressed curiosity was fleeting and casual.

"The C and FL office is just ahead, on the left," Duff pointed out to Pete.

"When we confront this man who is passing himself off as my son, I'll be most interested in seeing his reaction," Pete said.

"Yeah," Elmer said. "I'm sorta lookin' forward to that my ownself."

When they reached the little building that was adjacent to Martin Gilmore's law office, they saw that the door was standing open. That seemed a little strange to Duff, but he didn't pay that much attention to it until, as he was looping Sky's reins around the hitching rail, he noticed something else. The C&FL sign had been removed. The office was empty.

Duff stepped into Gilmore's office. "The office next door is empty," Duff said. "Would you be for knowing where the man who has been calling himself Poindexter might be?"

"I don't know where he is. I was meeting with an out-of-town client, so I arrived late this morning and was surprised to see the office empty and . . . wait a minute. What do you mean when you say 'the man who has been calling himself Poindexter'? Are you suggesting that he isn't Poindexter?"

"Martin Gilmore, I would like for you to meet Preston Poindexter," Duff said.

"Preston Poin—" Gilmore started, then, obviously surprised, he paused for a moment. "My word, are you *the* Preston Poindexter?"

"I prefer to be called Pete, but since I am the principal of the Poindexter Rail and Maritime Corporation, I suppose I would have to answer yes to that question."

"There is a picture of the real Jake Poindexter hangin' in Pete's office," Elmer said. "'N this pimple here, who's been tellin' ever'one that he's Jake Poindexter, for sure ain't him."

"What's the imposter's name?" Gilmore asked Pete.

Pete shook his head. "I'm sorry. I don't know the answer to your question. I just know that he is an imposter."

"You have no idea what happened to him?" Duff asked.

"No, I have no idea at all. I can tell you this, though. When I came back and saw that he had taken everything from the office, I was convinced that his departure is permanent. That's why I took the sign down."

"Aye, that there was nae sign is the first thing I noticed."

"Mr. Poindexter, since everyone is convinced that the man who so recently occupied the office next door isn't your son, may I, as a lawyer, offer a little advice, *bono*?"

"Yes, of course you may."

"The bank has a rather substantial amount of money on hand for use by the C and FL Railroad, and the fake Jake Poindexter has access to it. If I were you, I would put an immediate hold on those funds."

"Yes, yes, that is a very good idea!" Pete said. "Duff, please take me to the bank."

"I'm afraid you are too late," Dempster said when Pete, accompanied by Duff and Elmer, made the request to freeze the funds that had been transferred to the C&FL account.

"What do you mean, I'm too late?"

"Mr. Poindexter withdrew every dollar that was in his account early this morning."

"How much was in the account?" Pete asked.

"There was a credit of ninety-seven thousand, six hundred and fifty dollars, which included forty thousand dollars in cash. He withdrew all the cash, and transferred the remaining credit to the First Bank and Trust in Cheyenne. He also redirected the one-hundred-thousand-dollar wire amount there."

"Good Lord, are you saying there's a wire transfer of another one hundred thousand dollars?" Pete said.

"Yes, sir," Dempster replied. "Of course, as you understand, that is credit only. No cash has actually transferred as yet."

"I want you to stop that transfer," Pete said. "In fact, I want the money to remain in my New York account."

"I'm afraid I can't stop it," Dempster replied.

"What do you mean, you can't stop it?"

"That transaction would have to be terminated by the authority who originated the transfer."

"Well, that authority would be me, wouldn't it? I own the company."

"No, sir," Dempster said as he examined his

books. "The originating authority would be one Norman Jamison."

Pete took a gasping breath, then reached out to the table near where they were standing. His face grew pale.

"Mr. Poindexter, are you all right, sir?" Dempster asked, worried by the way Pete looked.

"You were right, Duff." Pete spoke the words as if he didn't want to admit it. "I thought I knew Norman Jamison better than anyone alive. I trusted him with my business, my son, and I would have trusted him with my life. Now I learn that the weasel has betrayed me."

"You said the imposter wanted the latest transfer to go to a bank in Cheyenne?" Duff asked.

"Yes, the First Bank and Trust of Cheyenne."

"Then that's where the blackheart will be going," Duff said.

"Not necessarily," Dempster said. "Since the transfer is a credit instead of actual cash, he would be able to access the money from anywhere. Denver, San Francisco, St. Louis, anywhere he goes."

"So he can be anywhere," Duff said.

"I'm afraid so."

"I don't care," Pete said, waving his hand. "Right now, first and foremost, is my son. Where is Jake? Is he still alive? I must know, and finding him is my top priority."

"We'll find him," Duff promised.

Chapter Thirty-five

A few minutes later, Duff, Elmer, and Pete were having coffee in Fiddler's Green, where Duff introduced Pete to Biff Johnson.

"Biff has an interesting background," Duff said. "He was a sergeant major with Custer."

"With Custer?" Pete said, surprised by the revelation. "I thought everyone with Custer was killed."

"True," Biff said. "What Duff means is, I was with Custer's column, but I was actually in the fight with Reno and Benteen."

"Oh, yes, I should have realized. I have read of those two gentlemen."

"They were officers and thus made *gentlemen* by an act of Congress. It took an act of Congress, because, believe me, neither one of those blatherskites are gentlemen," Biff replied. "As far as I'm concerned, they abandoned Custer, Reno because of cowardice, and Benteen because of hatred."

Duff chuckled. "As you can see, Biff is a man of opinion."

"I can see that," Pete said, also with a chuckle.

"So, you've come out here to check on how your son is doing, have you?" Biff said.

"He isn't my son," Pete said.

"What is he, your nephew or something? I thought Jake Poindexter was your son."

"Jake Poindexter is my son, but the man who has been passing himself off as Jake Poindexter is a phony," Pete said.

"I'll be damned. So you mean there ain't goin' to be a railroad after all? That's sure goin' to disappoint a lot of people."

"No, there will be a railroad, once I manage to get control of things again. My son came out here to build the railroad, but the man who claims to be my son has been doing nothing but stealing money from the company."

"You say your son *did* come out here?" Biff said.

"Yes, and I'm very worried about him."

"Then that's who it was!" Biff said with a snap of his fingers. "It has to be! And that would explain where Kay is."

"What are you talking about?" Duff asked.

"Just a minute and I think we can figure it out. Addie, come over here for a moment, would you?" Biff called out to the girl who had waited upon them earlier.

"Yes, sir, Mr. Johnson. More coffee?" Addie asked.

"No, we want to ask you a question."

Addie was clearly confused, and a little concerned, by Biff's comment, and it showed in her face as she approached the table.

"Addie, tell these gentlemen what Kay told you about overhearing some of the railroad police talking."

"She didn't say too much about it. Just that she had overheard some of them talking and she was curious about what they said."

"What did they say?" Duff asked.

"Only that they were watchin' over someone. Kay said it sounded to her like they were keepin' someone a prisoner, 'n since they are police themselves, she was wonderin' why they wasn't keepin' whoever it was in jail."

"If the man whose been tellin' ever'one that he's your son ain't really your son, 'n you say your son did come out here, then it could be—"

"The real Jake Poindexter is the one they're guardin' somewhere," Elmer said, interrupting Biff.

"Where?" Pete asked.

"I don't know where he is now, but I'm pretty sure I know where he was," Biff said. "You see, Kay spoke to the marshal and Charley Blanton about it, and damn if she didn't go off by herself to look into it."

"What did she find out?" Elmer asked.

"Well, I don't know for sure, but when she didn't come back after a few days, Charley and I figured out where the cabin was and we went to see for ourselves. That's when we found one of the railroad policemen, shot dead. I think it was Butrum."

"Did you ask the imposter about it?" Duff asked.

"No, Charley said that since we didn't find Kay there, talking about it might bring more danger to her."

"Aye, 'tis probably true," Duff said.

"But, whoever was being held there is gone, as well. And now, with you telling me that the real Jake Poindexter is actually out here, I would be willing to bet a hundred dollars to one that he was the one being held in that line shack. And with him and Kay both gone, I think they killed Butrum and made their escape. There's no doubt in my mind but that if we find Kay, we'll find your son."

During the conversation, Addie had stood by quietly listening as the men discussed her friend Kay and whoever might be with her. Then, realizing that her presence might be considered an intrusion, she asked sweetly, "Would anyone want more coffee?"

"Nae, lass. 'Tis late enough in the day. I believe I'll have a wee bit o' my scotch."

"Duff's special bottle is under the bar," Biff said.

"Yes, sir, I know which bottle is his," Addie replied with a pretty smile.

When Charley Blanton came into the saloon a short while later, he saw that Duff and the others were deeply engaged in conversation. He saw, also, that there was an older man who he had never seen before. Every chair at the table was occupied, but Charley, considering that freedom of the press extended to freedom to butt in, took an empty chair from one of the other tables and pushed it in between Elmer and Biff.

Just as Charley had not waited for an invitation to join them, neither did he wait for an introduction to the man who was a stranger to him. Before he sat down, he stuck his hand across the table. "I'm Charley Blanton, owner, publisher, editor, and reporter of the local newspaper, the *Chugwater Defender*."

"Preston Poindexter. Pete, if you will," Pete replied.

"Preston Poindexter?" Charley looked toward Duff.

"Aye, *the* Preston Poindexter," Duff validated.

"Well sir, all I can say is, you have some nerve coming here now, with all the damage your son has done to our community."

"The brigand who did all that was nae his son," Duff said. "We believe the real Jake Poindexter was captured by the imposter, and now we're trying to find Pete's son."

"Oh," Charley said contritely. "Mr. Poindexter, please forgive me. I had no idea."

"There is no forgiveness due, Mr. Blanton. As you said, you had no idea that the man doing all the damage wasn't my son."

"Do you know the name of the man who is impersonating your son?"

"I'm afraid not."

"Well, what does he say about all this? Have you confronted him?"

"Nae, for the brigand is gone."

"So, you are looking for the real Jake Poindexter, you say? Where are you looking?"

"Charley, I was tellin' that you and I may have almost found him."

"The line shack!" Charley said. "Yes, you're right, Biff! I think he may well have been the one who was being held prisoner, the one Kay went to check on."

"What did you find at the line shack?" Duff asked.

"The man who had been guarding them, Butrum, we believe it was, was dead, and Kay and the real Jake Poindexter were gone," Charley said.

Duff smiled. "Pete, if they were able to escape, 'tis

my thinking that they're both still alive 'n making their way to someplace safe."

"I pray that you are right, Mr. Blanton. That it was my son who was being held there, and I pray that you are also right, Duff. That they are both somewhere safe now."

Chapter Thirty-six

Wang Chow saw Zack Clark as soon as he stepped into Lu Win's Restaurant.

"There is your friend," Mae Win said.

"Zack, come and join us," Wang called out, speaking in English.

"Jīntiān wǒ bùshì Zack. Wǒ shì Lǎohǔ."

Zack spoke the words in a guttural tone that even the few Americans in the room and didn't understand the language, recognized as an implied threat.

"Why did he say that today he isn't Zack, he is Tiger?" Mae Win asked.

"I think he has come to challenge me," Wang said.

"Challenge you? Do you mean he wants to fight you?"

"Shi."

"Are you ready, my friend?" Zack asked, switching back to English.

"Not in here. I have no wish to bring damage to this place and the fine people who own it."

"In the street, then, *Dào sǐ*," Zack said, again, making a guttural challenge of the last two words.

"Dào sǐ," Wang replied as calmly as if he had just been asked to share a drink.

"To the death?" Mae Win gasped, horror-stricken by what she had just heard. "But no! You are friends! Why, Tiger? Why do you wish to fight to the death?" She asked the question in Chinese.

"It is a matter of honor," Zack replied in the same language.

"It is honorable for a friend to kill a friend?" Mae Win's words were filled with anguish and confusion.

"Wang Chow brought dishonor to the Temple of Changlin. Dowager Ci'an has issued a decree ordering his death, so as a priest of Changlin, I am honor bound to kill the man who was my friend."

Even though they spoke Chinese, the others in the restaurant realized rather quickly that there was about to be a fight, and that this fight would be like none they had ever seen before.

As Clark and Wang Chow left the restaurant, the others, including Mae Win, the employees, and even Lu Win himself, left the restaurant to follow the two men out into the street.

As Duff and the others continued their conversation in Fiddler's Green, someone stepped in through the batwing doors and called out. "Come quick! That Chinaman 'n another feller's about to have a fight in the street!"

"Wang?" Biff asked.

"It must be," Duff replied and his table, as did every other table, and even the bar cleared of customers as everyone rushed outside.

Already the street was filled with citizens of Chugwater as they gathered to see what was about to happen.

"That's a white man goin' up against Wang," Biff said. "What kind of fool would do that?"

"It's Zack Clark," Duff said. "He trained with Wang when they were boys." Duff knew of Zack's history.

"I thought they was friends," Elmer said. "What they fightin' for?"

"I don't know," Biff said. "But I've got an idea it's goin' to be a doozy."

Wang knelt before Zack and removed Zack's shoes. Then Wang stood as Zack knelt before him, removing Wang's shoes. With bare feet the two men stood in the middle of the street, facing one another. Putting their hands together, prayerlike, just under their chin, they made a slight bow of their heads toward each other.

With all the preliminaries out of the way, both men assumed a fighting stance, and the more observant of those who were gathered for the fight saw that the way they stood, and the way they held their feet and hands, were mirror images.

Approaching each other, they began making thrusts and jabs, but to no effect as they were mutually avoided or blocked. Then Zack took Wang down with a sweep of his leg to Wang's leg. As Wang was getting back up, Zack, with a yell, charged toward him and brought down a wicked chop toward Wang's neck. Wang moved to avoid the chop, and Zack's hand smashed through the thick hitching rail, breaking it into two pieces.

"Damn! Did you see how he broke that hitchin' rail? It must be four inches thick," someone called out, impressed by what he had just seen.

Wang rolled quickly out of the way and regained his feet. Again the two men made wicked thrusts toward each other, the kind of thrust that would have instantly brought down the average man. But neither of these two men were average.

Wang spun around and kicked his leg out, catching Zack in the chest. Zack went down but was immediately on his feet. Closing on Wang, he hit him on either side of the head, his cupped hands on Wang's ears stunning him for a moment.

Zack took advantage of that and hit Wang with a two-hand thrust that again knocked him down. Wang fell where the two pieces of the hitching rail hung from the end posts, making a *V* with the point at the ground.

Zack grabbed one of the pieces and, ripping it free, raised it over his head. With a loud shout, he started down with the large club, intending to deliver a killing blow to Wang's head.

Just before Zack could bring the club down, Wang shot his arm up, and the heel of his hand caught Zack on the tip of his nose. The blow caused Zack to drop the club as the splintered bones entered his brain. He fell backward on the street where he laid faceup, his arms out to either side of him. He wasn't moving.

Wang knelt beside him, placed the tips of his fingers on Zack's neck, then reached out to gently close Zack's eyes. He bowed his head and remained quiet and unmoving.

"What the hell?" someone said. "Is he dead?"

"He ain't moved a muscle since he went down, so he must be."

Finally Wang got up, walked over to put his shoes back on, then he got Zack's shoes and to the surprise of everyone, put Zack's shoes back on his feet as well, doing it in a way that could almost be described as reverent.

Duff went over to put his hand on Wang's shoulder. "Are you all right, Wang?"

"*Shi. Lǎohǔ* was a friend from my youth. I am saddened by what happened here."

With Jake and Kay

As all of Chugwater was buzzing with excitement over what they had just witnessed, Jake and Kay were just approaching something that had their hopeful attention. At first, it looked like nothing but little hillocks rising from the prairie before them, but as they drew closer they realized what they were seeing was a town.

"Jake, you did it!" Kay said. "You led us to a town."

Jake chuckled. "If it is Bordeaux, I led us to it. If it is some other town, it was a matter of blind luck and we merely stumbled across it."

"At this point it makes no difference. It is a town with a blacksmith shop, I hope. And a restaurant and a hotel with a means of taking a bath."

"Yes, but all those things cost money," Jake replied. "And here I am, the son of one of the wealthiest men in America, without a cent to my name. My hosts took all my money from me when they decided to make me their guest."

"Yes, they took my money as well."

"Then we are paupers who will be forced to beg, or attempt to convince them that I am who I say I am."

"Well, we aren't complete paupers," Kay said with a lilting laugh.

"What do you mean?"

"The pistol isn't the only thing I took from the late

and unlamented Mr. Butrum. I also took all of his money, one hundred and two dollars."

"Uh, Kay, forgive me for asking what I'm sure must be a very dumb question. But is one hundred and two dollars much money?"

Kay laughed out loud. "Only someone who is very rich could ever ask a question like that. Yes, honey, one hundred and two dollars is quite a substantial amount, especially under our current circumstances."

"You have made me a happy man."

"Ha, you mean I can buy you with one hundred and two dollars?"

"No, I mean because you called me *honey*."

Kay started to say that the word *honey* came easily from her lips as she, and all the other hostesses, used that word with just about every cowboy who came into Fiddler's Green for a drink. But she said nothing.

A few minutes later they rode into the little village.

WELCOME TO

BORDEAUX

Population 215

~Obey our Laws~

"Well, it would appear that it *is* your brilliant navigation and not merely a stroke of luck that brought us here," Kay said.

"Pa would be proud," Jake said with a little laugh. "I can't wait to tell him of my skill as a navigator."

At first glance, Kay saw that the town of Bordeaux seemed to be about one half the size of Chugwater. There was only one main street, running north and south, and it was intersected by two cross streets. The business establishments of the town appeared to be on both sides of the main street.

A single wagon was rolling up the street, coming toward them, and at least three horsemen were on the street, riding away from Jake and Kay. There were a handful of pedestrians on the walks and just as they were passing the Red Dog Saloon, a couple of patrons came through the swinging batwing doors.

"Well I'll be damned! Would you look at that?" one of the two men called out. "There's a man who's a-ridin' sidesaddle, 'n the woman with 'im is a-ridin' astride. I ain't never seen nothin' like that in all my borned days!" The man punctuated his observation with a loud guffaw.

"I guess you can see who wears the pants in that family," the other saloon patron said, laughing as loudly as his friend.

The strange sight of a man riding sidesaddle and a woman riding astride caught the attention of a few other pedestrians as well and though they stared in unabashed curiosity, no one, other than the saloon patrons, made any comments. Or, if they did make any comments they were so quiet that neither Jake nor Kay heard them.

What they did hear was the welcome, ringing sound of steel on steel, a blacksmith at work.

"Do you hear that?" Kay asked happily.

"Oh yeah, I hear it," Jake replied.

The blacksmith was standing in the open door of his shop when Jake and Kay rode up, and just as had the other citizens of the town he looked in surprise at the strange scene of a man riding sidesaddle and a woman riding astride. But, when he saw Kay helping

Jake dismount, and saw the leg irons on Jake's ankles, the mystery was solved.

"Ten dollars," he said as Kay walked and Jake hobbled toward him, speaking before either of them had said anything.

"What?" Kay asked.

"I reckon you're a-comin' here to get them things offen your ankles, ain't you?"

"Indeed, I am," Jake replied.

"That'll be ten dollars," the blacksmith repeated.

"Isn't that a little steep?" Kay asked.

The blacksmith shook head. "No, it ain't cheap at all. Lookin' at his ankles there, I reckon it ought to be worth five dollars to have them leg irons took off. 'N I'm goin' to have to be just real careful so's I don't hurt 'im none. 'N the other five dollars is for not never tellin' nobody about it."

"Why should I be concerned if you tell anyone about taking off my leg irons?" Jake asked.

The blacksmith pointed to the leg irons. "Them things you got on your ankles there is what they put on prisoners to keep 'em from runnin' away whenever they are transferrin' 'em from one jail to another. I figure that's what you are, but somehow your lady friend here helped you to escape." He chuckled. "I have to hand it to you, lady, comin' up with the idea of takin' a sidesaddle with you so's he could ride with them things. Ten dollars," he repeated.

Kay took the money from her dress pocket and handed him a ten-dollar bill. "All right. We're paying for your labor and your silence."

The blacksmith took the money. "Come back here.

I've got a place for you to sit on a stool where you can put your feet up so's I can get at them things."

After the blacksmith made quick work of removing the ankle cuffs, their next stop was the apothecary.

"You say you got some chafed skin? Well sir, there ain't nothin' no better than Vaseline to use on that," the druggist said. "'N it just so happens I got some, right here." He held up a small blue jar.

"We'll take two jars," Jake said.

"Now, before you use this, you need to make certain that the affected area is very clean."

"We'll rent a hotel room and get a bath," Kay said. "I must say I'm looking forward to it, and I don't have any chafing at all."

"What good will it do to take a bath if we have to put these same dirty clothes back on?" Jake asked after they left the apothecary.

"We can take care of that, too," Kay replied as, with a smile, she pointed toward a mercantile.

Jake and Kay stood at the front desk of the only hotel in town. They were clutching in paper bags the change of clothes they had just bought.

"You folks is mighty lucky on account of we only have one room left," the clerk said as he turned the registration book toward Jake.

Jake looked at Kay and, with a smile, she gave him a little nod. He signed the register *Mr. and Mrs. J. Poindexter.*

"Do you have provisions for a bath?" Jake asked.

"Yes, sir, we have a bathing room at the end of the hall on the first floor. There is a tub and a pump to provide water. Should you wish the water to be warm, there is a stove and a bucket for your convenience. And, I am proud to say that the stove uses coal oil instead of wood, so it'll heat up just real quick."

"Thank you," Jake said as he took the key. "Ladies first." He pointed toward the end of the hall as he unlocked the door to their room on the first floor—convenient to the bathing room.

Chapter Thirty-seven

An hour later both were bathed and wearing clean clothes—Kay a matronly dress, and Jake denims and a red shirt.

"Well now, don't the two of us look like we just came in off the ranch?" Kay teased.

"I'll fit right in," Jake said.

Kay chuckled. "I'm sure you will," she said sarcastically. "I need you to take off your pants and lie on the bed," Kay said.

"What?" Jake replied, surprised by the request.

Kay held up one of the little jars of Vaseline. "I'm going to rub some of this on your ankles."

"Yes, yes, thank you."

For the next half hour Jake lay on the bed under a cooling breeze that came in through the window. Kay's hands worked magic, and as she applied the petroleum jelly he felt some relief from the chafing for the first time in several weeks.

"You aren't going to go to sleep on me, are you?" Kay asked.

Jake opened his eyes and smiled. "You don't know

what a miracle you have just worked. You have hands of magic."

"Well, I had a little help," she said, holding up the Vaseline jar.

"What do you say we go to a restaurant? And please don't think I'm casting aspersions against the prairie chicken and the rabbit you cooked for us. But, I would like to eat a meal at a table, with my feet free of any encumbrances."

"I would love to have lunch at a restaurant. I'll buy. As a matter of fact, you buy. Here's the money." She held the rest of the money out toward him.

"No, I don't want to take your money," Jake said, holding up his hand in refusal.

"Don't be silly. It isn't my money. It's Butrum's money, but he won't be needing it anymore."

"No, I don't suppose he will. You know what, we should have gone through the pockets of Hawken and the man who was with him, too," Jake said.

"We couldn't take the chance that there might have been some others who would have heard the shooting," Kay said.

"Yeah, you're right. Let's go eat."

The Palace Café had a more grandiose name than the café itself delivered, but it was clean and, though the menu was limited, the food was good. The proprietor was a woman named Alma Shannon, and her somewhat obese frame was the best advertisement for her cooking.

"Have you a bill of fare?" Jake asked.

"A what?"

"A menu, a listing of what is available."

"You ain't from around these parts, are you?" Alma asked.

"No, I'm from back East," Jake said without being more specific.

"Ha! I thought so! I could tell by the way you was a-talkin', all dignified 'n such. Anyhow we ain't got nothin' like that. We only cook one thing for dinner, 'n most o' the times that's what we serve for supper, too. But seein' as it's dinnertime, you'll get it while it's still fresh."

"That sounds good enough to me," Jake said.

Alma walked back to the kitchen and a moment later returned with two steaming plates.

Jake stared in confusion at the plate that was put before him.

"What is this?" he asked after Alma walked away.

"Why, Jake Poindexter, do you mean to tell me you've never eaten chicken and dumplin's before?" Kay asked. "I doubt this will be as good as my mama's, but all chicken and dumplin's are good."

Jake took a hesitant bite, then smiled. "You're right. They are good."

Chugwater

The P R and M account was in the New York Bank for Savings, and upon learning that an additional one hundred thousand dollars was in the process of being transferred, Preston Poindexter sent a telegram to the bank.

RESCIND TRANSFER OF ONE HUNDRED
THOUSAND DOLLARS TO FIRST BANK
AND TRUST OF CHEYENNE STOP MAKE

NO FURTHER TRANSACTIONS OF ANY
KIND WITHOUT MY PERSONAL
AUTHORITY STOP
PRESTON POINDEXTER

Within an hour of sending the telegram, Pete, who was in Fiddler's Green at the time, got a response from the bank.

"They are going to call back the money they sent to Cheyenne?" Duff asked.

"Not yet." Pete showed the telegram to Duff.

REQUIRE AUTHENTICATION IDENTITY OF
SENDER THIS TELEGRAM BEFORE ACTING
UPON DIRECTIONS

"*Och*, and how will you be for provin' you are who say you are?"

"Biff, do you have paper and a pencil?" Pete asked.

"Sure thing," Biff said, going into his office. He returned a moment later.

Taking the pencil and paper, Pete began to write. When he was finished, he chuckled.

"Sure 'n 'tis quite a man who can laugh in the face of such adversity," Duff said.

"Or perhaps a man with just a touch of insanity," Pete said. "But this should be all the authentication I need." He showed it to Biff, Duff, and Elmer.

Cooper

"Cooper?" Biff asked after he read the note. "That's all it'll take to tell him who you are?"

"I'm sure this will be as confusing to the bank as it

is to you, so it will be taken to the president for further instructions, and he will approve it."

"That's all it'll take?" Elmer asked.

"The president of the bank is Keith Dunaway, and at a party given by Cooper Investments, Keith got drunk and started getting a little forward with one of the serving girls. He's a decent man and wouldn't have done such a thing if he hadn't been drunk. He is married and an important businessman and it would have been very embarrassing if it had gone on any further. I got him away from there before he made a bigger fool of himself, and even though the young girl didn't know who he was, I gave her one hundred dollars never to mention it. As a result of that, Keith experienced no embarrassment."

"Sure, 'n 'tis a good friend you are," Duff said.

About an hour later the Western Union boy returned to the saloon with a one word response.

AUTHENTICATED

Pete laughed. "It pays to have friends. Now, I must send another telegram."

After Jake and Kay finished their meal, they located a telegraph office so that Jake could send a telegram back home. Jake told Kay. "It'll be expensive because it's going to be a long one, but I'll arrange for my father to pay for it. He will be more than happy to do so, because I'm quite sure he has wondered why he hasn't heard from me in all these weeks."

The Western Union office was in the bank.

"My name is Jake Poindexter. I would like to send a telegram to my father, Preston Poindexter, at the P R and M Corporation on Fifth Avenue in New York. And please arrange for my father to pay the charges."

"*The* Preston Poindexter?" the telegrapher asked, impressed by the information.

"Yes, *the* Preston Poindexter."

"Very good sir. Would you like to dictate the message, or would you prefer to write it out on a tablet?"

"I'll write it out for you."

With a yellow-lined tablet, and a pencil, Jake composed the message.

Pa, for the last five weeks I have been held prisoner, betrayed by Ed Collins, a man I met on the train. Collins is in Chugwater passing himself off as me. No doubt he has made demands against the credit line that was established for the C&FL Railroad. Send no more money to the imposter.

I am free now, thanks to the efforts of a very courageous and wonderful woman who I intend for you to meet.

> *Love, your son,*
> *Jake*

P R and M Corporation, New York

Norman Jamison read the telegram, his irritation growing. Not more than an hour earlier he had received a telegram from Ed Collins.

RECEIVED WORD PRINCIPAL NOT IN
CHICAGO AS THOUGHT BUT IS AT HAND
STOP SUGGEST ONE FINAL TRANSFER OF
FUNDS THEN TERMINATION OF
PROGRAM

Jamison had been the one who developed the
C&FL program, specifically picking Chugwater because of its isolation. And though Jake didn't realize
it, it was a few hints and suggestions from Jamison
that caused Jake to decide to go to Chugwater for his
adventure. After that, it was easy to get the senior
Poindexter to authorize building a railroad through
the town.

Jamison had plans that would not only transfer another million dollars from the P R and M but also
transfer into another entity all of the land they had
thus far confiscated under the guise of building a
railroad.

A change in circumstances meant there was going
have to be a rapid change of plans. Somehow Jake
Poindexter had escaped his confinement. Jamison
had kept him alive intending to, through Collins,
demand a ransom for his release. But with Jake free
and sending telegrams, and with Preston in Chugwater, the project was going to have to come to an end.

Collins was right. The situation called for one last
major transfer of funds, and Jamison planned to do
just that, but not the way Collins expected. Because
of Jamison's position as executive secretary, he knew
that although Preston Poindexter was one of the
wealthiest men in America, the P R and M had only a
little over a million dollars remaining in liquid assets.

The major wealth of the company was in its holdings—
active railroad lines, rolling stock, ships, and real
estate.

Jamison decided to transfer one million dollars,
but not to Chugwater or Cheyenne. He would transfer
the money to the Merchants Bank of San Francisco,
and he would make himself the only person with authority to access the account. He would also keep the
existence of the San Francisco account secret from
the others.

"I'm sorry, Mr. Jamison, but I can't honor this request," the head teller said when he saw the draft
requesting the transfer of one million dollars to the
Merchants Bank of San Francisco.

"What do you mean, you can't honor this draft?"
Jamison asked, sputtering in anger. "I am the executive secretary of P R and M, and I know perfectly
well how much money is in our account. We have
sufficient funds to cover this transaction, and I am
authorized to draw from it. Mr. Poindexter has a business deal ongoing in San Francisco, and we must have
operating funds locally available in order to comply
with all the terms."

"I'm sorry, sir. But I cannot honor this request," the
head teller repeated.

"Then I demand to see the president of this bank,
and I demand to see him at once!"

"Yes, sir," the teller replied. "If you'll just wait here
for a moment, I shall tell Mr. Dunaway you're here."

"Be prompt about it," Jamison demanded. "I am a
most busy man, and I have no time for inefficiency."

"Yes, sir."

While Jamison waited, and fumed, the head teller stepped back to Keith Dunaway's office. As the door was open, he stepped inside.

"Yes, Dan?"

"Mr. Jamison is here."

"And?"

"It is just as you said, sir. He is attempting to transfer a large amount of money."

"How large?"

"One million dollars."

Dunaway let out a quiet whistle. "Yes, I would say that is quite a large sum. All right. Hold him for a few minutes then send him back here, and I will deal with the situation."

Dunaway took out the last telegram he had received from Pete.

JAMISON GUILTY OF EMBEZZLEMENT AGAINST MY COMPANY STOP IF HE ATTEMPTS ANOTHER LARGE TRANSFER PLEASE INFORM POLICE AND FILE CHARGES

Earlier, Dunaway had shared the information with the police. He called them. "Hello, Captain Burns. The man I told you about in our last conversation is in the bank now. Please send some officers to deal with it."

Dunaway knew that the nearest precinct was but two minutes away, so, after waiting for one minute, he stepped out of his office. "Mr. Jamison, you may come back now."

"It's about damn time," Jamison replied angrily. "Dunaway, your bank tellers need to know just who they are dealing with. P R and M is your biggest depositor, and I am the executive secretary with full banking authority." Jamison strode quickly, his irritation growing even as he walked. It had reached its peak by the time he stepped into the office.

"Dunaway, what is this?" Jamison demanded. "How dare you refuse a bank draft from us? And then make me wait around like some beggar from the street before you would even see me to deal with it." The words were spit out in one long, angry stream.

"Come on in and have a seat and we'll talk about it," Dunaway invited.

Jamison accepted the invitation.

"Would you like a cup of coffee?"

"Coffee? No, why would I want coffee? I came here for money."

"Yes, for one million dollars," Dunaway said. "And this, on top of several other recent and very large transfers."

"Why does it matter how much money has been transferred?" Jamison removed a piece of paper from his pocket and read from it. "As of this morning, P R and M has one million, ten thousand, six hundred and twelve dollars in its account."

"Yes, P R and M has that much money, but at this moment, we have insufficient cash on hand to handle a transfer that large. I'm afraid you will have to give us time to accumulate the assets so we can comply with your request."

"Are you telling me that the bank doesn't have that much money?" Jamison asked incredulously.

"Of course we do, but I'm sure you know how a bank works. We have loans, investments, and dispersed funds rather than keep all our assets in one place. It will take a little time to gather that much cash."

"How much time?" Jamison demanded.

"Oh, I'm not—"

Before he could finish his comment Dan, the teller who had dealt with Jamison, stepped through the door. "Mr. Dunaway, they are here."

"Send them in, please."

"Who is here?" Jamison demanded. "How dare you see someone else while we are discussing business?"

At that moment two uniformed policemen came into the office.

"What are the police doing here?" Jamison asked, his belligerent attitude replaced by one of apprehension.

"Officer, I am Keith Dunaway, president of the bank, and as agent for Preston Poindexter, our largest depositor, I am filing charges of bank fraud and embezzlement against this man, Norman Jamison."

"What?" Jamison replied, stunned by the sudden turn of events.

"Mr. Jamison, you are under arrest. Please come along quietly," one of the police officers said.

Chapter Thirty-eight

Chugwater

Duff, Meagan, Elmer, Vi, Wang, Mae Win, and Pete were having dinner in Lu Win's Chinese Restaurant.

"It's quite simple, my dear," Pete said as he was explaining to Vi how to use chopsticks. "You keep the bottom stick pressed up against your thumb so that it doesn't move. The other stick moves with your forefinger so that the sticks become, in effect, your thumb and forefinger. That way you can pick something up as easily as you can with your fingers."

"Oh, yes!" Vi said after she tried. "Why, that's marvelous."

Elmer chuckled. "Now she'll be serving her apple pies with chopsticks."

They had gathered for the dinner to commiserate with Wang, who was feeling remorse for having killed the friend of his youth. Both Mae Win and her father, Lu, had assured him that he had no other choice, but expressed their understanding of his regret.

"All here are my friends," Wang finally said. "I have

lost one friend, but I have gained many. I thank you for sharing my sorrow, but now my sorrow is ended."

"To friends, new and old," Pete said, raising his glass of wine.

As they drank their toast, the Western Union delivery boy came in, walked over to the table, and handed a telegram to Pete. He read it, smiled, then passed it around the table for others to read.

NORMAN JAMISON IN JAIL FOR ATTEMPT
TO DEFRAUD THE BANK STOP WILL FACE
EMBEZZLEMENT CHARGES WHEN YOU
RETURN STOP HE WILL BE IN JAIL FOR
VERY LONG TIME STOP THANKS FOR
COOPER STOP
KEITH DUNAWAY

Shortly after the Western Union delivery boy left, Biff came into the restaurant.

"Biff, 'tis a fine thing you have decided to join us," Duff said in greeting.

An enormous smiled played across Biff's face. "It's a finer thing than you can know." He stepped back to the door, then made a motion to someone.

Jake and Kay stepped in through the door.

"Jake!" Pete shouted, standing so quickly that the chair tumbled over behind him.

"Pa, you're here?"

"I thought you might appreciate the surprise," Biff said as father and son met halfway between them in a warm and welcome embrace.

"Pa," Jake said after the greeting. "This is Kay Greenly. She is the young woman who saved my life."

"Miss Greenly," Pete said warmly.

"No, Pa, it's *Kay*," Jake said. "If she's going to be my wife, don't you think you should call your daughter-in-law by her first name?"

Cheyenne

"What do you mean you can't honor my draft?" Collins demanded after the teller at the Cheyenne Bank and Trust refused the transaction. "I know for a fact that I have almost two hundred thousand dollars in my account."

"Perhaps you had better speak to our president, Mr. Walker," the teller said.

"I damn well will speak with him."

"Mr. Poindexter, I'm afraid your account has been withdrawn," Robert Walker said.

"Withdrawn? Who the hell withdrew it?"

"It was withdrawn by the New York Bank for Savings. There is no money in your account." Walker grunted what might have been a laugh. "Actually, there isn't even an account anymore."

"What are you talking about? I deposited forty thousand dollars, in cash, no more than two days ago! Are you telling me those funds aren't available?"

"I'm afraid they aren't.

"You mean we've done all this for nothin'?" Caldwell asked when Collins informed the others that there was no money to divide.

"It has to be Poindexter," Collins said bitterly. "Somehow that miscreant has closed the account."

"If we still had him we could maybe force 'im to put the money back," Mitchell said.

"'N if a frog had wings, he wouldn't bump his ass ever' time he jumps," Nichols said. "Either Hawken 'n Flannigan has already kilt Jake, or he's kilt them the way he done Butrum. It don't matter which. We don't have him no more."

"I know how we can get the money," Streeter said. "I've done it before, 'n I was by myself. With five of us, it'll be easy."

"If you're a-talkin' about robbin' this bank, they ain't goin' to be nothin' at all easy about it," Caldwell said. "It's on the busiest street of the biggest town around here. Why if we was to try, they'd be on us like ducks on a june bug."

"I ain't talkin' about this one. I'm talkin' about the one in Chugwater."

It was just after ten o'clock in the morning when Meagan heard the door of her shop open.

"I'll be with you in a minute," she said, her words somewhat muted because she was on her knees pinning up a dress and some of the pins were in her mouth. She heard someone coming toward her.

"Hell, I ain't in no hurry, miss," a man said.

Looking up from her task, Meagan saw one of the men who had been passing themselves off as railroad police. He was holding a pistol.

"I'm not sure which one you are," Meagan said. "Hawken?"

"Nah, we ain't found 'im yet, but that skunk is more 'n like lyin' dead somewhere. The name's Caldwell, if you really want to know."

"What do you want with me, Mr. Caldwell?"

"My friends is goin' to be doin' some business down at the bank in a few minutes then when we leave town we plan to take you with us. We figure that'll stop anyone from shootin' at us while we're leavin'."

"While we're waiting, you don't mind if I finish pinning up Mrs. Underhill's dress, do you?"

Caldwell laughed. "You're a calm piece of work, I'll give you that."

At that same moment, Collins, Streeter, Nichols, Dixon, and Mitchell came riding into town.

"Streeter, since I've never done anything like this before, for this operation you will have tactical command," Collins said.

"All right. Ever'body keep your eyes open," Streeter said. "Make sure there ain't no one that's takin' a particular interest in us."

"There's a couple of old men over there playin' checkers," Nichols said.

"Yeah, and there's a couple more men over there, sittin' out on the porch in front of the store," Mitchell added.

"Yeah, well, the checker players is too old, and them other men is more 'n likely waitin' out front while their wives is inside spendin' their money," Streeter said.

"There's the bank," Mitchell said, pointing to the building ahead.

"Ain't no need for you to be a-tellin' us that, Hank. We've all seen the bank before," Streeter said.

The four men rode down Clay Avenue, the hoofbeats of their horses making a hollow, clopping sound.

"Gentlemen, I don't mind telling you, I have a most disquieting feeling about this," Collins said.

"Collins, you're the damndest talker I've ever knowed," Streeter said. "What does that mean, you're feelin' quiet?"

"*Disquieting.* It means that there is something about this that's bothering me."

"What?"

"I don't know," Collins replied.

"Well we ain't goin' to back out, are we? I mean, we are goin' to do it, ain't we?" Mitchell asked.

"Yes, we're going to do it," Streeter said. "And remember what I told you. When we leave, start shootin' up the place. We'll stop long enough for Caldwell 'n the woman to join us, 'n that'll give us cover as we ride out."

At that moment Duff was riding up Lone Tree Road, coming into town to discuss the reorganization of the C&FL Railroad with Pete and Jake. As soon as he got into town, Lone Tree Road became Clay Avenue, and he saw Collins and three of the railroad police at the far end. At first he wondered what Collins was doing back in Chugwater. Was he unaware that Jake was here and had exposed him for the fraud he was? Then he saw them ride up to the front of the bank and swing down from their horses, handing the reins over to Collins, who remained mounted.

As soon as Streeter and the others were inside the bank, they pulled their pistols. Streeter shouted, "This is a holdup! You, teller, empty out your bank drawer and put all the money in this bag!" He handed the bag to the teller.

"There's no need for you to start shooting," the teller said as he began putting the money in the bag. "I've been told to cooperate if anything like this ever happens."

"Who told you?" Streeter asked suspiciously.

"I told him," Dempster said, stepping out of his office. "I told him that if we are ever robbed, to cooperate fully. We can replace money, but we can't replace a life."

"Yeah," Streeter said. "That's just real smart of you."

A moment later the teller handed over the sack filled with money.

"Let's go," Streeter said as, with guns drawn, he and the three men with him backed toward the door, then turned and stepped outside.

They saw that Collins had dismounted and was holding his hands in the air. Duff was there, holding his gun on Collins.

"I'll thank you lads to be for dropping your guns, laying the money bags down, 'n comin' with me to the jail."

"Do as he says, men, my life is at forfeit," Collins said.

* * *

"Damnation!" Caldwell was looking through the window toward the bank and saw Duff confront the men as they were leaving the bank.

"You," he called to Meagan. "Come with me."

With his gun held to Meagan's head, Caldwell stepped outside. He mounted his horse then ordered her into the saddle just in front of him. Holding his pistol to her head, he rode toward the bank.

Sensing the movement, Duff looked toward the approaching horse and, for just a moment, he thought Meagan was coming toward him. Then he saw someone behind her, and he knew she was being used as a shield.

"All right, boys, pick up the money 'n get mounted," Caldwell said to the others. "MacCallister ain't goin' to do nothin', long as I'm holdin' on to his woman."

"Good job, Caldwell," Collins said.

Caldwell waited until the others had retrieved their guns and the money. "Get mounted. Not you, Collins," he said as Collins approached his horse. "We don't need you no more, 'n with you gone we'll have one less to divide the money with."

"What? See here, I am in charge of—"

Collins's protest was interrupted when Caldwell shot him.

"Ha! I never did like that windbag!" Streeter said.

"Now, Duff!" Meagan shouted.

Looking toward her, Duff saw her slide off the horse, leaving Caldwell exposed.

He was the first person Duff shot. Then, taking advantage of the confused surprise of the others, Duff shot two more of them. Marshal Ferrell, who had come up when he saw what was developing, shot the remaining two.

When all the shooting was over, Collins and what remained of the phony railroad police lay dead on the ground in front of the bank.

Epilogue

Six months later

The entire town turned out to welcome the arrival of the first commercial train to run on the newly laid tracks of the Cheyenne and Fort Laramie Railroad. Cong Sing and the Chinese workers whose physical labor had built the railroad were honored guests of Lu Win.

"Here she comes!" Fred Matthews shouted, but no human announcement was necessary as the approaching train made its presence known by the two-tone whistle.

The locomotive that rolled into the station was a 2-2-0 Baldwin with a green boiler, brass banding, red driver wheels, and a cab of polished cedar. The first car behind the coal tender was a private car, the *Emma Marie*.

"Oh, look!" Meagan said. She took hold of Duff's arm. "Duff, wasn't our time in there the most elegant of anything we have ever experienced?"

"Aye, lass, that it was."

When the train stopped, the first person down from the *Emma Marie* was Preston Poindexter himself.

His arrival was applauded by all, even by the ranchers such as Dale Allen, David Lewis, and others whose initial setbacks with the C&FL had been made good by Jake, once he took over and started the actual construction of the railroad.

"Ladies and gentlemen," Pete said. "I appreciate the welcome, but now I would like introduce the man who oversaw the building of the C and FL, my new executive secretary, Jake Poindexter."

Everyone looked expectantly toward the car, but Jake didn't appear.

"Pa," Jake called from within the car, "you didn't finish the introduction."

"Indeed, I did not," Pete replied with a little chuckle. "Ladies and gentlemen, may I introduce my son and daughter-in-law, Mr. and Mrs. Jacob Poindexter!"

Jake and Kay stepped down onto the brick platform of the brand new Chugwater Depot of the C&FL Railroad.

"Oh, Duff, isn't she just the most beautiful thing you have ever seen?" Meagan asked.

"Nae, lass, 'tis yourself that's the most beautiful thing I've ever seen."

She tightened her grip on his arm.

**Keep reading for a special excerpt
of *The Backstabbers*!**

National Bestselling Authors
WILLIAM W. JOHNSTONE
and J. A. JOHNSTONE

THE BACKSTABBERS
A Red Ryan Western

FIRST RULE OF JOHNSTONE COUNTRY:
TRUST NO ONE
*No one knows the dangers of driving a stagecoach better
than Red Ryan. Especially when the passenger's a dead
man, the payoff's a gold mine, and the last stop is death . . .*

SECOND RULE: WATCH YOUR BACK
Red Ryan should've known this job would be
trouble. The first stop is a ghost town—in a
thunderstorm—and the cargo is a coffin. But things
start to look a little brighter when Red and his stage
guard, Buttons Muldoon, deliver the corpse to a
ranch run by the beautiful Luna Talbot and her
gorgeous crew of former saloon girls. Luna asks the
boys to help them find the Lucky Cuss Gold Mine,
using a map tucked inside the dead man's pocket.
Buttons can't refuse a pretty lady—or the lure of gold.
But Red has a feeling they're playing with fire. Especially
when the map leads them straight into the crossfire of
a ferocious range war and the path of a 400-pound
load of pure evil known as Papa Mace Rathmore—and
his backwoods clan of sadistic, kill-crazy hillbillies . . .

Look for *The Backstabbers* on sale now.

Chapter One

Beneath a black sky torn apart by a raging thunderstorm, the side lamps of the Patterson stage were lit as Red Ryan and Patrick "Buttons" Muldoon approached the town of Cottondale, some sixty miles east of El Paso, Texas.

Buttons drew rein on the tired team and shouted over a roar of thunder, "Hell, Red, the place is in darkness. How come?"

"I don't know how come," the shotgun guard said. Red wore his slicker against the hammering rain. "The place is dead, looks like."

"Maybe they ran out of oil. Long trip to bring lamp oil all this way."

"And candles. They don't have any candles."

"Nothing up this way but miles of desert," Buttons said. "Could be they ran out of oil."

"You said that already."

"I know, and that's still what I reckon. They ran out of oil and candles, and all the folks are sitting in their homes in the dark, sheltering from the rain."

"Or asleep." Red said.

Lightning scrawled across the sky like the signature

of a demented god, and for a second or two, the barren brush country was starkly illuminated in sizzling light. Thunder bellowed.

"Buttons, you sure we're in the right place?" Red yelled. Rain drummed on the crown of his plug hat and the shoulders of his slicker. "Maybe this isn't Cottondale. Maybe it's some other place."

"Sure, I'm sure," Buttons said. "Abe Patterson's wire said Cottondale is east of El Paso and just south of the Cornudas Mountains. Well, afore this storm started, we seen the mountains, so that there ahead of us must be the town."

Red said. "What the hell kind of town is it?"

"A dark town," Buttons said. "Remember the first time we seen that New Mexican mining burg, what was it called? Ah, yeah, Buffalo Flat. That looked like a dark town until you seen it close. Tents. Nothing but brown tents."

"With people in them as I recollect." Red said. "Well, drive on in and let's get out of this rain and unhitch the team."

"Yeah, the horses are tuckered," Buttons said. "They've had some hard going, this leg of the trip."

"So am I tuckered. I could sure use some coffee."

Buttons slapped the ribbons, and the six-horse team lurched into motion. Lightning flashed and thunder banged as nature threw a tantrum. As it headed for a town lost in gloom, the Patterson stage was all but invisible behind the steel mesh of the teeming downpour.

Cottondale consisted of a narrow, single street bookended by rows of stores, a hotel, a saloon, and a livery stable. A large church with a tall bell tower dominated the rest. The town was a bleak, run-down, and windswept place. The buildings huddled together like starving vagrants seeking comfort in each other's company. It was dark, dismal, and somber. Silent as a tomb, the only sound the ceaseless rattle of the relentless rain.

Buttons halted the team outside the saloon. A painted sign above the door, much faded, read THE WHEATSHEAF. "We'll try in here."

Red shook his head. "Try in here for what? Buttons, this is a ghost town. It's deader than hell in a preacher's backyard."

"Can't be. Ol' Abe said we have a passenger . . . what the hell's his name again? Oh yeah, Morgan Ford. He's got to be here and a whole passel of other folks."

Thunder rolled across the sky.

When it passed, Red looked around and said, "Then where the hell are all them other folks?"

"Sleeping the sleep of the just, that's where. There's a church in this town, and God-fearing folks go to bed early." He angled a look at Red. "Unlike some I know."

Red reached under his slicker and consulted his watch. "It's only eight o'clock."

"Farmers," Buttons said. "Farmers go to bed early, something to do with all that plowing they do at the tail end of a horse. All right. Let's try the saloon. Day or night, you ever seen an empty saloon? I sure as hell haven't."

The saloon was as empty as last year's bird nest. Cobwebbed and dark, the shadows were as black as spilled ink. The mahogany bar dominated a room with a few tables and chairs scattered around a dance floor. A potbellied stove stood in a corner. Red thumbed a match into flame and held it high. The guttering light revealed pale rectangles on the walls where pictures had once hung, and the mirror behind the bar had been smashed into splinters.

"Ow!" The match had burned down and scorched Red's fingers. Irritated, he repeated, "Like I said . . . we're in a damned ghost town."

Buttons had been exploring around the bar and his voice spoke from the murk. "Three bottles. All of them empty." Lightning flared as Buttons stepped toward Red in the dazzle, and he flickered like a figure in a magic lantern show. "We've been had. This is what they call a wild-goose chase."

"I don't think the Abe Patterson and Son Stage and Express Company is one to play practical jokes," Red said. "Abe never made a joke in his life."

"You're right. Abe wouldn't play a trick on us," Buttons said. "But it seems somebody is, and if I find who done it, I'll plug him for sure."

"Unhitch the team and let the horses shelter overnight in the livery stable. I'll get a fire going in the saloon stove and boil up some coffee."

"Fire will help us dry off. Damn, Red, this was a wasted trip."

Red smiled, "It's on the way back to the Patterson depot in San Angelo. We didn't lose anything by it."

"Except a fare," Buttons said.

"Yeah, except a fare. But I reckon Abe Patterson can afford it."

Buttons closed his slicker up to the neck and stepped toward the door. Red lingered for a few moments and decided that the chairs would burn nicely in the stove. He craved coffee and the cigarettes he could build without the downpour battering paper and tobacco out of his fingers.

Button's voice came from the doorway, sounding hollow in the silent lull between thunderclaps. "Red, you better come see this. And you ain't gonna like it."

Red's boot heels thudded across the timber floor as he walked to the open door. "What do you see? Is it a person?"

"No, it's that," Buttons said, pointing.

A hearse drawn by a black-draped horse stood in the middle of the rain-lashed street. Just visible in the murk behind the large, oval-shaped windows was a coffin, not a plain, hammered pine box, but by all appearances a substantial casket made from some kind of dark wood accented by silver handles and hinges.

"What the hell?" Red said.

"I don't see anybody out there," Buttons said. "Who the hell is in the box?"

"Maybe our passenger."

"Red, don't make jokes," Buttons said. "I'm boogered enough already."

"Let's take a look out there. A hearse doesn't just appear all by itself."

Red Ryan and Buttons Muldoon stepped into the street that was suddenly illuminated by a flash of lightning that glimmered on a tall, cadaverous man who wore a black frockcoat and top hat and seemed uncaring of the rain that soaked him. The man's skin was an ashy gray, as though he spent too much time indoors, and he held a hefty Bible with a silver cross on the front cover in his right hand, close to his chest.

"Well, howdy," Buttons said. "Who the hell are you?"

Lightning shimmered, turning the rain into a cascade of steel needles, and thunder boomed before the man spoke. "I am the Reverend Solomon Palmer of this town. You have come for our dear, departed brother Morgan Ford, have you not?"

Rain ran off the brim of Buttons's hat as he shook his head. "Not the dear departed Morgan Ford, mister. The alive and kicking Morgan Ford."

"Alas, Brother Ford passed away two days ago," Palmer said.

"From what?" Buttons stepped back, alarmed. "Nothing catching, I hope."

"From congestion of the heart," Palmer said. "I watched his pale face turn black and then he gave a great sigh and a moment later he hurried off to meet his Creator." The preacher clutched his Bible closer. "He was a fine man, was Brother Ford."

"He was a fare," Buttons said. "And now he isn't. There ain't no profit in dead men for the Abe Patterson and Son Stage and Express Company."

"Ah, but there is," Palmer said. He smiled, revealing teeth that looked like yellowed piano keys. "Come with me . . . Mister . . . ah . . ."

"Muldoon, but you can call me Buttons. And the feller in the plug hat is Red Ryan, my shotgun guard."

"Come with you where?" Red asked. "Me and Mr. Muldoon are not trusting men."

"I will do you no harm," Palmer said. He glanced up at the black sky where blue lightning blazed. "Only the dead are abroad on a night such as this."

"Cheerful kind of ranny, ain't you?" Buttons said. "I'll have to see to my horses before I go anywhere, and I'll take care of your hearse hoss." He shook his head. "I don't believe I just said that."

"Hearse hoss," Red said. "It's got a ring to it."

"Yes, I'd appreciate it if you'd take care of my mare," Palmer said. "I think you'll find hay in the livery, and perhaps some oats."

"And where will you be?" Buttons said.

"Right here, waiting for you." Palmer looked stark and grim and bloodless as the storm cartwheeled around him, putting Buttons in mind of a corpse recently dug up by a resurrectionist.

The horses were grateful to get out of the storm and gave Buttons and Red no trouble as they were led to stalls and rubbed down with sacking before Buttons forked them hay and gave each a scoop of oats.

Buttons had been silent, deep in thought as he worked with the team, until he said, "Red, what do you make of that reverend feller?"

"He's a strange one."

"You mean three pickles short of a full barrel?"

Red nodded. "Something like that."

"He said that there's profit in the dead man. Did you hear him say that?"

"More or less."

"Do you believe him?"

"Enough to listen to what he has to say."

"Here," Buttons said, turning his head to look behind him. "He ain't a ghost, is he?"

"A what?"

"A ghost, a spook, a revenant . . . whatever the hell you want to call it."

Red smiled. "No, I think he's just a downright peculiar feller. Man must be crazy to live in a ghost town."

Buttons pointed a finger. "See, you said it, Red. You said *ghost*."

"I was speaking about the town, not the preacher. Let's go hear what he has to say."

Chapter Two

The Reverend Solomon Palmer led Red Ryan and Buttons Muldoon to a cabin behind a tumbledown rod and gun store that still bore a weathered sign above its door. The thunderstorm had passed but had left a steady rain in its wake and when Red and Buttons stepped inside, their slickers streamed water onto the dirt floor.

Palmer lit a smoking oil lamp, and a mustard-yellow glow filled the cabin. Red noticed that a well-used Winchester stood in a gun rack and hanging beside it a holstered Colt exhibited even more wear. He decided right there and then that there was more to the Reverend Palmer than met the eye. The man might be a parson now, but that wasn't always the case . . . unless the firearms belonged to someone else.

A log fire burned in a stone fireplace flanked by two rockers. A small dining table with a pair of wooden chairs completed the furnishings. Above the mantel hung a portrait of a stern-looking man in the uniform of a Confederate brigadier general. The old soldier had bushy gray eyebrows and a beard that spread over his chest, and he bore a passing resemblance to

Palmer. The cabin had an adjoining room, but the door was closed. The place smelled of pipe smoke and vaguely of blended bourbon but had no odor of sanctity that Red associated with the quarters of the clergy.

"Help yourself to coffee," Palmer said, nodding to the pot on the fire. "Cups on the shelf." The man removed his top hat, revealing thinning black hair. He set the hat down on the table. "Are you sharp set?"

"We could eat," Buttons said, a man who could always eat.

"Soup in the pot, bowls on the shelf, spoons on the table," Palmer said. "Eat and drink and then we'll talk about Morgan Ford."

The coffee was hot, black, and bitter, but Red found the soup surprisingly good. "Good soup," he said after he'd finished his bowl.

"I spent some time as a trail cook for old Charlie Goodnight," Palmer said. "I learned how to make bacon and beans and beef soup because it was one of Charlie's favorites."

A cook could acquire a Colt and a Winchester, but Red figured he'd never use them the way Palmer's had been used. He still put a question mark against the reverend's name.

Buttons burped more or less politely and then said, "Tell us about the dead man in the box."

"Brother Morgan Ford came to Cottondale ten years ago, hoping to outrun a reputation as a gunman, and in that quest, he succeeded," Palmer said. "He built the saloon, but when the town died, Morgan took sick and died with it. Him and me, we were the only two left. I remained to take care of him in his last weeks, as was my Christian duty."

"How come the town died?" Red said. "Looks like it was a nice enough place with a church an' all."

"At one time it was," Palmer said. "But then the farmers who wanted to grow cotton here discovered that the cost of irrigating the land ate up any profits. One by one, defeated by the desert, they pulled stakes and left until only Morgan and me remained. Three days ago the heart trouble finally took him and he gasped his last."

"And lost me a fare," Buttons said.

"You still have a fare, Mr. Muldoon," Palmer said. "When Morgan lay dying he told me to contact his only living relative, a niece by the name of Luna Talbot, and ask her if she would bury him. Needless to say, I was surprised that Brother Ford had a niece, but using El Paso as my mailing address, since mail is no longer delivered to Cottondale, I wrote to her and she replied and said yes. She wants his body and will pay to have it sent to her. Apparently, Mrs. Talbot has a successful ranch due south of us on this side of the Rio Bravo. In every way, she seems to be an admirable young lady."

"And you want us to take the body to her? Is that it, Reverend?" Buttons said.

"Yes, I do. That is why you're here. I contacted the Abe Patterson company in San Angelo and made all the arrangements."

Buttons shook his head. "Nobody made arrangements with me that involved picking up a dead man. The Abe Patterson and Son Stage and Express Company doesn't carry corpses and if it ain't there already, I plan to write that down in the rule book."

"Five hundred dollars, Mr. Muldoon," Palmer said.

"Huh?" Buttons said.

"Five hundred dollars, Mr. Muldoon." A heavy cloudburst rattled on the cabin's tin roof, adding to the reverend's suspenseful pause. "That is the amount of money the grieving Mrs. Luna Talbot is willing to pay for the safe delivery of her loved one."

"I reckon that from here it's around two hundred miles to the ranch you're talking about," Buttons said. "That's a fifty-dollar fare."

"And indeed, you are correct, Mr. Muldoon. The Patterson stage company gets fifty and you keep the rest." The reverend smiled slightly. "Because of the unique nature of the . . . ah . . . delivery, Mrs. Talbot is prepared to be generous."

"Red, what do you reckon?" Buttons said.

Before Red could answer, Palmer said, "I have a sufficient length of good hemp rope to lash the coffin to the top of the stage. We can make it secure so that brother Morgan can take his final journey in peace."

"Without falling off, you mean?" Red asked.

"Precisely," Palmer said.

Buttons and Red exchanged a glance, and finally Buttons nodded. "Get the rope, Reverend."